The Fence

The Fence

Bill Morales

Writer's Showcase
New York Lincoln Shanghai

The Fence

Writer's Showcase
an imprint of iUniverse, Inc.

iUniverse books may be ordered through booksellers or by contacting:

iUniverse
2021 Pine Lake Road, Suite 100
Lincoln, NE 68512
www.iuniverse.com
1-800-Authors (1-800-288-4677)

ISBN-13: 978-0-595-17820-9 (pbk)
ISBN-13: 978-0-595-72168-9 (ebk)
ISBN-10: 0-595-17820-0 (pbk)
ISBN-10: 0-595-72169-9 (ebk)

Printed in the United States of America

"*None of us can help the things life has done to us. They're done before you realize it, and once they're done, they make you do other things until at last everything comes between you and what you'd like to be, and you have lost your true self forever.*"

Eugene O' Neill

CHAPTER ONE

"We've crossed the *fence*, lights out. We'll be in Steel Tiger East in fifteen minutes," Chris Andrews broadcasted over the intercom as the AC-130A Gunship crossed the *Mekong River* along the Thai-Laotian border.

"What are we playing tonight, Chris?" asked Major Marks, while he donned his flak helmet.

"Tonight's request is brought to you from the I.O. gentlemen." Chris Andrews inserted the 'Sam & Dave' tape into the mission tape recorder, channeling *Give me Some Lovin'* into the aircraft intercom system. Willie Santiago, the I.O., and the Spectre flight crew became aroused, driven in concert by the rhythmic beat as they headed toward another major supply route on the eastern border of *Laos*. Booth sensor operators impatiently searched for benign targets on the ground to boresight the 40-mm and 20-mm guns in preparation for another night stalking operation.

"Three Wolfpacks on station at 15,000 feet at our six," the navigator interrupted the rhythmic moment for a mission update.

Major Stuart Marks, the aircraft commander, was attuned to the needs of his fourteen man crew so that they functioned flawlessly, centering their skills and training during the arduous five hour missions. Who gives a shit about regulations, and how the mission recorder was used before a mission, he thought. He wanted his men pumped-up and on the edge, ready to waste the motherfuckers on the trail. If music got their adrenalin pumped to kick *North Vietnamese* ass, so be it, he thought.

Ralph Aguilar, The flight engineer, extinguished the interior lights of the AC-130A from his control panel, illuminating the crew cabin and cargo compartment with an eerie, low-intensity red light. The gunners and the illuminator operator were accustomed to the low-light levels and could easily maneuver around the crowded compartment without bumping into each other or into the munition racks filled with 40-mm and 20-mm shells. A small trailer-type compartment, known as the booth, was manned by three officers that operated and housed sophisticated high-tech electronic equipment that literally was the eyes and ears of Spectre. The sensor operators thought they were hot-shit, often claiming that they could distinguish between warm elephant shit and farts from the NVA. They were good, but they also had lots of U.S. technology behind them. A computerized fire-control system linked the guns and sensors that made Spectre extremely deadly. A Forward-Looking Infrared sensor enabled the Spectre to detect heat from vehicles even after they had turned off their engines. Its sensitivity could even pick up heat emissions from a cigarette at ten thousand feet. And the Low-level light TV could see in the dark by amplifying moon and star light. Then there was the Black Crow, an impressive ignition detection system device that could hone-in on moving vehicles along the trail then relay the data to the other sensors for target acquisition. The digital fire control system then integrated inputs from the three sensors providing position and attitude data to the pilot, allowing him to place the aircraft in a search or attack orbit. Input from the fire control system drove a bead in the pilot's gunsight, which represented the target. When the fixed reticle in the gunsight was aligned with the bead, the pilot was then ready to shoot at its quarry.

The Forward Looking Infrared, Black Crow, and Low-Light-Level-Television operators began calibrating their equipment in preparation for the evening hunt, while the navigator made sure that the videotape recorder was functional and ready to confirm the evening's kills for the Intelligence assholes who questioned every kill during the mandatory debriefs once they returned to *Ubon*. The electronic warfare officer made final checks and adjustments, and made sure that all was ready and operational in the event of a surface-to-air missile, better known as a flying telephone pole, was launched at them. Chaff tubes which hung under the wings were armed and ready to jam enemy radar.

Marks and his crew had a reputation throughout the base as a hard-nosed bunch. And it was usually an individual without much intelligence or who was inherently stupid that would dare question Marks' crews' sense of manhood or lack of balls without getting their face smashed in, even by an officer. They were never known to go about their business the easy way, like letting the F-4 fighter escorts take out the triple-A batteries when they were under attack. They preferred, and mostly enjoyed, doing it themselves.

#   #   #

A hard rain began to fall as *Le Thanh* sat stoically beside his camouflaged 57-mm antiaircraft weapon. His pith helmet made of pressed cardboard covered with a thin cloth was hardly a shield against the dense sheets of rain that slowly advanced through *Binh Tram* 37 in eastern *Laos*. *Thanh* would occasionally look skyward, intently listening for the RF-4's that regularly patrolled the northwestern sector of Route 12 and 15 of the *Mu Gia* mountain pass that ran south into *Laos* from *North Vietnam*. The steep mountainous jungle terrain surrounding the *Mu Gia Pass* provided excellent cover for the rapidly moving supply convoys under the protective triple jungle canopy. Its deep mountain caverns and limestone karsts' caves were a superb natural camouflage for antiaircraft batteries and for storing large quantities of supplies for the planned 1972 spring offensive. B-52's were unable to destroy or dislodge them from the caves after many years of carpet bombing, while resourceful *North Vietnam*ese road repair teams cleverly used the massive craters for storing supplies, then camouflaging them.

Thanh had taken note that unarmed photo reconnaissance flights had recently intensified. What he didn't know, was that the flights were precipitated by the emitting signals of seismic and acoustic sensors that were implanted over hundreds of miles along the enemy's logistical transportation routes. Tree branch-like sensors would relay data to a ground station at *Nakhon Phanom*, a Royal Thai Air Force Base in eastern *Thailand* by two specially equipped EC- 121's that continuously orbited the enemy's infiltration routes. Two IBM mainframe computers in air conditioned trailers at NKP worked 24-hours a day deciphering the information, trying to get a fix on the enemy's location and movements. It wasn't long before intelligence agencies began receiving signals from various locations at the start of the dry season as the roads and passes had been cleared by NVA road teams for the convoys. *North Vietnam* was escalating their logistical supply flow through the *Ho Chi Minh* trails in mid-December in their attempt to supply their forces in the South.

Thanh grinned. He knew that the increase in traffic meant they would soon be visited by more ominous night-flying aircraft to interdict their convoys at critical choke points once a positive identification and location of the vehicles had been made. "Spectre will be out tonight," he thought out loud, while sixty Russian built ZIL 157 trucks idled under the jungle canopy waiting to be fueled and continue their trek through the narrow pass into *Laos*, then into *South Vietnam*. Zil's were Spectre's favorate prey. AC-130 gunships had been specifically developed and deployed by the Air Force in 1968 to deter the transportation of munitions and supplies during the start of every dry season. ZIL's were an incredibly reliable and durable vehicle. Each six-wheel drive transport carried five tons at 40 mph over the most prohibitive roads in Southeast Asia. It could inflate or deflate its tires while moving, literally adjusting to the various terrain changes and road surfaces. *Le Thanh* felt a slight measure of apprehension as his stomach muscles tightened, slightly from hunger but mostly from anxiety in anticipation of the pending battles soon to come. No fight was ever like another, *Thanh* thought pensively. Each was unique in drama and climax. He sensed the butterflies in the pit of his stomach begin to stir before a battle. With the torrid monsoon rainy season over, the skies would be clear and movement on the ground would be much easier to detect by enemy aircraft. With an average of one-thousand trucks out on the trail every evening, there was a good probability that some of them may have been detected approaching the fuel depot that was well hidden under the jungle canopy.

The RF-4's had indeed spotted the convoy, and reported the sighting to the ABCCC, the Airborne Battlefield Command and Control Center. Code named Moonbeam, the modified C-130 assigned and directed combat aircraft throughout the theater of operation. Two opposing forces would soon engage in a violent exchange of flesh-ripping steel.

A surge of joy and pride flowed through *Le Thanh*, sensing the war had been already won when the Americans had chosen to fight a prolonged war of attrition instead of attacking its center of gravity in Hanoi with its superior weaponry. For *Thanh*, the Americans were already defeated, lacking the moral conviction to inflict the horrors that were usually required to *win* wars and force the will of one over the other, the real objective of war, he reasoned. And their defeat had already been set into motion when their political objective was not to *win* but to prevent the South from being overtaken by the North. Little did the Americans know that they were being manipulated by the North, drawn into fighting a revolutionary war, frustrating them by denying them the ability to fight with all of their strength. Unknowingly, the protesters in the United States had been instrumental in forestalling an all out attack on their sanctuaries in *Cambodia* and *Laos*. When the Americans finally decided to go after the sanctuaries,

the *Viet Cong* and *North Vietnamese* had already established other locations and transportation corridors to hide from their pursuers.

Hanoi was quick to respond to the Christmas bombing halt
announcement by redeploying its Russian-built 57-mm antiaircraft
weapons with gun laying radar along the *Mu Gia Pass*, as they prepared
for another major offensive to win the war militarily in 1972. *Le Thanh*
knew that the slow moving converted C-130 aircraft was vulnerable to
antiaircraft fire. The 57-mm was a deadly weapon when employed
properly. It had an effective slant range of 13,000 feet with optical sighting and its effectiveness increased to 20,000 feet with radar. *Le Thanh*
affectionately stroked the cold 57's barrel, assured that it would find its
mark when Spectre was in its sight. But nearly two thousand trucks had
been destroyed in his sector during the last dry season. It was pure car-
nage. Spectre would somehow find its prey through the thick jungle
canopy and attack unmercifully at the defenseless supply vehicles and
troops traveling south. Tonight, the rules of engagement would be
changed with the radar capability, *Le Thanh* thought confidently,
though in awe that Spectres could detect the heat emission of their
vehicles.

He shrugged his shoulders as if to brush away the fear that would
easily overwhelm a soldier in the field; never knowing if he would ever
go home again. *Le Thanh* no longer reflected on death, or his future. For
Thanh, death would just be an abrupt inconvenience from completing
his mission. *Thanh* had spent the last three years in the jungle as part of
a *Binh Tram*, a subordinate unit to the 559th Transportation Group that
controlled a portion of the NVA's logistic network in *Laos* and *Vietnam*.
There were a multitude of *Binh Tram's* throughout the NVA's logistical
lines of transportation, whose prime responsibility was to make sure
the trucks and supplies kept rolling. Defense of the trail was divided
among the 37th Antiaircraft Battalion in the north and the 45th in the
south. *Le Thanh* was responsible for the defense of his quadrant and
parts of the 37th. The whole Trail was managed by the 559th

Transportation Group with its rear headquarters in the *Ha Tinh Province, North Vietnam*, and forward headquarters in *Laos*, west of the *A Shau Valley*. U.S. intelligence agencies had estimated that there were nearly thirty-thousand personnel assigned to the group to keep the Trails open and passable. Critical *Binh Tram* stations were known to have between two to four-thousand personnel, which included engineering battalions and a couple of bulldozer companies, and many men and women using shovels to clear the trails. *BT37* was suspected to have two infantry battalions, four engineering battalions and one artillery battalion.

Thanh longed for a cigarette as he contemplated revenge and his first Spectre gunship as he scanned the night sky in search of his prey. He turned his back to the sky and cupped his hands tightly to conceal the illumination of the match. Years of war and suffering had slowly hardened him, learning at a young age to exist and fight on meager subsistence levels and a steady diet of worn-out cow dung Party slogans. *Thanh* despised the incompetent Party elitist bureaucrats along with the stinking foul breath Russian advisors who'd never spent a night in the jungle or had to hunt for another starving animal for their next meal. The bureaucrats were conscientious only in assuring that they had an adequate supply of ammunition but never concerned with providing a decent meal. Their speeches were jaded words that often employed blundering, ill-conceived military plans that only led his people to slaughter. Ten thousand of his comrades had already been killed in defense of the trails. *Thanh* rested his head on his arm while he leaned on his weapon.

The night sky was luminous. A perfect backdrop for a decorated nineteen years old antiaircraft gunner who had shot down three RF-4's and was looking forward to avenging the deaths of those who had fallen victim to Spectre's wrath. A single 37-mm round exploded in the sky five miles from Le Thanh's position, a warning shot that gunships were in the area and heading his way. Without much of a reflex, *Le Thanh* loaded the gun breach and looked for the familiar spiral search patterns of Spectre.

"We have a mover at ten o' clock with his lights on," the FLIR operator eagerly notified the crew as his sensor locked onto the heat emanating from the still vehicle. The other sensors honed-in on the target as well, while the human scanners searched the moonlit night for enemy ground-fire. Chris Andrews abruptly ejected the tape from the recorder and replaced it with the one intended for the mission.

"He must have stalled out and can't get it started," the LLLTV operator added as the three sensors collectively began to feed target data to the fire control system. Major Marks ordered the flight engineer, Aguilar, to arm the 40-mm Bofors since his only intention was to get a little target practice and gun alignment before continuing to the assigned area of operation he had received earlier from Moonbeam. He was more interested in the bigger game five miles away.

"I'm rolling in," announced Marks as he rolled the Spectre into its familiar thirty degree attack pattern, orbiting over the ill-fated truck. Marks quickly aligned the pipper with the fixed reticle in his gunsight and anxiously waited for Moonbeam to give them the clear to fire order.

"How long does it take those assholes to give us clearance?" Marks' was obviously frustrated, but it normally took anywhere between ten and fifteen minutes for approval from the ABCCC.

"Maybe they want us to pull the *pendejo* over and validate his *Ho Chi Minh* driver's license and vehicle registration," Aguilar whispered sardonically into the intercom.

"You're cleared to fire, Major," the navigator responded. Marks quickly tightened the Spectre into its thirty-degree bank attack orbit and prepared to reacquire his target for an easy kill.

The words "*No Fear*" were scrawled in large white letters across Willie Santiago's flak-helmet. Santiago positioned himself several feet out the ramp door, casually scanning the twelve to six o' clock aircraft position through the protective bubble face-shield flak helmet. Known for his

perpetual smile, Santiago leaned out a little further to get an unobstructed panoramic view of the Spectre and the threatening terrain
below, looking for muzzle flashes and the familiar red tracer signature
of 37-mm antiaircraft fire. Santiago's view of the war was through the
narrow window of his plastic bubble face shield. Almost dangling above
the battles, I.O.'s observed the larger conflict rather than the piecemeal
chaos seen by the ground-pounding grunts on the ground. But funda-
mentally they shared much of the same intense excitement and fear;
smoke and gunfire, explosions and rushes of bewilderment and terror.
With over two-hundred missions behind him that included two-crash
landings as well as parachuting over enemy territory when enemy
ground fire blew-off the right wing of his aircraft. Despite the close calls
and near death experiences, Santiago remained dauntless and uncon-
cerned about his luck, or thoughts about packing it in and going home.
Santiago was fearless, and for that reason alone Marks had recruited
him to watch his 'six.'

Marks patiently scanned the darkened landscape searching for a defiant target for his shit-hot crew that knew how to take it to the *North
Vietnamese*. They were competent at their craft. And the only difference
between his crew and the others was really simple, he thought. We
looked for the shit, other crews would just run into it. Major Marks was
enamored with his crew and thought about the special bond that
existed between men in the midst of adrenaline-stress-filled war. Their
closeness was not tied to the usual things you would have expected
under the current circumstances, like patriotism or duty. They simply
had vowed they would always protect each other's back, since
Washington could only find ways to *expose* it.

Willie Santiago was not anticipating any antiaircraft fire since if there
was anything of value near the doomed vehicle, antiaircraft batteries
would have lit-up the skies immediately. For what must have been less
than a fraction of a second, Santiago turned around to draw a gumdrop
which he kept on the side of the aircraft fuselage in his flight bag to keep

his throat moist during the long arduous missions. As he turned, Santiago caught the reflection of an intense red glow off his flight bag of what appeared to be a bright flash that could have only come from the ground, and outside the aircraft's orbit, its most vulnerable position.

"Triple-A, two to six o'clock," reported Santiago calmly. "No threat, hold what you got." The setup had been planned for several weeks. Le Thanh's battery had planned to bait a Spectre into interlocking fire, luring it into a trap with what appeared to be a helpless truck caught in the Spectre's firing orbit. His team ran the engine for several hours, flashing its lights on and off, aware of Spectre's sensors ability to detect engine noise, as well as movement and heat. Spectre 15 was now in the snare. To the surprise of the co-pilot and right scanner, seventy perfectly spread 37-mm red tracer rounds were in pursuit toward Spectre outside its orbit. *Le Thanh* had flawlessly orchestrated the antiaircraft batteries' assault by layering their fire above and below the gunship, denying it from rolling above or below the flak curtain, closing off any escape routes while pushing it to a predestined location in the darkened sky. *Thanh* knew all too well, if you were going to receive triple-A, it was always preferable from inside the orbit because you had greater maneuverability to avoid the barrage.

Having spotted the triple-A, the Wolfpack escort flight leader was cleared by Marks to suppress the guns with cluster bombs. CBU dispensers were filled with spherical bombs that contained steel buckshot type pellets. When the dispenser was ejected from the aircraft, a timer opened it and the bombs were spread across the jungle floor. Spectre's flight crew took a long deep breath as the pleasant looking but deadly red tracers exploded into bright orange glows narrowly missing the aircraft by less than thirty feet.

"I'm rolling out. Let's get the fuck out of here for a few minutes," fumed Marks, violating communications decorum as he distanced the gunship from the triple-A batteries but further into Thanhs ambush. Marks could feel his hands sweating inside his Nomex flight gloves, not from fear but more from the enemy's tactical surprise. The adrenaline surge filled him. Wolfpack delivered the cluster bombs in an even pattern covering about a two-mile area, silencing the 37's.

"I have a radar lock," shouted the Electronics Warfare Officer from the booth, his mouth was suddenly dry from stress and fear.

"What direction Pete?" asked Marks calmly.

"It's from inside the orbit, about two miles, Major," responded the EWO.

"Keep your eye's open, Willie. I'm going to take her down to four thousand feet. I want the 20's online now" ordered Marks. Santiago responded in the affirmative by keying his microphone switch twice, acknowledging receipt of the order. "It's time to get some" the Major articulated in a smooth yet threatening tone.

"The 20's are armed," barked the flight engineer Aguilar as he engaged the toggle switch arming the Vulcan 20 mm cannons that could fire twenty five-hundred rounds of high explosive incendiary shells per minute.

"Clear," broadcasted the front gunner who maintained the 20-mm Gatling guns, as well as the 7.62 miniguns. The 20-mm tracer rounds could literally spew tongues of red steel across the jungle floor with just a minor dip of the left wing. Marks had a sixth sense as to where the gun emplacements and radar vans were hidden and believed he could destroy them by spraying the area with the Vulcans. The tree line was stockpiled with several months' worth of supplies and ammunition intended to make their way south. Marks had a knack, or an instinct, if you will, in finding the exact location of the supply caches and hidden antiaircraft emplacements. He thought of it as a special gift, but now was focused with taking out the 37 mm emplacements and radar vans that were pinpointing his location in the sky for the triple-A batteries. They were Spectre's nemesis, and Marks had a special hard-on for them.

Sensor operators eagerly searched the jungle terrain for hot gun barrels that would pinpoint the location of the gun emplacements. Spectre

15's crew could feel the warming in the cabin temperature as the aircraft descended rapidly to four thousand feet.

Sgt. Willie Santiago suddenly saw a muzzle flash and the bright orange signature of a 57-mm round. They say when one is about to face death it is surprisingly accepted calmly, without as much as a whimper. As the radar guided 57-mm raced toward its prey, Santiago immediately knew that his life was to come to a sudden end and calmly cursed at his misfortune, "Fuck me."

As Marks rolled the aircraft into its thirty-degree firing pattern, the 57-mm round ripped through the aft fuselage and upper ramp door raining shrapnel throughout the cargo bay and through Willie Santiago's body.

"Mayday! Mayday! This is Spectre 15, we've been hit by triple-A. We're heading west on heading two-zero-five," screamed the navigator into the emergency frequencies as Major Marks struggled to regain control of the gunship out of an uncontrollable climb. Bracing the control column completely forward, Marks ordered the crew members up to the flight deck, hoping to bring the nose of the aircraft back down. Willie Santiago was dying, dangling from the restraining harness out in the slipstream.

As if hell itself had decided to participate in the frenzy, the sky lit-up with hundreds of successive air bursts exploding around the aircraft, pelting it with shrapnel as hungry antiaircraft batteries attempted to complete the task *Le Thanh* had incited. Spectre 15 was hanging together by a thread. Its utility hydraulic system was failing, along with the booster system. The rudder, elevator trim, and autopilot were inoperative as well.

Le Thanh smiled wryly momentarily at the sight and sounds of the crippled Spectre. He knew that the gunship would try and make it back to *Ubon* if it could, or bail-out over the Thai Laotian border. He had hurt them. Spectre would be kept out of his sector for several weeks, *Le Thanh* thought. But it also meant that they would eventually pay dearly for their victory. His sector would most likely be given priority by the Air Force planners which meant constant bombardment...Arc light bombings from B-52's.

Spectre 15 limped back to *Ubon*. As they neared the base, Major Marks ordered the nonessential crewmembers to bail-out. As soon the rest of the crew had exited the aircraft near the western Laotian town of *Savannakhet*, Ralph Aguilar manually lowered the landing gear. When he was done, he went to the booth to look at Santiago who had been lowered from his restraining harness by the crew before they had bailed out. Santiago's body was cold and torn to pieces with shrapnel. His life source flowed along the floor of the booth, mixing with the wounded aircraft's crimson hydraulic fluid. Tears of hate flowed from Aguilar as he covered Santiago's body with his flight jacket trying to somehow comfort him.

"We're cleared to land Major," the navigator conveyed looking into his eyes, hoping to draw strength from Marks. As Spectre 15 approached *Ubon*, the Major reduced the aircraft's power as it rapidly plunged toward the 9,000 ft. landing strip. The gunship hit the ground hard and bounced violently as it raced quickly toward the end of the runway. Marks' attempt to reverse the three-bladed Allison T-56 turbo-prop engines failed to slow the aircraft after two-thousand feet, and it suddenly veered to the right despite Marks efforts in applying additional thrust to number three and four engines. The right wing sheered off as it hit the runway, ripping the polyurethane supported fuel tanks that protected them from exploding if struck by ground fire. JP-4 fuel was now engulfing Spectre 15. Crippled, the Spectre erupted into flames as it came to a violent stop off the runway. Fire trucks and ambulances rushed to the dying aircraft.

"Let's go," ordered the Major in an amazingly tranquil tone, quickly unfastening his seat belt and shoulder harness. But Ralph Aguilar dashed madly to the booth to get Santiago's body. Marks couldn't stop him in time as flames reached the flight deck. Marks, the co-pilot, and the navigator narrowly escaped the aircraft through the flight deck hatch.

Ralph Aguilar and Willie Santiago were lost in the flames and the explosion of burning ammunition. Marks silently wept as emergency crews struggled to extinguish the flames. The rest of Marks crew was recovered on the Thai Laotian border the next morning by a Sikorsky HH-53 Super Jolly Green Search and Rescue team.

Le Thanh prepared himself to sleep his accustomed dreamless night in the cold winter confines of a well-fortified cave as fifty Zil's approached the strategic pass, patiently waiting their turn to refuel and continue their journey south. In his hand, *Le Thanh* clutched a half-faded picture of a farm and family, now a nameless place of features, from another time. *Thanh* had no hope for life; *he was there for the duration.*

CHAPTER TWO

"You're my first and last breath," Ray Vaquero whispered as he stared at Suzanne Logan's photograph, clinging to a painful past that wouldn't let go. It was a blustery cold night in New York City as Ray Vaquero waited to board a bus at the Port Authority that would take him to Kennedy Airport. Vaquero gazed momentarily at the silver moon and the multitude of pulsating stars that glistened and throbbed on a frosty winter night. He inhaled deeply into his cigarette, hoping it would get rid of the chills running through him. His thoughts wandered ten thousand miles away pondering once again his decision to return to the war. He shuffled his feet, attempting to shake out the bitter cold and nervousness. Vaquero detested the cold weather and was looking forward to spending the next twelve months in a warm climate, sucking tropical winds while hanging out the back of an AC-130 Spectre gunship at seven thousand feet.

Festive holiday music by *Tito Puente* blared through the cabin as it finally surged toward the airport with a full load of passengers in high spirits looking to spend the holidays on the island of enchantment, *Puerto Rico*. The briskness in the air had momentarily left Raymond Vaquero as he absorbed the rhythmic Latin sounds, casually glancing at the passengers scattered throughout the bus. They were mostly G.I.'s like himself, anxious to get home to their family for Christmas before shipping out to various bases in Vietnam. He reclined his seat, and lit another cigarette; his thoughts wandered momentarily before they focused in on Suzanne. "You threw your money away again, shithead," he whispered out loud. Vaquero could have flown straight home after AC-130 Gunship Training at Hurlburt Field, Eglin AFB, Florida, but decided instead to try to see Suzanne Logan one more time before leaving for *San Juan*. But when he finally got enough nerve to call her from a deserted Gulf gas station in West Nyack, New York, two miles from the Logan's home, Suzanne's parents told him that she was out celebrating her recent engagement with her fiancé Michael Collins. Her mother, Jeanny Logan, cordially wished him a Merry Christmas. And after a long and uncomfortable silence, Mrs. Logan said, "goodbye, Ray." Vaquero folded his hands and momentarily rested his head on them fighting back the heartache.

"Let it go Ray; *let her go*," he pleaded with himself. Fragments of a Rod McKuen poem filtered through the grief as he thought of Suzanne Logan.

I stood watching as you crossed the street for the last time. Trying hard to memorize you. Knowing it would be important. The way you walked, the way you looked over your shoulder at me. Years later I would hear the singing of the wind and that day's singing would come back. That time of going would return to me every sun-gray day. April or August, it would be the same for years to come...

Mental fences again fortified themselves, mercifully denying him the painful conclusion to the poem. It don't mean nothing, Vaquero mused, as he fought back the sensation of nausea. His stomach muscles tightened into taut little knots as the thought of Suzanne Logan in the arms of another man sickened him. He released a long and painful, audible sigh that caught the attention of several passengers close to him. It was not unlike the sounds of a dying man in the waning moments of life before his life spirit let go, moving on to a better place. Vaquero's heart was suddenly empty and indifferent as he sat silently, staring blindly toward nowhere.

Thoughts of stalking an enemy under the cover of darkness added an eerie, although twisted measure of excitement and anticipation now, as seeds of retribution began to sow in his heart. It reminded him of the times when, as a teenager, he dared to venture to the north side of the apartment complex with his friends through a maze of passageways that connected all the buildings. The adrenaline would surge through their veins in anticipation of the trouble that would be waiting for them.

The Italian gangs were known as the Lords of the north side, and the Puerto Ricans, new to the territory, resided in the south. They had no fancy names, only the misfortune of living in a neighborhood where they weren't welcomed. His best friends, Manny Rodriguez and Cano Rincón, would eagerly look for ways to piss off the Lords with regular incursions into their territory. There was nothing more the Lords hated than knowing that Vaquero and his friends were stalking through their neighborhood undetected, especially Cano, a handsome, fair-skinned, blond-haired Puerto Rican who always attracted women like a magnet. Cano loved women, and no *fence* was going to deny his stinky-finger tonight, even if it meant battling the Lords. It was a cat and mouse game in which Vaquero, Rodriguez and Rincón knew they were always the hunted. There was a tall wooden picket fence that served as a territorial demarcation line that divided the two rival groups. The rules were explicit. An ominous warning was written on the wall to all that ventured beyond the wooden divide. And although they were not familiar with the author, they knew that it was meant primarily for the brown skinned Puerto Ricans:

"The rain has such a friendly sound
To those who are six feet underground"

The Lords

Vaquero stared blindly out the window of the Greyhound, deep in thought and reflection. It wasn't just the excitement or danger that lured them to venture over the *fence*. The wall was a constant reminder of the divisions that existed in the *barrio* with its daily challenges and confrontations. Being poor and living in a neighborhood that didn't want them there in the first place.

Fuck them…they're nothing but a bunch of *maricones*. Faggots, Ray thought, now seething as he found little humor in his past and the shit-hole neighborhood in Parkslope Brooklyn where he grew up. *One day*, they would make it out on their own terms, not the Lords. His temper and heart rate began to soar as Vaquero relived one particular incursion over *the fence*, as he drew deeply from his Lucky Strike.

Sprinting back toward the *fence* one night after being spotted by the Lords, Vaquero and Rincón ran side by side, praying under their breath for spiritual guidance to help them back over the *fence* before the Lords had a chance to catch up to them. Rodriguez was bringing up the rear, shouting insults at the Lords, communing with his maker as he tried to keep up with his accomplices. They could hear the Lords' heavy foot-steps pounding the pavement in rapid succession. Shit, Vaquero thought, they're out in force tonight. The sounds of a mob echoed in the streets, and if he hadn't feared for his life, Raymond Vaquero wanted to laugh his ass off.

"I'm going to kick your motherfuckin Spic ass, Manny." A white, foamy spit spewed from the sides of Lupo's mouth as he labored to get closer and prevent them from getting away. With her underwear hanging around her ankles, Lupo Constantino had caught Manny Rodriguez fondling his sister April, a couple of weeks earlier in the rear of the apartment complex. Manny had gotten away then, but not this time.

"*Maricón*, faggot, you asshole! I humped your sister tonight, you sack of shit, and it was *muy bueno*!" Responded Manny. Tears formed in Ray and Cano's eyes trying to hold back the fear, and laughter. Don't laugh, Vaquero commanded himself, attempting to moderate his breathing patterns and direct all his power and energy to make it back over the *fence*.

Manny delayed his jump to allow Ray and Cano to get over first, covering their rear. As Cano rolled over the wooden barrier, his T-shirt got caught on the picket fence. Manny frantically turned around and saw that the Lords were just about on top of him. One of the Lords suddenly ran straight at him and Manny instinctively sidestepped and caught him with a right cross that landed squarely on his face, sending him reeling backwards, landing hard on his back. Instead of making a desperate lunge over the wall to save himself, Manny jumped as high as he could and detached Cano's shirt from the picket. Ray and Cano could see Manny through the cracks in the *fence*, surrounded. He stood impassively while the Lords began to encircle him. Ray and Cano heard Manny calmly whisper, "I'm fucked," under his breath. He smiled then winked at Ray and Cano then calmly turned around to face the Lords.

"Let's go, which one of you *pendejos* want a facial tonight?" Manny danced around comically in an Ali style shuffle, attempting to gain confidence and not think about the beating he was about to endure. Although it was customary for the junior members to initiate the fight, Lupo's rage and thirst for Manny's blood prevented him from waiting until it was his turn. He wanted Manny all to himself and none of the other Lords would dare deny him. Lupo Constantino's blood lust was at its pinnacle.

"Hey Ray, Cano, I know you can hear me. I suggest you stay real close so that you can carry this sack of shit over the fence once we're done with him, that is, what's left of him." Lupo smiled a sadistic grin at Manny, self assured that his quarry could not get away since his gang blocked any chance of escape over the *fence*. Lupo stared and grinned at Manny, as he reached into his boot and pulled out a knife. Manny was not easily frightened, but he was definitely surprised since weapons had not been used before. All Manny could think of was getting sliced and diced by Lupo.

"Hey Ray, Cano, the faggots out number me twelve to one and he pulls a knife on me! What a *pendejo!*" Lupo quickly lunged at Manny with vicious slashing motions from left to right. Manny swiftly dodged and weaved, narrowly avoiding Lupo's deadly thrusts as they circled the perimeter of the arena. Ray and Cano were gripped with fear, terrified of the violence that ensued before them. Ray Vaquero suddenly leaned back from the wall as the cold reality of the situation finally struck him. Lupo Constantino had no intention of letting Manny get away alive. Ray grabbed Cano Rincón by the shoulders and spun him around abruptly. Cano was shaking and almost in tears.

"Listen to me," Ray ordered firmly. "Does your old man still have the .38 in the closet?" Cano nodded in the affirmative, still shaking. "Run as fast as you can and bring it back here, Cano. Do you hear me, man? It's the only chance we have to save Manny. Now run!" Cano Rincón took off like a bat out of hell. Ray just assumed he would come back with the weapon. The hard part was getting back out of the house once Cano got his hands on the pistol.

Ages seemed to have passed from the last moment Vaquero had checked to see how Manny was holding out.

"Hang in there, Manny," Ray whispered to himself.

Manny continued to dance around, ducking Lupo's ruthless lunges toward his face and chest. Manny got in an occasional jab to Lupo's face, which would then enrage him further. Both combatants were drenched in sweat and were beginning to show signs of exhaustion.

Lupo suddenly put his knife away and leaped toward Manny. Lupo outweighed his opponent by at least forty pounds, which made it difficult for Manny to maneuver at close range. Lupo viciously drove his fist into Manny's midsection and the fifth blow sent Manny reeling into the other Lords. But the harder the blow Lupo delivered, Manny would somehow find the strength and get up, enraging and frustrating Lupo further. Ray and Manny both knew that it was just a matter of time before Lupo would attempt to carve Manny again.

"Keep moving, Manny," Ray encouraged from over the *fence*. Manny defiantly got up from his knees after Lupo had slammed him on to the ground. Manny began to coax Lupo to come forward and engage him. He was a master at anticipating an opponent's move as Lupo obliged him, lunging quickly toward Manny then suddenly coming to an abrupt halt as he walked into Manny's guided fist. A ferocious jab caught Lupo's chin, followed by an instantaneous right-cross that nailed Lupo squarely on his nose. Blood showered the other Lords as it began to flow in a steady stream; Lupo staggered to regain his bearing, slowly rising from the ground. Lupo went ape-shit. He lowered his head like a bull and charged toward Manny like a man possessed. Manny tried to cushion the impact by bracing his hands against Lupo's shoulders, but the force of Lupo's rush slammed both of them against the *fence*, splitting the center board.

Ray kept looking over his shoulder, looking for Cano to return. Where the hell is he, he thought. There was no other alternative, as it suddenly occurred to him that he would have to go over the fence and help Manny despite the odds or the consequences; They had pledged to look after each other.

Physically exhausted, Manny suddenly ceased to fight back as Lupo had pinned him against the *fence*. All Manny could do was hold on as blood bubbled from his mouth with each hammering blow. His spent body stood slightly slumped to one side as he held on to his broken ribs bracing himself for the next blow.

At the moment Ray had decided to go back over the *fence*, he heard the rapid sounds of footsteps. At the same time, Lupo pulled his blade from his boot again, raising it above his head in full display of the other Lords. A piercing loud roar came from Lupo's gang, signaling approval for the final act. Lupo's right arm was extended at shoulder level when Cano Rincón fired the first round blindly into the *fence*. And in one steady fluid motion Cano leaped, propelling himself off a neighboring trash-can like a diving board flying over the *fence* like an insane man. A surge of electricity charged through Ray as he stood up and began yelling wildly, thinking to himself, "what the fuck," as he followed

Cano's path over the fence. Vaquero prayed that Rincón had more
rounds in the remaining chambers. At the moment Cano had fired,
Lupo Constantino had begun a savage upward thrust directed to go
through Manny's stomach and up toward his rib cage. Manny coldly
stared at his assassin, impassively…and braced himself against the
fence. Cano's errant shot had torn into Lupo's upper right shoulder,
exited, striking one of the Lords in the stomach. Cano landed besides
Lupo, who was now screaming uncontrollably from the pain. Cano's
cold stare froze the other Lords; now paralyzed, shocked and frightened.

Ray Vaquero ran over to Manny Rodriguez to see how he was. Manny
just looked up at Vaquero and grinned his shit eating grin as if to say
they finally got the upper hand on the Lords this time. Cano Rincón,
now gloating with pride at his heroics, turned toward the Lords twirling
his .38 and secured it partially through the top of his jeans. "You guys
are a bunch of *pendejos*," a degrading insult which meant worthless.
Cano had his bogeyed, crazy expression on. If you didn't know him, you
would find his insane stare intimidating. Ray and Manny worked hard
not to laugh at Cano's antics. The Lords nodded their heads in agreement when he called them *pendejos,* and with no idea what it meant.

"What took you so long *mano*, he was going to design me a new asshole," Manny Rodriguez whispered with a raspy voice. He tried to laugh
but it hurt so much that he spasmed and coughed thick drops of blood,
spraying Vaquero's shirt. Vaquero noticed Rodriguez battered face in
the dim moonlit night. His lip and chin quivered, ashamed that he had-
n't gone over the fence sooner. Rodriguez looked at him through the
narrow slit of his swollen eyes, sensing Vaqueros' pain.

"Hey, there wasn't anything you could do. If you had come over earlier, you'd be laying next to me." Rodriguez reached up with his right
hand and gently pressed Vaquero's arm. "You were there when I needed
you, man. That's all that really mattered, *mano. I would have done the
same for you.*" Rodriguez grinned, "*Anytime, anywhere.*"

Drenched in perspiration Ray Vaquero suddenly woke up as the bus shuddered as it drove over a large pot hole. Then, like a vision he sensed *her*, a premonition. Vaquero frantically reached for his wallet where he kept a picture of Suzanne taken while she intensely studied in his room at Columbia University. He carefully flipped it over to read her words for probably the millionth time.

> *When you look at this, I hope you*
> *remember all that we've shared -*
> *books, beds, train rides to Columbia*
> *University, sleepless nights and love;*
> *packs of cigarettes, and bottles of wine.*
> *When we first met in Physics class,*
> *philosophy tests, and tears in our own*
> *private cloakroom.*
> *Thank You,*
> *I love you*

Anguished, and full of sorrow, Vaquero wiped the tears with his coat sleeve. Someone like Suzanne comes only once in a lifetime, and he just walked away…abandoning her. And it was all because of foolish pride and self-pity, and his unwillingness to let go, and let her into his heart, completely. Vaquero had drifted aimlessly, unable to motivate himself, struggling academically and unable to admit that his head wasn't ready for college. He would have left Columbia much sooner, but around the time he was considering dropping-out, he had met Suzanne. The stigma of failure was gnawing him, which explains why on impulse one day, instead of going to class he took the subway to the Air Force Recruiting Station in the middle of Times Square in New York and enlisted. Ray Vaquero needed a stage to prove his worth, although at this moment, it felt like punishment for his stupidity. "What macho bullshit," he blurted out loud, full of self-pity, and uncomfortable with himself when he played the victim, a role that was clearly uncharacteristic of him. "Fuck it. It don't mean anything now anyhow," Vaquero remarked sarcasti-cally. But, in truth, it did *mean* something in the bigger scheme of things. You lose much when you hold back in love, he remembered someone telling him once. Ray drew heavily from his cigarette and silently waited for the bus to finally pull into Kennedy airport. But like a thief in the night, a whispering voice finally pierced him during his momentary calm, cutting through his lowered defenses, and McKuen's poem painful conclusion.

These long years later it is worse; for I remember what it was, as well as what it might have been.

"...Last breath," he whispered. Ray Vaquero began to sweat on this very cold and unsympathetic moonlit night.

CHAPTER THREE

As the bus raced toward JFK Airport, the highway lights seemed to explode. Bright beams of light refracted and expanded on the fogged windows. Thoughts of exploding antiaircraft fire entered his mind as the Greyhound bus rushed by the tall highway lights, and it occurred to him for the first time that it was possible that he might not make it back alive. He stared out the window again with a reflective gaze, thinking how he would have traded his vacation and meager sergeant's pay for just one hour with Suzanne. But Ray also knew that he needed to put her behind him for now, but it was difficult forgetting someone that embodied everything that he ever wanted.

On military leave as well in Puerto Rico, he hoped Manny and Cano would raise enough hell around the island to anesthetize the wounds. Cano Rincón and Manny Rodriguez were members of the elite Marine 7th Force Recon Company that fearlessly ventured into enemy base camps tracking *North Vietnamese* Army troop movement through hundreds of miles of triple-canopy covered trails to determine their strength. Three to six-man teams would secretly go behind enemy lines to monitor logistic and supply operations, shadowing the NVA along hidden roads and passes that were difficult to spot with airborne FAC's requiring closer Force Recon team scrutiny. Once the enemy's strategic depots and camps had been found, Manny and Cano would meticulously map the uncharted trail and call the find to a Forward Air

Controller who would then radio in tactical air or artillery from a local fire support base to rain hell over the poor NVA bastards. They code-named their team after the native Indian of Puerto Rico, the *Taino*.

They were known to look for assignments that were considered unusual and different and relished the opportunity to attempt something new and dauntless. Like the time they noiselessly walked through an NVA base camp, faces camouflaged, dressed in NVA clothing very early one morning to ascertain NVA strength in the infamous *A Shau Valley*. Everyone in the camp had been asleep, except a man and woman that were engaged in intercourse in one of the outlying bunkers one steamy Asian morning. The NVA guards were supposed to have been watching the trail, except *Taino* observed the couple for twenty minutes as they lustfully consumed each other. Monkey love, thought Rincón, as he grinned and envied them. *Taino* left them undisturbed, for the moment. The camp would inevitably be hit by tactical air strikes once its location had been forwarded to the Fac and team *Taino* was securely out of the area.

Ray yearned to see his best friends again.

Kennedy Airport was buzzing with Christmas travelers as the bus finally screeched to a halt in front of the Pan Am terminal. The airport was packed with Puerto Ricans' waiting for the next plane to transport them back to the *Isla*. Vaquero looked out into the distance and reminisced about how excited he'd get when he would visit Puerto Rico as a young boy with the family each summer when he was growing up in Brooklyn. Vaquero and his sisters couldn't wait to get to the sultry tropical beaches of the Caribbean, particularly *Luquillo Beach* near *Fajardo*, on the eastern part of the island. It was the only time he could remember when the oppressing humidity and heat didn't phase him. It's funny, he thought. After so many visits he still felt like a foreigner. The islanders and local family members never failed to remind him when he would go visit them that he was a "New York Rican," implying that he could never be a true *Boriqua*, a native, and never fully assimilate to the native customs and language. As Vaquero walked over to the departure gate, his attention was drawn to the sounds of Latin music coming from a group of homesick Puerto Rican soldiers singing, "*Mi Viejo San Juan.*" It was a popular island melody about a native's love affair with the *Isla*, the island, and its people. It was a patriotic song equivalent to the national anthem; an ache to be back home again, all wrapped up in one melody. Ray fought back the tears, filled with emotion now as he listened to their heartrending song. The words became a spiritual connection to his people; a sharing, a common bond of land and birth.

They are truly from the *Isla*, he thought. And he envied them. Ethnically, he was just like the others but never completely assimilated. For the first time in his life Ray Vaquero coveted their affinity for the island where he was born, but never genuinely knew. Torn between two cultures yet simultaneously drawn to both. Tumultuous approval roared through the terminal as the musicians concluded their serenade. The multitudes that had gathered around the soldiers dispersed, and began to collect their belongings as the boarding announcement was finally broadcasted for the flight to *San Juan*. Their holiday spirits were lifted, and excited anticipation grew as they began to board the 747 aircraft. In three hours they would reach *San Juan*.

Vaquero was captivated by the music, and for the moment, was not concerned about convoys or *Vietnam*, but was mesmerized by the memories of sensual island mystic sounds as he boarded the aircraft. Vaquero quickly settled into his seat on the 747 and stared out the window, as uncontrollable thoughts of Suzanne flowed into his consciousness again and he began speculating whether she ever thought of him and how much he loved her. He fell asleep in his thoughts, unaware as the 747 lifted up into the wintry night. Awakened two hours later by his growling stomach, someone gently touched him on his right shoulder as he contemplated what flavorful dinner he had missed. Vaquero hadn't noticed the elderly man now occupying the aisle seat when he first boarded the aircraft. He was smiling at him and asked, "*Queres un trago mijo?"* The stranger pulled a small brown paper bag from his coat pocket and surreptitiously unveiled a small bottle of Barcardi rum. He couldn't help but laugh to himself as he stared into the old man's concerned paternal face. The stranger had noticed that Ray had slept through the meal service and wanted to offer him some refreshment. Ray didn't want to drink on an empty stomach but he didn't want to hurt the old man's feelings either.

"Me llamo Raymond Vaquero, como se llama usted?", Ray asked, embarrassed at not being sure if he had phrased the question, what is your name, properly.

"Me llamo Victor Santana," he responded cordially. He must have been in his early sixties, weather beaten from too much sun and overexposure. A myriad of sun spots, and moles covered his sun baked ripened face. Victor Santana was on his yearly pilgrimage to the island for the holidays, Vaquero guessed. It was a sure bet that he had exhausted his meager savings to pay for his trip. Christmas was always preferably celebrated on the *"Isla,"* rather than freezing your ass-off in the city. The trek was a yearly pilgrimage to the island made by thousands of New York Puerto Ricans, and no cost was spared. Chances were that he had saved just enough from his social security checks together with a loan from a neighbor to purchase his ticket.

Ray nodded and said, *"si, como no señor,"* and swallowed long and deep into the smooth warm rum. Vaquero smiled, and returned the bottle in the same covert manner as he quivered at the alcohol's obvious kick. He could see it made Victor feel good when he accepted his offer. They smiled at each other, clearly overjoyed that they were going home again to celebrate the holidays and be with *la familia.* The Christmas holiday was truly a special time for Puerto Ricans. Good natured, loving people, Ray thought, as the rum began to take effect, wondering now, what genetic influences the original island natives the *Taino* Indians, played in the development of the islanders' personality over the course of time. *"Boricua,"* the name given by the Taino's to the island of Puerto

Rico, was now a phrase commonly used by anyone with an affinity with it. The holidays were a season of parties that would last through February; singing *Alguinaldo's*, traditional Christmas carols that have been passed down through the generations. The custom included the traditional Christmas holiday, including the Three Kings that visited Jesus at the Manger.

"I too was, in the Army," Victor exclaimed. "I fought the Germans during World War II." He leaned back in his seat reflecting on his past as if it were just yesterday. "Did you know that the great majority of Puerto Rican units in service during WW II were stationed in the Canal Zone, and throughout the Caribbean, guarding vital U.S. installations?" Victor gave him a serious stare, making sure that Vaquero was listening. "Few were allowed to fight in the front, Puerto Ricans weren't really trusted. I was one of the lucky ones," he exclaimed proudly. Vaquero knew the history. Over 65,000 Puerto Ricans had served in the U.S. armed forces during WW II.

"I grew up in a poor *Barrio,* Ramon, military service in the armed forces was a way out of the dirt, filth, and poverty. *Yo era un jibaro*, without a job or future." A jibaro was a common designation for a rural Puerto Rican, a hillbilly. Ray listened attentively. "The military attracted many unemployed youth in the island searching for opportunity, and an avenue out of the *Barrio*. But they wouldn't allow many Puerto Rican officers either. Are you an officer?" Victor suddenly asked.

"No," Ray answered, as Victor leaned back in his seat and slipped back to his time.

"Most Puerto Rican officers were 'Americanos' back then, since some of the generals didn't trust us. Although some of us had fought in Europe, the word had gotten around that Douglas MacArthur had refused to use us in his operations, reflecting an official distrust of the Puerto Rican soldier. I had served with the 69th regiment, composed solely of Puerto Ricans, which made significant contributions to the defeat of the Nazi's," Victor said proudly. "What we did back then gave our people much credibility and respect." Victor, now a bit melancholy, looked at Ray with pride and a smile as he tried to stay awake. The warm rum had finally taken its toll on Victor Santana, and he fell asleep.

Vaquero remembered similar stories he had heard from his uncles, who had fought in the Korean War when the U.S. Army was short of troops and it had to turn to its National guard regiments. The 65th Infantry Regiment of Puerto Rico was put on alert, and brought to full strength and shipped out. The regiment's first assignment was to protect the main supply routes and engage North Korean guerilla units. But MacArthur had ignored intelligence reports and overstretched his defensive lines. The Chinese came down in great numbers and surrounded the First Marine Division in the vicinity of the Chozin Reservoir. The 65th Regiment went to the rescue and formed a corridor to relieve the besieged Division. Many individual acts of heroism were carried out by the Puerto Rican soldiers during that war. The regiment, nicknamed "*The Borinqueneers*," fought with great determination and valor but paid a high price in casualties. The troops, which General MacArthur had not trusted in World War II, had given a good account of themselves and saved his ass.

Vaquero was awakened by the jolt of the landing gear of the 747 as it touched down, and a simultaneous roar of exhilaration permeated the aircraft as the passengers celebrated a safe landing and the anticipation of being reunited with their loved ones. Vaquero was excited as well, though his parents wouldn't be there to pick him up at *Isla Verde* Airport. He just hoped that Manny and Cano would be sober enough to drive. If not, he knew the way home.

#   #   #

The aroma of *Asopao*, a Puerto Rican rice-based stew made with beef, permeated the bedroom. Ray scrubbed the sleepers away from his eyes as he struggled to read his watch. It was almost lunch time. He brushed his hair back and winced slightly as his head throbbed from a giant hangover. A warm ocean breeze stirred the curtains as it calmly blew through his window. It felt good to be home again, he thought.

For the moment, Ray didn't remember much after Manny and Cano picked him up at the airport along with several female companions. His head was about to explode, and the hunger pangs in his stomach growled reminding him that he hadn't had a decent meal for almost two days. Ray lit a cigarette and walked over to the window, and closed his eyes to listen to the distant sounds of waves as they crashed along the shores of *Luquillo Beach*. A sudden breeze covered him with the scent of tropical waters. He smiled as he reminisced on lost innocence and the fun he had at *Luquillo,* the endless hours of play until he would almost drop from exhaustion. Looking at the serene surroundings made him feel like he had grown up on a different planet. Brooklyn was never like this. Rosa and Miguel had finally made the right decision when they moved back to the island, Ray thought as he extinguished his cigarette.

About last night, Rosa would surely try to fill in the details as Ray laughed and struggled to put on his shorts. Real or imaginary, she would remember the how, when, and what condition he was in when he had arrived last night with those, as she called them, *"Cornu* friends," or better known as....cock hounds. Ray heard footsteps, then a knock on the door.

"Are you awake, *hijo*?" It seemed like an eternity since he'd last heard her voice, yet it sounded no different from when he was fifteen and she'd come into his room and coax him to get up to go to school.

"*Si mami,* it's OK to come in, I'm already up," Ray said happily wanting to see her. He met her halfway and put his arms around her, squeezing her tight as he picked her up and swung her around the room. Rosa was barely five-feet tall on her toes and weighed only a hundred and two pounds, but in that little package lived a huge and compassionate heart. Rosa laughed and squealed like a little girl. She always had a great sense of humor and it never took a lot of effort to get her to smile. Rosa could never tell a joke. She would uncontrollably laugh in anticipation of the punch-line. At that point, everyone would crack up in laughter without ever getting to the punch-line. She has gone through a lot of shit in life, Ray thought, as he looked into her cheerful, yet elderly eyes. Rosa knew how to keep her sense of humor, he mused, as he continued to swing her around the room.

"*Hijo*, put me down. You're going to make me throw-up, *por favor!*" Rosa laughed hysterically as he swung her around. "Your father will be home any minute, and he'll want to eat when he gets back. Please put me down," she pleaded. "You know how he gets when he hasn't eaten. He was waiting for you to get up to have his lunch." Her small feet gently touched the ground as Ray carefully held on to her. She grabbed his face and kissed him softly on the cheek. "It's good to see you again *hijo*." She looked into his eyes with adoration, and smiled a smile that mothers reserve only for their sons.

"*Vente*, into the kitchen, we'll talk there."

"Where's *Papi*?" Ray asked, expecting him to have been there when he had gotten up. Miguel Vaquero was always on the move, working, fixing, toiling. He never cared much for being idle. Ray would never hang around him too long because Miguel would find something for him to do, or worse, ask him to help him out at his upholstery store.

"He went down to the *bodega* to buy you some *Pan de Agua*. He knows that's your favorite with *Asopao*." *Pan de Agua* was a crisp crust bread that was only made on the island and difficult at best to duplicate back in the States. And when you ate it hot, it was a religious experience.

"*Hijo*, would you like to help me with the *plátanos* for the soup?"

"Sure, tell me what you want me to do." She took the *plátanos* out of the pan. They had just been fried and were ready to be rolled into ball size shapes and sprinkled with salt. Rosa knew just the right amount of olive oil mixed with garlic to pour into the *plátanos* to give them their unique savor.

Ray heard Miguel's voice outside the house, talking to one of the neighbors. "It's Dad, Mom, I'm going to go outside to greet him."

"*Vete*, go, hurry outside, he's been waiting to see you." Rosa began to sing so loud that the neighbors looked out their windows to see what all the excitement was about at the Vaquero home. She was in a festive mood, thanking Jesus and all the *santos* for her son whom she had almost lost at childbirth, was safe at home and with his family. It was moments like these that we were created, she thought. Rosa celebrated life, *la familia* and the joy it brought to her heart.

"*Oye papi*, where have you been?" Ray said jokingly, walking over quickly to him to embrace him.

"Where have I been? I was going to get one of the rats that lives under the house and put it in your bed if you hadn't gotten up by the time I came back from the store," he said with a half smile. Miguel was never comfortable showing affection, but Ray knew that he was beaming inside with joy.

"I was tempted to have your *pendejo* friends arrested last night for not bringing you straight home from the airport as they had promised," he said, feigning anger in his voice. His arms waved in all directions for emphasis. "They woke-up the neighbors with their *relajo* and giggling women in the car last night. Men will be men, but, don't let your mother know what you were doing with those women," he said wryly. "She'll keep me up all night, pestering me to explain what a nice boy like you was doing with those women at that hour of the night."

"Nothing happened, Pops, I swear. As a matter of fact, I don't even remember!" They both laughed uproariously as they embraced each other and headed back to the house.

"Here." Miguel handed him the bread. It was still hot. "I bought you three loaves, I know it's your favorite. They don't make this in Thailand, you know. This is the best bread in the world." The best was always from the *isla* for Miguel. He had a strong affinity for the island, and was proud of Puerto Rico and everything it symbolized. But on a global

scale Puerto Rico was still an impoverished American commonwealth
struggling to overcome wrenching poverty in the midst of glitzy hotels
and Vegas style nightlife for the tourists. Without a significant industrial
base to free it from its dependence on the States for economic support,
it was forever snared on its reliance on the U.S. government. For Ray,
the island continued to struggle to find its niche in the global scheme of
things while engulfed with the needs of the impoverished. But, as far as
Miguel Vaquero and the majority of its inhabitants of the island were
concerned, they were happier there than living in the shithole apart-
ments of Brooklyn. Miguel had always said that the size of the stage you
stood on in life was not of any significance. It was the character you
choose to play that was genuinely consequential to one's lot. There were
no illusions or fences that blurred Miguel's view of reality. Ray wasn't
going to try and convince him otherwise. He was right anyway. It was
also Miguels' way of expressing his concern about Ray's decision to go
back overseas. And although Ray hadn't told him specifically that he'd
be flying combat missions, he sensed Miguel knew he wasn't telling him
everything. His father also chose not to probe.

Rosa came out to the porch with her hands on her small waist, and
with a fretted look on her face.

"You two are worse than two gossiping whores on a street corner,"
she said mockingly. "The soup and the *plátanos* are getting cold! Don't
complain to me if the lunch is not the way you like it. I'm not going to
cook anymore today. *Se acabo!*" She was looking for sympathy and some
appreciation for her labor of love. Ray and Miguel looked at each other
and spontaneously began walking effeminately back toward the house
and babbling away, mimicking what jabbering whores would look like.
Upon their approach she made a bee-line back into the house laughing
hysterically at their gay performance.

"*Carajo, mami, esta sopa esta buena como tu,*" Miguel blurted. Ray
busted out with laughter too. The food was incredible. Rosa wasn't satisfied until they had finished the whole pot. Ray was happy to oblige

her, cleaning the bowl with the last piece of the crusty bread. When they were through Ray and his father helped her with the dishes so she could relax and sit to watch her favorite Puerto Rican *novelas*. While she was glued to the T.V., Ray and Miguel sat out on the porch catching up on local gossip, the family, the latest news from Brooklyn, and his Miguels' favorite topic, the Mets and why the Dodgers ever left Brooklyn.

Miguel never ceased to surprise Ray, when he would show certain sides of himself that was still new and unknown to him. Under that image of a tough-skinned, short-tempered Latin stereotype was a calm side that he'd seldom seen, and was often disquieting to Ray since he was unaccustomed to this delicate side. His father loved to listen to Spanish classical music by Andre Segovia, and his favorite, "*Bolero*" by Ravel. He would go into almost a trance-like state as he rocked in his rocking-chair out on the porch. As the melodic evening sounds resounded in harmony with Segovia's trilling guitar, Miguel had rocked himself to sleep. Ray kissed him on his head then headed back into the house.

Rosa was in the bedroom rolling back the sheets preparing to call Miguel to come to bed. She couldn't see her son who quietly watched her in the darkness. She had sacrificed a lot for him, Ray thought. Life had not been easy on Rosa and Miguel. Rosa would toil at a local garment district sweat house with corrupt bosses and unions that would tax her already meager wages with questionable union dues and medical benefits that were nonexistent. The family couldn't even afford to get sick since there was no way to pay for the expenses. Ray thought about other disillusioned Puerto Rican immigrants hopes that were extinguished in those rat-infested, shit-hole garment sweatshops. But no matter how bad things were, Rosa would always look at the bright side of things and say, "*Darle gracias a Dios*," thank God for our blessings. Life was difficult in the *Barrio*; a tough place to start out in life, compounded by the worries of trying to raise two daughters and a son. Miguel hadn't fared any better with his job in the city, and the daily constant bickering with his supervisors would take its toll on the family when he'd come home from work after a twelve-hour shift. Ray and his sisters would often dread his arrival, and often pray at times for their father should leave the family. Miguel would usually arrive in a bad mood and take out his frustrations on the family. Ray would raise his ire further by staying in his room in the dark, ignoring his father all together.

It was only now that Ray began to understand how difficult it was for Miguel to make ends meet. With just a sixth grade education, there was not much hope, or money, to afford to get out of the city. But one day, they gathered enough courage to say, "We're leaving."

"*Mami*, I'm going to bed. I'll see you in the morning." Ray walked over to her and kissed her on the cheek. "I love you, Rosa." Ray whispered. He wanted to tell them that he was sorry for disappointing them.

"What are your plans for tomorrow, Ray?"

"Manny and Cano are taking me to the Dorado Beach Hotel, and hang out at the beach."

"Why Dorado? You have such a beautiful beach here in *Luquillo*," she asked.

"Cano's uncle is an assistant manager at the Dorado, and he wants to have us over for lunch and to just basically hang out Mom." Her inquisitive nature was getting the best of her now. Ray knew what she was getting at, so he thought he'd get to the point. "We plan on checking out the girls along the beach," Ray said, looking at her with a wry grin, laughing now, unable to maintain a straight face. She laughed too, knowing better than to pursue the subject further. She knew that such activities were "men" things, and it was only natural that young men chased young and attractive women. It was nature's way of reminding us of our youth and innocence; their urges were only natural, she reasoned.

"Be careful with those friends of yours," she said in a threatening manner. "They can sometimes get a bit wild."

"Don't worry *mami*, we'll be okay," Ray said, as he started to head for the bedroom. "I'll see you in the morning, Mom. Goodnight."

"Goodnight, Ray," she said, as she went outside to get Miguel up and coax him back into the house and into bed.

The evening air was cool and damp as the sounds of *Coqui's,* a toad like amphibian, echoed throughout the surrounding forest. Ray lit a cigarette, and took a deep drag looking for the subtle little high of nicotine. The smoke refused to move in the still dank air. It just hung there unnaturally. The frantic buzzing of a mosquito caught his attention, as it orbited above Ray's head. His eyes adjusted to the darkened room, and he could see the mosquito frantically searching for a way out of the choking haze. Ray was enjoying its suffering. It would suck him dry if it got the chance, Ray assured himself. He wondered how it could see in the dark and thought that maybe it had Forward-Looking Infrared like a Spectre. Ray laughed halfheartedly. Suddenly, the little shit darted out of the cloud and headed toward the back of the bed.

"Great, just fuckin' great." Ray said, pissed-off now that he hadn't splattered the little shit when he had the chance. Now he'll be pestering me all night. "I hope a *Coqui* eats your blood-sucking ass," Ray whispered, as he cautiously got into bed and pulled the sheets over his head.

The morning came quickly as Ray Vaquero began to stir and listen to the sounds of the farm animals Rosa and Miguel nurtured, excited and looking for their morning breakfast in the back yard. The fragrance of mangos ripening in the warm Caribbean sun permeated his bedroom. Ray would climb up the eighty-year-old tree as a child to eat its succulent fruit and play on the massive branches for hours. Rosa's chickens cackled nervously as the head rooster swaggered out of his coop besides its harem, keeping them in line and ready to attack any intruder that threatened his domain. Boy, did he have it made, Ray pondered with a broad grin. Unlimited guilt free sex. Ray jumped out of bed excited that he was home, and a bit more relaxed than he had been the last few days. He needed to put the negatives in his life behind him for now, although he would never have considered his relationship with Suzanne as a negative. Things could have worked out between them, he thought again, unconvinced that it needed to end the way it did. "Fuck it," he blurted, releasing some of the anger and tension, resisting the temptation to put all the blame on Suzanne for giving up on him so quickly. "Shit happens, that's all."

"*Hijo?*"

"*Si mami*, hold on a second." Ray took a quick glance below his waist to make sure he didn't have one of his "early risers." It was so common place that he usually never gave much thought except when he was around women, and never quite understood what caused it or why it would happen in the first place. If nothing else it assured him that he was alive and functional at twenty-two years old. But for now he didn't want to embarrass himself. It was safe. "*Entra mami.*"

"You must have been really tired, *hijo*, it's almost twelve o' clock," she said with her maternal smile as she leaned back against the wall, admiring her son who was once a little boy not so long ago, she thought, had suddenly become a man. *Como se van los anõs*, she thought, reflecting how quickly the years had gone by, and how precious the little time you have with them before they leave the nest. You never lose by loving too much, you lose by holding back, she use to say to her children.

"Yeah, I must have been, I slept like a rock," Ray chuckled. "What's *papi* up to this morning?"

"He's down in the *pueblo* buying me some groceries. You know him, he'll take forever getting there and back. He'll stop and talk with everyone he knows and then say that the cashiers were slow." Rosa giggled. "What would you like to eat for breakfast, *hijo?*"

"I'm really not that hungry, but some of your specially brewed coffee would be just great right about now," he exclaimed. She would manually grind the fresh coffee beans in an old coffee bean grinder that had been in the Vaquero family for decades. Rosa Vaquero loved to cook, and got great satisfaction watching her family and visitors eat. It was usually difficult to depart from a Vaquero home on an empty stomach. "I'm sorry, but I promised Manny and Cano I'd go down to Dorado with them, remember? Cano's uncle Victor works there, and he's going to treat us to lunch," Ray explained.

"Will you be back in time for dinner? You know your father doesn't wait for anyone when it comes to having his meals on time," she said jokingly.

"It's OK," he said. "If I'm not back by five go ahead and eat, I'll have something later." Ray was also trying to factor in the probable mischief Manny and Cano were brewing once they got to Dorado.

The familiar melody of *"La Cucaracha,"* blared through Manny's quad-horns as he cornered slowly onto Ray's street in his 1965 red convertible Mustang. Manny bought the car with his re-enlistment bonus money last fall back at Camp Pendleton, in California, and wanted it to be in mint condition after he got back from his last tour. It made Ray think of his 68' yellow convertible, Pontiac Le Mans he had left in storage near Travis AFB outside of Fairfield, California.

"Buenos dias Señora Vaquero," Manny Rodriguez and Cano Rincón politely uttered in unison like two little school boys. Rosa suspiciously glared back with a lukewarm smile, acknowledging their presence.

"Hey Ray, are you ready to go? "Manny nervously looked at his watch. "It's getting late, and we're supposed be at Dorado by 3:00 p.m. If we hurry, we should make it in time for a late lunch." Manny was obviously anxious to get going, not wanting to explain their exploits to Rosa Vaquero.

"Sure, I'm ready. Let's go, "Ray said, eager to bail Manny out, but more importantly, Ray was ready to party hardy. "Tell Dad I'll see him later. Don't wait up for me." Ray jumped into the back seat of the car next to Cano's saxophone case.

Rosa hesitantly waved goodbye as the bright red Mustang turned onto the main road in the direction of Highway 3 toward *San Juan*, with its radio blaring Latin music at maximum volume. Despite her misgivings of Ray's friends, Rosa was overjoyed that her son was home on leave for the holidays. She knew she wouldn't see him again until morning. Rosa also knew that her son was in great pain. She had seen the torment in his eyes the morning she had walked into his room. It was that familiar dark hollow-eyed stare that revealed many sleepless nights full of anguish. But she had promised herself not to probe, lest she open wounds in him that had not yet healed. A mother can feel their children's pain as if they were their own, she thought. We forget many things in life as we grow older, but never a great love. Ray's love for Suzanne Logan was great, she thought. Rosa could see it by the change in his countenance whenever he spoke of her. Or in his reflective gaze as he stared into the distance in thought. Or in the softness of his voice and by the look in his eyes, full of infinite love and adoration. *"Great love overcomes great obstacles,"* she whispered. Rosa straightened her apron and turned back to the house, singing a Christmas *aguinaldo*.

Raymond Vaquero was taking it all in as they cruised down the highway heading toward Dorado Beach, just west of San Juan. The tropical scent in the air filled his senses, and it pleased him. For the first time in a long while Ray felt relaxed and was beginning to enjoy himself. Cano passed out bottles of the local Corona beer as Manny maniacally raced down the highway.

"Hey Cano, what's with the Sax?" Ray asked inquisitively.

"Manny's uncle, Victor, might let me play along with the band tonight." Cano said eagerly. "It all depends how shitfaced I get. The more plastered I am the hotter I play!"

"You take requests *mano*?" Ray asked jokingly.

"Anything you want Bro," Cano said confidently. "You name'z it, I'z can play'z it!" Ray and Cano laughed and punctuated the remark with the Latin version of the Dap handshake. They were in a festive mood as they sang along to *Carlos Santana* music, "I ain't Got Nobody to Depend On," as Manny anxiously raced toward Dorado.

It was the peak tourist season when travelers from the mainland would come to the island in winter in search of sun and fun and the lush island atmosphere with its nearly three hundred miles of coastline. The *isla* terrain was magnificent to look at from either the ground or the air. *Luquillo Beach* to the east near *Fajardo*, *La Parguera's* phosphorescent bay in the southwest part of the island, the lush central island mountain lakes, waterfalls and famous teak forest along with the dramatic karst mountains covered with limestone earth, pocked with deep conical sinkholes. The only sightseeing they had on their minds had to do with the female anatomy.

"Hey Manny," Ray yelled into his ear, trying to get his attention above the blaring music.

"Yeah man, what is it Ray?" Manny responded.

"Can we detour through the city? I haven't been through San Juan in ages. Would you mind?" Ray asked.

Manny smiled and nodded. "Sure *mano*. We should all take one more look before we leave. It'll be a while before we'll come back here," Manny said pensively, realizing that they all had another tour of duty ahead of them. "Better get a year's worth of an eye-full. It's going to be a long twelve months."

San Juan was filled with historic colonial buildings that had been restored to their original splendor. Some were almost five hundred years old, influenced by Spanish architecture, with wood balconies and pastel painted buildings. "I love this place!" Ray Vaquero screamed out loud as they left the city and headed toward Dorado Beach.

"Might as well go all the way guys and get Valet parking and let the *Mami's* know we have arrived!" They laughed as Manny pulled up to the main entrance and told the attendant to be careful parking the car. Manny slipped him a few dollars just to be sure his Mustang would receive special care. Manny led them to the manager's office and introduced himself to the attendant. Within minutes Manny's uncle, Victor

Cruz, arrived to greet them, then led them to a table by the pool that had been reserved for the special guests.

"Order whatever you want, gentlemen, compliments of the Dorado. If you need to spend the night, I've reserved one of the Executive suites for the three of you. There's no need for you to drive back home if it gets too late. I'll be in the office if you need me. Enjoy yourselves."

"Thank you for everything Mr. Cruz," Ray said, reaching over to shake his hand. Cano and Manny did likewise, appreciative of his hospitality. Victor Cruz, smiled then headed back to his office.

"Great guy, Manny. Have you always been this close to him?" Ray asked.

"I knew his son, Angel, pretty well. Victor would send him to my folk's house in the States during the summer months. He wanted to expose him to city life in case he ever wanted to live there as well as spend time with his other relatives who had left the island to find a better life in the city. We'd room together and share stories of growing up in the city and the island. Angel was a good kid."

Manny downed his beer then stared into the distance for a moment. "Victor lost his son in the *A Shau Valley* in the of Spring 1969. Angel was Special Forces, and his outpost was overrun after the Viet Cong and NVA were not too keen on the outpost's presence in their area of operation. His unit monitored the NVA lines of communication through the *Ho Chi Minh Trail* in *A Shau* and their supply operations in I Corp. There were no survivors." Manny paused for a moment, fighting back his anger. "Even wasted the fucking Montagnards women, children and animals in the Camp to punctuate their displeasure. Victor holds no hard feelings against the U.S. about what happened, you know. This is his way of showing appreciation to guys like us who are caught up in this shit. But I'm sure Victor is bitter that we're not trying to win this war and get the fuck out. This country thinks that by taking a defensive posture we'll win eventually. No fucking way man." Manny was seething now. "The NVA doesn't give a shit about how many of their people are sacrificed in order to achieve their objectives. The end justifies the means, literally. You know what I mean? It burns my ass when I think about the protesters bitching that we should stay out of it, and how the *Vietnam* war is a people's war. It's total bullshit!" Manny's voice started to get loud, and some of the hotel guests began to stare at them.

"Calm down Manny," whispered Cano getting in Manny's face for emphasis. Cano didn't want to get thrown out of the Dorado. But Manny Rodriguez was going to have his say and vent his anger because he gave a rats' ass. Manny stared down those who glared at them.

"Okay, I'm calm," he said in a whisper, but he wasn't through. "The fucking Party in Hanoi pays lip service to the people about sacrifice for the cause except it's always someone else putting their ass on the line for the Party. I bet if we had delivered some Cluster Bombs up the Party's ass in Hanoi in 1968, this war would be over years ago…and Victor's son would be here today."

"Manny, you're right," Ray Vaquero calmly interjected. "But the three of us accepted the risks, especially the fact that we're fighting a war with one arm tied behind our backs. And despite our governments miscalculations and blunders, it doesn't change the fact that we choose to be here." Ray paused long enough to look into their eyes. "Let's agree on one thing," Vaquero stretched his hand across the table. "Let's agree that we all come home. No one stays behind." Manny and Cano nodded in silence as the three joined hands.

"Agreed," blurted Cano, breaking the silence. "All this talking has made me thirsty." Cano then guzzled his beer. Ray and Manny laughed. "Fuck the Party." Cano stood on the table to make a toast with an empty glass. Manny and Ray stood for the ceremonial proceedings with their right hand over their heart.

"*Ho Chi Minh* is a faggot," The three of them repeated as hotel guests stared at them through their sunglasses. Ray and Manny lifted Cano from his chair and flung him into the pool.

"Come on, Cano, let's go." Manny and Ray pulled Cano out of the pool and anxiously headed for their room.

Vaquero stood out on the balcony of the ninth floor suite gazing at the cloudless azure sky while Manny and Cano changed into their bell-bottom and platform shoes.

"What's on your mind, Ray?" Cano asked as he towel dried his hair.

"Nothing really. This is all so, surreal. I could easily forget where I'm going in two weeks and get totally wrapped around this island," Ray said nostalgically, but also with a sense of guilt.

"Yeah, I know what you mean, Ray," Cano responded. "Just making love to your main squeeze in the heat of the day…have mercy!" Cano howled at the thought of becoming entangled with a willing partner. "Did you leave anyone back in the States, Ray?" Cano asked.

"Yeah, I did." Ray let out a long breath as if it were a hidden secret held in his soul. "It's over now though. It's better not having any attachments in light of where we're going. I don't want to be thinking about some guy trying to pork my girl while my ass is being shot at."

"Fucking-A Ray. If you worry about your squeeze you're bound to mess up, and the *pendejos* back home will get the girl in the end anyway when you're six feet underground. Put all the emotional shit aside *mano*. Live one day at a time." Cano offered a reassuring smile as he combed his hair in the mirror.

Not surprisingly, they had the best table in the club. And like radar, Ray, Manny, and Cano immediately scanned the club for prospective targets for the evening. Manny, not known for being shy instantly walked toward a table where three females were seated and asked one of them, a short brunette with huge breasts to dance. Cano and Ray were busting up in laughter as they watched Manny grind dance with his partner. She soon excused herself and went back to the table before the music was over.

"Gee, Manny, *que paso*?" asked Ray, shaking his head at Manny's crude exploits. "Not too smooth, *mano*."

"Just give it time," Manny said confidently. "There's always one out there that appreciates the fine art of grinding."

The band played a mixture of contemporary tunes from the island and the States to the delight of the crowd. Ray Vaquero had not asked anyone to dance yet, and Manny and Cano were too absorbed with their new partners to have noticed. Slow music set the mood as the lights were dimmed in the club. A figure approached Ray from the right side of the table.

"I've been watching you for some time now, and you look like you're not having any fun at all." A tall slender female smiled warmly at Ray as she pulled out the chair next to him and sat close enough to where her knee pressed against his thigh. Ray felt a sudden rush as he noted that her miniskirt had shortened as she crossed her legs, exposing further the details of her firm shapely figure. "Would you dance with me? I love this song. By the way, my name is Carrie."

"Hi, I'm Ray." He obliged her without reservation. 'When a Man Loves a Woman,' played as Ray and Carrie walked on to the crowded dance floor. Manny and Cano gave Ray a thumbs up in support of his decision to participate in the festivities. Carrie caressed the back of his head as they slowly swayed across the wooden floor in fluid motion. Ray was embarrassed as he was aroused by the smell of her perfume as she pressed her firm body up against his, but made no effort to distance himself from her. Beads of sweat formed on Ray's forehead as Carrie gently pressed her waist against his in rhythm to the passionate love song. Vaquero struggled to repress the emotion that was stirred by the love song and how it reminded him of Suzanne Logan. When the lights were turned back up Ray saw that Carrie had auburn hair, large almond green-yellow eyes; just like Suzanne's he thought. Shit. Her hair hung slightly below her shoulders and her penetrating eyes made him stare at her more so.

"Thank you," she said with her infectious smile. "Do you have a last name?" she probed, while she toyed with his hand.

"Vaquero. Ray Vaquero," he said sheepishly. He felt a little nervous and it made him uncomfortable.

"Do you mind if I sit with you?" Carrie asked.

"Sure." Ray pulled out the chair for her as the barmaid came by to take their order.

"You don't look like you're from around these parts Ray Vaquero. Are you?" Carrie asked wanting to know more about the stranger.

"I'm not a permanent resident, but I was born here. My parents live about 25 miles from here, in *Fajardo*. My friends and I are on military leave for a couple of weeks before we go back overseas for a tour of duty. I was raised in Brooklyn New York, but my roots are here. Any other questions?" Ray thought he handled that well without getting defensive about his past or the war.

"So, you're looking for a good time." Carrie pursed her lips, smiling, thinking that she had cornered him with a loaded question.

"Yeah, in a way," Ray replied pensively. "I want some good times, to remember when there are bad times." Images of Suzanne surfaced as he stared at Carrie, who was now fidgeting with his fingers. He nervously lit another cigarette.

Manny and Cano approached the table dangling from their female companions, totally shitfaced. "Hey Ray, how's it going man! I want you to meet Nancy, she's down here on vacation from L.A." Manny had his hands all over her ass, squeezing and massaging as if rolling dough. He'd make a great baker, Ray chuckled to himself.

"And this is Julie." Cano loved his women tall and thin.

"Hey Cano, when am I going to hear you play?" Ray asked, more interested in getting absorbed in sentimental music than dry conversation. There wasn't anything particularly wrong with Carrie, but his thoughts and sense of faithfulness, was elsewhere. Cano pulled his arm away from his female companion.

"What would you like me to play?" Cano asked Ray as if he owed him a favor.

"Well, my favorite, very favorite tune is, Jr. Walker and the All-Stars, 'What Does it Take to Win Your Love for Me,' and 'Shot-Gun.' But can you handle it in your condition?" Ray asked Cano, knowing that the question was posed as a challenge and not a query. Cano was being dared.

Cano unfurled his wry grin, performed a military about-face and headed for the bandstand looking for his saxophone. The club was silenced as its attention was drawn to Cano and the saxophone's introductory wail. The other musicians joined in and supported Cano as the audience rocked and clapped their hands to the rhythm of the beat. Carrie stroked Ray's arm, examining him with her all knowing smile and penetrating eyes.

The audience gave Cano a standing ovation as he stepped off the stage and headed back to Ray's table. "That was good Cano, I mean, really good." Cano was sweating profusely. While Cano and Manny were planning their next move with their companions, Carrie slipped her room key into Ray's hand.

"Excuse me, I'll be right back." Carrie said as she took her purse and left the club. As she reached the door, Carrie looked back at Ray with her captivating smile. Manny and Cano had noticed the nonverbal exchange directed at Ray.

"Why you sly dog," commented Manny. "All the while we thought you weren't having a good time. I can see you're about to go out on your own patrol, huh?" Ray just grinned and casually flashed the room key that Carrie had surreptitiously placed into his hand. "Well, so much the better," Manny declared. "Now we'll have the suite to ourselves," he said to Cano, grinning from ear to ear.

"I'll check with you…later?" Ray remarked, knowing that they actually wouldn't see each other again until the next morning. Although, Ray wasn't sure whether this was something he wanted to do, except for the part of his brains that resided below his waist was urging him on; he was about to explode.

"Sure, let's stay in touch." Manny laughed as they gathered up their things and started to leave the club. Ray settled in his chair for a moment pondering his next move. He finished his beer then headed toward the elevator. When he knocked on the door to Room 324, there was no answer. Maybe she decided against it as well, Ray thought, although a part of him wanted her to be there. Ray used the key. The room was dimly lit with one of the night lights by the bed on. Ray felt a breeze coming through the balcony, carrying along with it Carrie's perfume. As his eyes adjusted to the faintly lit room, Ray could make out Carrie's image out on the balcony.

"Well, you finally made it," she said jokingly. "I thought you were going to get cold feet and change your mind at the last second. I'm glad you decided to come, Ray." Carrie's eyes glittered in the moonlit night. She was dressed in a thin black silk robe, exuding passion, as she stared at Ray with sensual eyes.

"It's a beautiful night, isn't Carrie?" Ray said, trying to continue a conversation yet consciously trying to avoid the inevitable. Carrie just smiled her gorgeous grin as Ray spoke, uninterested in his discussion of the universe. She gently placed her hand on his mouth, moved closer, and kissed him in a way to impart a response, and he responded willingly. She cautiously led him back into the dimly lit bedroom. They embraced as long lost lovers often do, infiltrating the other's shattered soul, rejoicing in the exhilaration of the moment and indulging themselves in the physical bond.

Carrie Holland had contrived her plan before she had ever set foot on the island. Depressed and tired of unfaithful and floundering relationships, the lies and broken dreams of long gone former lovers. For once in her life she was doing something out of her own volition; totally without hope or false pretenses. She was bent on screwing her brains out for revenge sake, and Ray Vaquero would be the instrument of her vengeance. She was delighted as she used and toyed with him for her own pleasure. Carrie guided him through all the empty avenues and voids of her essence, littered with anguish, anxious yet goading the pending force beneath her. She exacted all of him, and he willingly responded to her instruction. Emotionally detached, yet yearning for fulfillment. Callous…yet tender. Throughout it all, Vaquero was totally mesmerized with thoughts of Suzanne Logan, oblivious to Carrie's form, whispering instead the name of his former lover.

"I didn't have any preconceived expectations about this evening Ray. I hoped I pleased you," Carrie said as her lips gently explored his neck. They were both physically spent. Ray Vaquero smiled assuring her that she had. "I hope you don't mind staying the night. I just don't want to be left alone," She pleaded. "I'm always a little nervous by myself in the dark. Are you?" Carrie asked, covered in perspiration, as she moved closer to him for warmth.

"No, not really," Ray remarked tenderly, trying to comfort her. "Sometimes what you can see is more disturbing. The dark is not necessarily all that bad," he said pensively. Vaquero turned around to face her and stared deeply into her green-yellow eyes.

"What are you going to do overseas Ray?" She asked inquisitively.

"Oh, just a job that someone has to do…in the dark," Ray whispered. As the hours of love making finally consumed them, Vaquero could no longer stay awake and fell asleep. Carrie drew closer to comfort him, as an evening tropical shower came upon Dorado Beach, cooling the evening air.

In the morning, Carrie had checked out of the hotel by the time Ray wakened. It was one o'clock in the afternoon. She had not left her address or phone number, but only a note that said, "You never lose by loving too much, you lose by holding back."

CHAPTER FOUR

It was 1:40 in the afternoon when the lumbering C-141 gently touched down at *Ubon* RTAFB. *Ubon* had been a sleepy agricultural province of 25,000 people, until the U.S. Air Force arrived in 1962. The base was strategically located in the eastern plateau of *Thailand*, too far for the *Viet Cong* or *North Vietnamese* army to antagonize, but ideal for the U.S. Air Force to launch punishing raids against *North Vietnamese* supply lines. The base strength had grown to 5,000 strong by 1971. When the bombing of *North Vietnam* was halted in 1968, the Wing's mission had turned to interdiction against the flow of supplies along the *Ho Chi Minh Trail*. But more importantly, to buy time for a hasty U.S. withdrawal since the United States would no longer politically support or bleed for South Vietnam any longer.

It was already a hot and humid day at *Ubon* Royal Thai Air Force Base. There wasn't a cloud in the sky when Ray Vaquero stepped off the rear of the cargo aircraft with a hundred new arrivals. The base was bustling with activity as his lungs filled with exhaust fumes as F-4's roared on the runway. Accustomed to the humidity of Asia, he didn't think twice about the perspiration that was already soaking through his flight suit. Scents long forgotten resurfaced in the warm, damp, Asian breeze. He shifted the duffel bag strap as it began to dig into his shoulder, while he slowly walked toward the main terminal. Ray instantly spotted the AC-130 gunships a short distance away. The left wings hung a bit lower to the ground due to the seven-thousand pounds of armor plating along the left side of the fuselage. They looked ominous covered in black-green camouflage as they rested, waiting patiently in their revetments as maintenance and munition crews readied them for the missions that began at dusk. *Thor,* the mystical god of war and thunder, was painted between the pilot's window and crew entrance door. A menacing figure grasping a 20-mm Vulcan Gatling gun with a half crescent moon in the background.

At the terminal entrance was a large welcome sign with the logo of the 8th Tactical Fighter Wing, better known as the *Wolfpack.* The Wing had four F-4D Phantom tactical fighters squadrons and other specialized detachments that were critical to the Wing's mission. Tactical air support along with weather and rescue units were essential to the total mission. Also assigned to the Wing was the 16th Special Operations Squadron that flew the AC-130 gunships.

"Yes, sir, this is Sgt. Raymond Vaquero. I just arrived, can I get a ride to the barracks?" Vaquero asked the duty officer.

"Sure, Vaquero, welcome to the 16th," the duty officer responded. "I'll have Walters drive by and pick you up. He should be there in a few minutes."

Within minutes a beat-up old jeep appeared. The driver, slammed on the brakes inches from Vaquero. James Brown music blared from the radio. "Hey man, you Vaquero?" The driver had a broad friendly smile.

"Yeah, that's me," Ray said, grinning back at the driver who was unfazed that he almost ran over Vaquero.

"Mike Walters, nice to meet you man," Walters extended his hand. "Just throw your shit in the back. I'm supposed to take you over to the barracks. Welcome to the Third World my man," the black buck-Sgt. said jokingly. Vaquero quickly threw his bag in the back of the open jeep and jumped in next to Walters. As the vehicle started to move forward, Walters spit a huge wad of tobacco juice toward the sidewalk that splashed onto a Thai MP's spit-shined boots. Ray looked back to see whether he would come after them, but he just stood there in total shock and amazement. Walters just grinned as he maneuvered around the narrow road toward the barracks.

"You just in from the P.I. man?" Walters asked.

"Yeah, spent a week in Jungle Survival School. Pretty mild shit compared to Basic Survival School," Ray said, pondering the mental stress he went through during basic survival school in Spokane, Washington, learning how to survive in the event he became a P.O.W.

"No shit." Walters blurted in agreement.

"You'll like your quarters," Walters commented. "The Illuminator Operators and Flight Engineers live in the same barracks, I.O.'s downstairs, flight engineers upstairs." Walters still had that wall to wall grin on his face. "I'm flying tonight, so I'll just be dropping you off. I need to get back for preflight and mission briefing. I might see you later this evening since I'm on the first flight out at 1700 hours. It's a great fuckin' job, Vaquero. The guys are great and so are most of the crews," he said happily. "Just make sure you find the right crew and you'll be all right. There's no other high like it!"

Walters suddenly slammed on the brakes again in front of a fairly modest looking two story building. He kept his hand on the horn until the occupants from the barracks finally came outside to see what all commotion was all about. "If you need a bunk, there's an extra in mine, room number two, last door on the right. You're welcome to bunk in with me. Just make yourself at home, Vaquero. You don't have to worry about doin' your laundry or shoes here either. We have a house boy named *Bai* that takes care of all that shit for 100 *baht* a week. That's five bucks my man, and it's worth every penny, especially if the head *Mamasan* throws in a little pussy." Walters cackled and spat another large brown wad on the grass as he got out of the jeep to help Vaquero with his duffle bag.

"Hi, I'm Scotty Wilson, but you can call me Scumbag." Walters laughed at Wilson's matter-of-fact introduction, as he poured an ice cold can of Olympia Beer over Vaquero's head.

"It's a pleasure to meet you…Scumbag." Ray responded, cringing from the ice cold beer.

"Watch out for that mothafucka, Ray. You'll learn soon enough why they call him Scumbag." Walters cautioned Vaquero, laughing and pointing a menacing finger at Wilson. Scotty Wilson chuckled along with Walters. "And make sure you sleep on your back and lock your door at night too. You never know what shit he's up to," he cautioned as Walters and Scumbag exchanged amusing evil eye stares with each other. Ten other I.O.'s introduced themselves and poured their beer over Vaquero.

"It's a tradition of the 16th that when a new arrival comes in that we take their picture just so after twelve months you can look back and see how much you aged in one year." Heads nodded in agreement through-out the group. "Who's got the fucking camera?" Wilson bellowed, as one of the IO's handed him a Polaroid camera and another positioned Vaquero in front of the barracks entrance. Several flight engineers casu-ally looked in on the proceedings from the top of the staircase on the second floor.

"Smile." Six large pails of water were simultaneously dumped on Vaquero from the roof of the barracks, staircase, and from a fire hose manned by three I.O.'s hidden from Vaquero when he had first arrived. Ray was knocked off his feet from the force of the water.

"Welcome to the 16th SOS Vaquero," Scumbag said with a snorting laugh at the look of surprise still frozen on Vaquero's face. Scumbag placed a Cuban *Cohiba* cigar in Vaquero's mouth. "You know what bunk you have?" Scumbag asked. Ray nodded in the affirmative. "In two or three days after you're done with your administrative bullshit, get your flight gear together ASAP and we'll get you some flight time and hope-fully on a crew within two weeks. Maybe sooner. It all depends how

soon we can arrange getting your ass shot-off." Scumbag leaned over
and lifted Vaquero's duffel bag and headed toward the barracks. "Give
Pappy Duncan a call at the Squadron once you're dried off. We all work
for Pappy around here."

Vaquero struggled to stay on his feet as he headed down the hall
drenched, leaving puddles on the floor after every step. Greetings were
extended as he passed by the rooms as others were hastily getting prepared for the evening's hunt. He changed into some dry clothes and
unpacked his things into his metal closet. Vaquero walked back down to
the middle of the barracks where there was a lounge with a bar, TV, and
a couple of very worn-out beer-stained tables that appeared to be frequently used for some very serious card games.

"Sixteenth SOS, Chief Master Sgt. Pappy Duncan, may I help you
sir?"

"Yes sir, this is Sgt. Raymond Vaquero, I just got in today. Uh, Scotty
Wilson thought I should give you a call." Ray was a little nervous, not
knowing what to expect.

"Hey Ray, welcome to the 16th," Duncan responded cordially. "Aren't
you a little early? We weren't expecting you for another week."

"I decided to come over a little earlier than planned, plus I was anxious to get over here." Ray hoped that didn't appear odd to Duncan.

"Well, that's shit-hot Vaquero, we'll just start your training earlier
that's all. We could always use the extra help." Duncan replied, eager to
have the additional help to carry the load. There was always someone
grounded with either an ear block or a severe cold. "There's an orientation briefing scheduled for tomorrow at 0800 hours at the Squadron
Operations briefing room. Have one of the guys point you in the right
direction in the morning. After you're done, stop by my office. We'll talk
for a while and I'll see what I can do to get you squared away." Vaquero
got a good feeling about Duncan. "And by the way, you can call me
Pappy. I'll see you after your orientation Vaquero." Ray smiled as he
hung up the phone.

Hunger pangs rumbled in his stomach. "Excuse me, can one of you tell me how to get to the chow hall?" Ray asked three individuals who were on the edge of their seat intensely watching an old 'Twelve O' Clock High' rerun.

"Hi, I'm Bob DeSena. How are ya? I'm going over there. Hold on a second, let me get my wallet." DeSena was a muscular individual, and stood about six feet tall with thick jet-black hair. "The chow hall is about a quarter of a mile from here, but would you be interested in going into town and getting some *Thai* food?" Bob asked, looking toward something more exotic than the daily ration of meat and potatoes.

"Sounds good to me," Vaquero replied, eager to savor some *Thai* cuisine again. "I'm game, let's go." *Ubon* looked no different from any other foreign U.S. installation that Ray had toured. At the gate were the impoverished selling anything to willing Americans. And those that had no commodities to sell made sure you took note of their deformity as they approached you with an extended hand. Vaquero and DeSena pushed through the crowd of humanity and quickly jumped into the waiting cab.

"*Thai Palace*," Tony DeSena instructed the cab driver as he tried to ignore the merchants and beggars attempting to get their attention, with outstretched arms reaching through the open window. The cab driver shouted some obscenities to the crowed as he made a U-turn leaving a trail of chocking red dust as the cab headed down the main road into *Ubon*. Within five minutes they were at the *Thai Palace,* an upscale *Thai* restaurant that catered primarily to the U.S. serviceman and well-to-do merchants of *Ubon.* Bob received a special greeting from the hostess; it was obvious he was a frequent patron of the restaurant. She was extremely striking, with large black piercing, almost round shaped eyes, dressed in traditional *Thai* attire. She stood about 5'7, tall for a Thai, and graceful as she made indirect eye contact with Ray Vaquero.

"Well, I already know what I want Bob," Ray said with eager anticipation.

"What might that be?" DeSena asked, not yet getting an opportunity to look at the menu.

"*Yum Nuah* and a big bottle of *Thai* beer." Ray was famished.

"What the fuck is *Yum Nuah?*" Replied DeSena. "I don't even see it on the menu, Ray. It better not be monkey meat or I'm going to get extremely pissed-off," DeSena cautioned Vaquero.

"Trust me." Ray smiled at DeSena, and turned to the hostess who was patiently waiting for the two patrons to order. "Two *Yum Nuah's* and we'll each have a bottle, make that two large bottles of *Thai* beer." The hostess gazed at Vaquero when he was not looking then lowered her eyes when he looked back at her. Her stares had not gone unnoticed.

"Hey Bob, stop complaining, I'll pay if you don't like it OK? I'll even buy you another dinner if that makes you happy, alright?" Ray retorted confidently. "Fair?"

"Fair," remarked DeSena.

"How long have you been with the 16th," Ray asked. The waitress arrived with what appeared to be quart size bottles of beer. She intentionally poured them slowly into the glass so that it wouldn't create a large head of froth. Bob DeSena waited until the waitress left before continuing the conversation.

"You can never tell who's listening," DeSena said calmly. "She's got a great body doesn't she? Her name is *Toi Dasananda*." Vaquero nodded affirmatively as they both licked the foam from their lips and watched *Toi* bend over to pick up some silverware that had fallen on the floor and thought how appropriate her name was. "You always have to be aware who might be listening or asking probing questions about the 16th and its mission. It sounds paranoid I know, but, you just never know." Vaquero listened attentively. "The NVA can't strike at us in force but you can bet they have their agents here picking up tidbits about the AC-130 capabilities and our mission. Little things that may seem harmless, like flying altitudes, munitions, number of crew on board, sensors. That kind of information might just be enough to give them the edge they need to shoot your ass out of the sky." DeSena glanced around the room to see whether anyone was paying any special attention to them. "I have a simple philosophy about this place Ray," DeSena said, looking intensely into Vaquero's eyes. "First and foremost, trust your instincts, it'll keep you alive." Sharp instincts and quick reflexes were far superior to conscious thought in war if one was to survive. DeSena momentarily remembered when Willie Santiago had shared the same words of wisdom with him. He guzzled his quart of beer in record time, then waved to *Toi*, pointing to his glass expressing that he needed a refill.

"You asked me how long I've been here, didn't you?" DeSena lit a cigarette and seized a long drag from his Marlboro. Scratching his forehead, there was a long introspective pause. "I just extended for a second tour." DeSena grinned. "I believe in what we're doing over here though it's for a lost cause. If we weren't out there every night slowing the supplies and challenging the NVA at every pass, the South would have been lost a lot sooner." DeSena was absorbed in thought and grappling with the reality that the U.S. military's hands were constantly tied with political restrictions, and not given a chance to win.

"Another reason why I extended is that *I love to fight*," DeSena said in a subdued tone and half smile as he glared back at Vaquero, gauging his reaction.

Toi finally arrived with their dinner. *Yum Nuah* was prepared with strips of beef marinated in a delectable Thai sauce that included garlic, celantro and hot chili peppers on a bed of fresh lettuce and tomatoes. Although DeSena shed a few tears over his meal due to the hot chili peppers, he grudgingly agreed with Vaquero that it wasn't bad. In the morning Bob DeSena would give his initial assessment of the new arrival to Pappy Duncan and figure out what crew Vaquero would be assigned to and determine whether he might be a liability. DeSena was good at assessing a man's character under casual settings. He could

immediately spot the ones with major insecurities or the dangerously
overconfident, young, dumb, and full of come types. Can't have a
swelled head or appear that you know all the fucking answers. DeSena
thought about Willie Santiago again, and how his life had come to a
sudden end. Nobody had their shit as tightly wrapped as Willie. But no
one was invincible in Vietnam, not even Willie Santiago. Everyone fal-
ters sometime along the way, DeSena thought as he reflected momentarily about the price one pays for failure, both in life and in war. In any
event, Bob DeSena truly relished the opportunity to kill *North
Vietnamese.*

"When the Viet Cong got the living shit kicked out them during Tet
in 68', it forced the North to send NVA regulars down south to replace
their losses and establish hardcore defenses over some of the more critical passages that needed to stay open at any cost. They had brought lots
of their favorite toys with them to just to let us know that they planned
to stay in business and keep their supply routes open." DeSena stopped
talking long enough to consume some of his dinner. "Rumor has it that
they are planning a major offensive in the Spring that would include an
attempt to go for Saigon in the process. They're not planning on making the same mistakes they made in 68, you know." The student listened
attentively, clinging to every word.

Vaquero and DeSena's stomachs were about to explode after almost
two quarts of beer and lots of spicy food. "My treat," Vaquero asserted,
as he waved to *Toi* to come over in order to pay for the dinner.

"Fucking chili pepper seed is stuck between my teeth," DeSena
exclaimed, as they laughed at his attempt to dislodge it. *Toi* began to
laugh while DeSena struggled to dislodge the burning demon seed nestled between his gums and teeth.

Vaquero and *Toi* gazed at one another for several seconds as DeSena
was finally able to pry it loose. Her smile was infectious and warm.

"Please come back and visit us again sir," *Toi* remarked in a gracious
tone.

"I promise, I'll be back," Vaquero said as she escorted them to the door.

The cab driver that had taken them to the *Thai Palace* was still parked outside the restaurant. "Back to base my man," DeSena commanded the taxi driver as they jumped in. He nodded and made one of his kamikaze U-turns in the mist of oncoming speeding traffic from both directions. Vaquero and DeSena howled in excitement at the maneuver and cowered at the moment they had crossed the main intersection expecting to be hit head on. The frenzied car maneuvers caused DeSena to belch and fart and fill the cab with the pungent odor of regurgitated beer mixed with Thai spices. The driver began to dry-heave as he fought back the desire to vomit due to the stench and was obviously cursing and pissed-off as he struggled to keep his head out the window and clear the vehicle of the foul odor that had consumed them. Vaquero had lowered his window, laughing uncontrollably while hanging halfway outside of the cab himself.

"What's wrong with you two?" DeSena said innocently. When they reached the base DeSena offered to pay for the cab and threw in a little extra tip for the unexpected accident. Vaquero and DeSena struggled again through the masses of humanity clustered around the gate at *Ubon*, as another Spectre was taking off and heading east across the *fence*.

#   #   #

"Good morning gentlemen, my name is Captain Carl Peterson, operations and mission planning officer for the squadron. Welcome to the 16th Special Operations Squadron, Royal Thai Air Force Base, *Ubon*." Peterson was a tall, lean fellow with glistening light brown hair and he reminded Vaquero of Robert McNamara, the Secretary of Defense.

"As part of your initial orientation this morning, I will be covering a brief overview on the mission of the 16th Special Operations Squadron and the unit history. Major Stuart Marks will cover operational objectives as well as anticipated enemy offensive this Spring. I understand that some of you just arrived last night, so please bear with us and we will try to complete the briefing as soon as possible and let you go back to the barracks and settle in." Peterson turned several pages in his briefing package until he found the page he wanted.

"On October 5, 1967, the 16th Special Operations Squadron came into existence with five aircraft. The 16th SOS was then put under the command of the 8th Tactical Fighter Wing at *Ubon*." A fairly large map hung in the background, covered with various color coded tape outlining enemy major supply routes, depots, staging areas and their defenses.

"One of the early challenges of the air war in Southeast Asia was to adapt existing aircraft in the American arsenal to the unique needs of this war. Since the early days of the conflict, the United States has possessed total air superiority in Southeast Asia. That has presented an opportunity to apply these advantages to support ground combat operations and to disrupt the *North Vietnamese* supply and troop movements into *South Vietnam*." Peterson walked over to a large map already on the stage, pointing to the myriad of enemy logistical supply routes.

"The Air Force high command had long been looking for an aircraft that could saturate the ground with fire power for interdicting enemy movements along the many roads and passes along the *Ho Chi Minh Trail*. Gunship theory was a simple one, gentlemen. As most of you learned at Hurlburt Field, by flying an aircraft in a banked left-hand turn to aim side-mounted guns at a fixed target on the ground provides you with the capability of keeping your side-firing weapons continuously pointed at the target. Swivel-mounted machine guns on World War I airplanes fired laterally at air and ground targets. Our initial needs' assessments determined that the aircraft had to be able to hit small moving targets in dense terrain, and through the thick Asian jungle canopies. Another important aspect of the development of the gunship was that it had to be survivable because it had to loiter for long periods of time over targets. But more importantly, it had to possess great firepower. Due to the nature of the *Vietnam* conflict, and dense tropical terrain, current Air Force combat aircraft have difficulty finding enemy targets at night or are obstructed by the dense jungle canopy, unable to use their enormous fire power at hand. Compounding the situation, the enemy often uses the cover of darkness and the difficult topography to mask their supply movements. After much research and development at the Air Force laboratories and testing at Eglin Air Force Base, the C-130 cargo transport had been selected for modification for combat duty, to eventually replace the Spooky AC-47's and Stinger AC-119 gunship and assigned the primary role of interdicting enemy supply movements from the north into *South Vietnam* during the hours of darkness. Of the three kinds of gunships the Air Force uses, the AC-130 has become the preeminent truck-killer of the war." Peterson paused for a moment, drank a glass of water, and asked, "Any questions?" No one raised their hand.

Capt. Peterson turned off the lights in the room and began talking from view graphs he had projected onto a screen. Seventh Air Force Operations Order 542-70 spelled out the mission priorities for the AC-130 Gunship, or as it was more commonly known as, 'Spectre.' Due to the variety of engagements for gunships, PACAF wanted Spectre to concentrate their firepower offensively. The orders from the Seventh Air Force delineated a priority mission statement for the Spectres:

- Night interdiction and armed reconnaissance to destroy wheeled and tracked vehicular traffic on roads and sampan waterways.
- Night interdiction of targets that have been bombed and then hit with fire suppression missions.
- Close fire support of U.S. and friendly military installations including forts, outposts, and strategic towns and cities.
- Search and rescue support.

- Offset firing in support of troops in contact by use of aircraft radar and ground beacons.
- Daylight armed escorts of road and offshore convoys.
- Harassment and interdiction.

"That concludes my part of the briefing, gentlemen. If you have any questions, please feel free to stop by my office down the hall next to the operations room. Thank you for your attention." Capt. Peterson looked to his left and nodded to a figure whose presence Ray Vaquero had not noticed earlier. Major Stuart Marks was a well-physiqued, red-haired fellow, about forty-five. As he approached the podium, the Major scanned the room carefully for a few moments as if looking for a familiar face or a long lost friend. His slightly weather beaten fair skin features told of multiple tours endured in the hot tropical climate of Southeast Asia. And although Peterson said nothing about the number of missions he had flown, Ray sensed that the major had flown a shitload. There was just an air about him that exhibited confidence, and a leadership quality that mesmerized Vaquero.

"Gentlemen, good morning. Light them if you have them. Just don't throw the butts on the floor, otherwise Colonel Roberts will have me working overtime tonight." Laughter filled the room as the Major cut the tension in the smoke filled room.

"I want to tell you that I had the honor of flying the original prototype and I'm proud to say that in the initial evaluation the first Spectre destroyed over 2000 vehicles, and an estimated 600 KBA *North Vietnamese* troops on their way to the south. No fighter aircraft can match the kill ratio of this aircraft." The Major exuded confidence and determination in his voice.

"During the monsoon season, we've taken advantage of the down time to upgrade Spectre's sensor, avionics, and armament capabilities and stay one step ahead of the enemy. Our six AC-130E's have been equipped with 105-mm Howitzers which obviously provides a bigger punch but also a higher flying altitude and distance from threatening triple-A.

The remaining six AC-130A models have also been upgraded with a digital fire control computer and improved sensors as well. Since the closure of the 1970-71 hunting season campaign, the *North Vietnamese* have been able to expand the *Ho Chi Minh Trail* by three hundred miles. The tempo of the conflict had been intensifying until the seasonal monsoons had come into play last year, and decelerated their logistical push to the south. This intensification is primarily driven by the *North Vietnamese* and Viet Cong requirement of a heavier flow of supplies to *South Vietnam* due to their dire need to supply their force's deep penetration and increased attacks into *South Vietnam*. Supplies are reaching the communist forces in *South Vietnam* over hundreds of roads in the Laotian panhandle." Marks pointed to the key infiltration routes.

"It is through *Laos* that they carry the greatest supply tonnage and troop infiltration. Wherever possible, they also transport cargo by river. The NVA have been busy during the wet season. Much of the road network has been upgraded for year-round use. It appears that due to the length of the monsoons, *North Vietnam* has changed some of their tactics and have made their logistical support work crews stay in the trail area through the wet season keeping the trail in repair year round. It didn't take them long to figure out that we're not able to strike back effectively twenty-four hours a day." The Major paused for a moment, lit a cigarette with his Spectre Zippo lighter and filled his lungs with nicotine before he continued.

"The NVA are primarily moving supplies during dawn and dusk. They're so cocky right now that we're hearing that they're actually traveling with their lights on. Specialized road repair crews have been restoring the Trail and constructing alternate routes when the main passages have been heavily bombed or impassable. Most of the roadwork and movement of supplies take place at night. You can also expect increased numbers of antiaircraft weapons defending vulnerable Trail points this year. Intelligence reports show that the *North Vietnamese* have expanded their protection of the trail with more accurate weapons. I'll get into the triple-A threats a bit later. Weather will also be pivotal in the interdiction effort. The Southeast Asian monsoon season generates seasonal periods of bad and good weather for air operations over the Trail. From May to November air operations over Laotian trails are poor due to bad weather but the enemy wasn't going anywhere either. He's been digging in and storing supplies along the way. With the northeast monsoon comes clear dry weather over *Laos*. November to May is characteristically known as the 'Hunting season' gentlemen."

"Let's see, have I missed anything?" Major Marks grimaced, going over in his head what he had briefed and assessing if he left anything critical out. "We are also supporting road watch teams who work with the indigenous supporters of the south. They look for the hidden trails, and determine main traffic routes that the NVA is using that we can't detect from the air. You will occasionally be in contact with them if they need close air support." Manny and Cano thought Vaquero, and the prospect of engaging the enemy with his friends.

"During the 1971-72 hunting season campaign we expect to concentrate our efforts in Barrel Roll, a northern *Laos* region, and Steel Tiger East, the eastern *Laos* panhandle which has the most important routes running from three major mountain passes. You'll get to know them as the *Mu Gia, Ban Karai*, and *Ban Raving*. We are also considering supporting the *Cambodian* theatre due to the enemy's increased efforts in utilizing the Mekong River as another avenue of transporting supplies into *South Vietnam*. *Khmer Rouge* insurgents have been attacking convoys traveling up the Delta. Seventh Air Force is evaluating that situation and considering Spectre support in escorting the convoys destined to *Phnom Penh*. Phase one of our strategy is to attack the enemy at key interdiction, or choke points at specific road segments where it would be difficult for them to detour when blocked or divert them to predictable alternative roads. B-52's will attack main interdiction boxes to setup choke points and channel the traffic to predictable locations." The objective was simple; force the trucks to travel over longer exposed distances.

"Tactical aircraft will also be used to pound critical mountain passes with laser-guided bombs. Phase two blocking belts will consist of aerial mines and sensors implanted across narrow road areas. Acoustics and seismic sensors will also be embedded over alternate bypass routes. Hopefully, the folks with their computers at NKP will be monitoring the enemy's movement and their attempts to avoid the mine fields and blocking belts. At that time Spectres will be directed to attack and destroy the traffic jams behind the blocking belts." Marks took a moment to light another cigarette.

"The plan is phased to the expected pattern of the NVA logistic efforts which entails heavy movement of supplies and troops through the *Mu Gia, Ban Karai,* and *Ban Raving* passes early in the dry season. Supplies have been stored at key route points known as *Binh Trams.* At these junctures, supplies would then be shuttled to other *Binh Trams* in *Laos, Cambodia,* then into *South Vietnam.* Abnormally low rainfall in August and September has accelerated an early start of truck movement along these passes. As you are well aware, you will be supported by flak-suppression 'Wolfpack' F-4D escorts to attack triple-A sites and vehicles along the main transportation corridors and along alternative routes. This will be your primary mission in life, men. Secondary missions will be seeking out truck parks and supply caches, fuel depots, and lastly to seek out and destroy whenever possible antiaircraft artillery.

Intelligence reports suggest that more than 10,000 trucks moved through the main corridor last month with an estimated 5,000 tons of supplies to prepare for the Spring offensive. They are planning something big this year, men. What they don't know is Spectre will be waiting for them."

"Operational channels for mission assignments come from the 7th Air Force through the 8th Tactical Fighter Wing to the 16th Special Operations Squadron. The 7th Air Force tactical air control center exercises battlefield direction through the airborne command and control center, known as Moonbeam for the Steel Tiger region, Alleycat for Barrel Roll, and with on location assistance of Forward Air Controllers and Road Watch Teams. In the final analysis men, we believe that the Communists are amassing men and supplies for a major offensive this Spring. We expect that it is to be carried out by a large conventional force. To impede this force, interdiction of these forces and their supplies has become a high priority mission for the 16th SOS." Marks paused again to drink some water.

"I want to say something now about triple-A. The *North Vietnamese* antiaircraft defenses are growing in strength and have improved in accuracy. Surface-to-air missiles are growing in number southward as they are now protecting their main transportation corridors, as I had mentioned earlier. We have estimates that there were about 800 antiaircraft weapons ranging from 23-mm to 100-mm with increased radar capability in place at the close of the 1970-71 dry season. We expect that antiaircraft weapons along the critical corridors will have increased by 25 percent by the start of this campaign. The NVA have gone through great pains in camouflaging their gun emplacement and have moved them to preplanned sites to avoid detection. It also appears that the guns and surface to air missiles have not been moved from their sites during the rainy season, and they have greatly fortified their positions." Marks grinned after his last remark.

"Well, there you have it. I also want to inform you that I have been asked to put together a crew for my third tour. I look forward to flying with some of you within the next month. Thank you for your attention, and remember," he said jokingly, "you got away with fucking up at Hurlburt. There were no triple-A threats in the Gulf of Mexico, or SAM missiles to worry about. But here...ah shit Peterson, I forgot to show the tape. Go ahead and roll the projector. I think the film will speak for itself." The Major had started to walk off the stage but then turned back quickly. He wanted to punctuate a point and drive a message home. He stepped away from the microphone and stood as close as he possibly could to the edge of the stage to emphasize his point.

"You know, what you're about to see would scare the shit out of most sound men," he said with a broad assuring smile. "But I want to impress upon all of you that our successes so far are not solely due to superior fire power or tactics, but as a result of teamwork and oneness. Remember, we're all one team on Spectre, one aircraft, one body. By the way, this film will also give you an appreciation for your I.O. who will be leaning outside the aircraft retained only by a restraining harness…make sure you take care of the I.O." The pain of Willie Santiago's death still haunted Marks.

"How many I.O.'s are in the room?" the Major asked. Vaquero raised his hand. His was the only one that was raised, and heard someone jokingly whisper "Dumbshit," from the back of the room.

"Take a look at him," Marks barked. "There's no technology around yet that can anticipate the direction of antiaircraft fire better than your I.O. He'll be watching your ass while you're smokin' Charlie on the trail." The briefing room was deadly silent. Vaquero fired the 'bird' in the direction of the snide remark as he lowered his hand. "Lets get the job done and end this war as soon as we can. Good day gentlemen."

The officers and enlisted men in the room rose to attention as Major Marks left the stage, smiling and waving at everyone, then casually looking in Vaquero's direction before leaving the room. All Vaquero could think of was how he was going to get assigned to Marks' crew and whether he would be given a choice in the matter. He estimated that it would be at least two weeks of training with an instructor before he'd be assigned to a flight crew. But then, there was no way that the Major would be interested in an unexperienced I.O. The room suddenly went black as Capt. Peterson turned on the projector. The film was a documentary on the *North Vietnamese* use of Russian and Chinese weaponry and their application throughout Southeast Asia in defense of their convoys. Ray was fascinated by the orchestrated fire power display. It was common for AC-130 Gunships to encounter multiple 37-mm antiaircraft guns with interlocking fields of fire when engaged on a hot trail in pursuit of a convoy. Trail gunners wouldn't look for a fight unless there was something of significant value for them to protect, Vaquero thought, frantically trying to instantly recall everything he had been taught at Hurlburt. Trail gunners weren't any different than himself Vaquero reasoned, as he watched the enemy employ its massive arsenal from ground level, a definite 9.5 on the sphincter-tightening scale. The trail gunners were possessed combatants when it came to defending their convoys. They had reason to be fearless. Vaquero was familiar with the stories about gunners that would chain themselves to their weapon or steering wheel of the truck so that they wouldn't run in fear. What balls, he thought, but stupid as well. There are times to fight, and there are times when it is far better to duck and try again another day. The thought of going out at night looking for a fight added to the suspense and the mystery of the hunt, and the knowledge that the antiaircraft gunners would be stalking him as well. It also brought back memories of venturing over the fence with Manny and Cano. Except over here, there wouldn't be enough of you to put in a body-bag after being blown out of the sky. Just enough for a late evening snack for all that squirms and crawls in the dark under the triple canopy jungle abyss.

CHAPTER FIVE

The Squadron area was bustling with activity as the operational staff planned for the evening missions. Behind the operations counter was a large white board that listed each aircraft's tail number, take-off time, and assigned crews. Vaquero had noticed that Major Marks had put together his crew, and he quickly scanned the board to take note of which I.O. had been delegated to Major Marks. "Duane Shaw," he whispered. Vaquero let out a long sigh of disappointment.

Vaquero walked slowly down the hall toward Duncan's office but was drawn to loud voices coming from the squadron's commanders office. He couldn't help but stick his head inside as the commander, Colonel William Roberts' and Major Stuart Marks were engaged in a heated discussion regarding Duane Shaw. Colonel Roberts was a short, stocky, well built individual with muscular forearms. The veins in his neck looked like they were about to explode as he jabbed his finger into the air for emphasis, while Marks calmly looked on, impervious to Roberts badgering. Both sensed another presence in the office and coldly glared at the intruder.

"Can I help you, Sgt.?" Col. Roberts asked sharply, with an icy authoritative voice.

"Ah, yes sir, I'm sorry, I'm ah, looking for Sgt. Duncan," said Vaquero nervously, embarrassed that he had been caught snooping.

"He's down the hall, last door on the left," replied Col. Roberts with a more cordial tone. "I haven't seen you around here before, son, did you just get in?" asked the Colonel.

"Yes sir, I arrived yesterday." Vaquero thought he stepped into some deep shit this time, and wanted to hide. "My name is Raymond Vaquero." He moved closer to shake Roberts hand.

"Well, I guess you've figured out who I am," he said with a broad smile. "Let me introduce you to Major Stuart Marks." Marks extended his hand and welcomed Vaquero to the 16th SOS. Vaquero sensed Marks deep penetrating eyes look through him, as if appraising the essence of the man before him.

"It's a pleasure meeting you both," said Vaquero. "I'd better be going now. Sgt. Duncan is expecting me." Vaquero saluted them and walked briskly down to the end of the hall.

Robert Duncan was on the phone with his feet propped up on the desk when Vaquero walked in the office. He waved at Vaquero to come in and pointed to a seat next to his desk as he continued his conversation on the phone. Pappy Duncan looked to be about forty-eight to fifty years old, with a full head of grey hair. A large flight schedule board hung behind him with the names of the squadron I.O.'s. Vaquero's name had already been penciled in next to Scotty 'Scumbag' Wilson, and was scheduled to fly the following night. Duncan hung up the phone and quickly walked toward Vaquero.

"Hi there, Ray, welcome to the 16th, we're glad to have you," Duncan said as he firmly shook Vaquero's hand. Duncan had a broad indulgent smile that was easy to warm up to. Vaquero could see why everyone called him 'Pappy.' "Come over here and take a chair. Let's talk for a few minutes before we walk over to the flight equipment hootch and get your gear all squared away." Pappy sustained his smile as he offered Vaquero a cigarette. He leaned over to light Vaquero's, then his, as he sat at the edge of the desk.

"Are you all squared away in the barracks, Ray?" Duncan asked.

"Yeah, I'm OK. I'm bunking with Mike Walters. He's quite a character." Duncan nodded, and smiled in agreement. "I had dinner last night with Bob DeSena."

"And how did that go?" Duncan asked.

"Just great. I could surely learn a lot from him. Tony filled me in a little on the squadron's mission, objectives, and what's expected of me."

"You think you're up to it, Vaquero?" Duncan suddenly interjected, with a mindful gaze.

"I think so." Vaquero thought his response was short and not a very reassuring one. Duncan's broad smile rounded his face again as he stood up and patted Vaquero on the back.

"Don't worry about a thing, you'll be ready by the time we let you go out on your own," Duncan assured him. "Let's go get your flight gear squared away."

The 16th SOS Squadron was next to the 8th Tactical Fighter Wing Operations building, and virtually on the flight-line. Aircraft exhaust fumes stirred the hot Asian air, elevating the already agonizing 98 degree temperature. Idling F-4D engines suddenly surged to a deafening roar as their afterburners kicked in to lift them off the ground with their lethal ordnance tucked under the wings. Vaquero and Duncan held onto their hats as they walked toward the flight equipment building.

"Hey shitheads, let's get some fucking service here," Duncan said calmly, pounding the counter with his fist, but with his patented smile. Two technicians were engrossed in repairing a survival radio Spectre flight crews carried when they were out over the Trail.

"Sure, Pappy, what can I do for you?" one of the technicians responded, obviously callous and unruffled by Duncan's remark.

"I need you to take care of this here new I.O., Sgt. Raymond Vaquero. He needs the same old shit, locker, helmet, oxygen mask, and a .38 pistol that doesn't shoot straight." Duncan winked at Vaquero while he lit another cigarette.

"How much?" Asked T.Sgt. Hunter.

"Five bucks," Pappy shot back. Pappy and Hunter would always bet on who could come closer to guessing the new arrival's helmet size. Hunter had a reputation and could accurately gauge anyone to within a half inch. But occasionally he was wrong, and Pappy hoped that this was his day. Hunter casually looked over the myriad of helmets stored in a box under a table. He glanced back at Vaquero then reached under the table behind his desk and coolly selected a flak-helmet that was within an eighth of an inch of Vaquero's head size. Pappy handed over the five, and with his index finger, beckoned Hunter to lean over the counter so he could whisper something belittling into his ear. Hunter laughed, enjoying the abuse as much as Duncan.

"Your locker is number 428," remarked Hunter. "Fourth aisle on the right." Vaquero signed for rest his flight gear that included his web-gear vest, oxygen mask and a blood chit. The blood chit was a silk scarf with an American flag with messages in several Asian languages inscribed on the waterproof material with promises to financially reward those helping in the escape and evasion of a downed airman and help return him to friendly forces. Radios and a .38 pistol would be issued during pre-flight. The web-gear was full of much needed equipment in the event Vaquero unexpectedly found himself running around in the jungle. Pyrotechnic flares, compass, water bottles, strobe light with an infrared filter to camouflage his whereabouts from the enemy.

Vaquero walked down to his assigned locker and hung his vest and oxygen mask on the metal rack. The small, square locker was used to store personal items prior to a mission. Dog-tags were the only form of I.D. permitted on a combat mission. Vaquero removed from his wallet one of two pictures of Suzanne Logan that he carried and wedged it into the upper right corner of the locker. Vaquero stared at the picture for an eternity, mesmerized by her beauty and his one-sided love affair. Her countenance was innocent, yet coy. Distant, yet attainable, he thought. It was a picture he had taken while she intently studied in his room in the Spring of '69. He desperately fought to repress emotions that centered in his chest, like a massive weight that shortened his breath whenever he thought of her. He gently touched her smiling face and faintly whispered, "I'll see you in my dreams…"

"Ray, are you done yet?" inquired Duncan as he quietly observed Vaquero from the center aisle.

"I'll be right there," replied Vaquero as he wiped his eyes, secured his locker and hooked the key onto his Dog-tags. Vaquero headed out the door with Duncan when T.Sgt. Hunter called them back in.

"Hey Vaquero, I'll make sure that someone on the next shift modifies your flak-helmet with a new face shield," remarked Hunter.

"Thanks Sarge," replied Vaquero, as he waved goodbye, then headed out the door back to Duncan's office.

"Let's see, what's left for you to do, Ray?" Pappy was thinking about what still needed to be done before Vaquero could legally fly.

"Go down to medical and get your foot prints and dental charts examined, then come back here and you'll fill out your SAR personal identification codes in the event you find your ass shot down," Duncan said with a broad grin. During a rescue operation there was a good probability that the enemy would be also monitoring the rescue attempt with captured U.S. radios. Some enemy radio operators spoke perfect English, and would attempt to draw the Search and Rescue operation into a trap and shoot it down. Each flight crew member kept in his personal file three questions the SAR team would ask prior to a rescue attempt. All you had to remember were the answers to your questions while your ass was all puckered-up waiting for someone to get you out of there. Foot prints and dental charts were necessary for I.D. purposes in the event your body was charred beyond recognition along with your dog tags. Your feet were probably the only parts that would be preserved, protected by the thick jungle boot.

Vaquero was drenched with perspiration by the time he got back to the barracks after a quarter mile hike. A cool blast greeted him as he entered the building. The barracks lounge reeked with the smell of stale beer as the I.O.'s were heavily engaged in several friendly card games. Mike Walters was the dealer in what appeared to be a serious game of Blackjack. Scumbag was seated at another table teamed with Bob DeSena and Pappy Duncan picking the pockets of two other cherries. Stale cigar smoke and loud music consumed the tiny lounge.

"Kiss my nigger ass!" Walters bellowed, "Blackjack! I win again." Walters was on a roll with several hundred dollars stacked in front of him. "I tell you what chumps, why don't you just co-sign your piddly-ass paychecks over to me cause I own your cracker ass!" Walters cackled loudly as he intentionally taunted those around the table hoping they'd be pissed off enough to want to get even and keep playing. Most of them just laughed at Walters' antics, but one of the victims sitting directly across Walters leaned forward and aggressively flipped him the 'bird,' a hair's length away from Walters face.

"What the fuck is that supposed to mean, mothafucka?" Walters asked, giggling at the same time. "Is that a number one? Oh, oh, I get it Shaw, you giva numba one blow-job," Walters exclaimed in an exaggerated oriental accent and protruding buckteeth. Everyone in the room roared with laughter at Walters' put-down and humiliation of Duane Shaw. With clenched fists and stiffened muscles, Walters prepared himself for a fight. He coldly gazed back at Shaw with a menacing stare, prepared to strike. "Don't let your mouth write a check your ass can't cash Shaw." Pappy Duncan, Scumbag, and Bob DeSena began to move away from the table, prepared to jump in and break up any skirmish. Vaquero took a step back as well.

"Fuck it. Fuck you Walters, and the horse you road on. I quit," a defeated Shaw huffed, then headed down the hall to his room slamming the door.

"Hey Vaquero, rookie, you're fresh meat and new from the world," queried Walters, obviously impervious to Shaw's remark. "Why don't you pull up a seat here, just where Shaw's fat ass was," he whispered under his breath. "You see all this money?" Walters spread his winnings which were now in excess of two-thousand dollars, across the table for Vaquero to see. "It can be all yours, all you have to do is take a chance, and play like a man. That's all there is to it." Walter's facial expression was sinister. His right eye brow was raised higher than the one on the left.

"Uh, no thank you. You're hot. Maybe some other time." Vaquero laughed. Walters was disappointed that Vaquero wouldn't give him a chance to pick his wallet. Ray grabbed two warm beers from a case on the counter then headed down to his room to get out of his flight suit. A cold shower was definitely in order. When he got to his room, the houseboy was sorting out his laundry. *Bai Simaphon* was a short, dark skinned, lean Thai barely five feet tall. His warm pleasant smile greeted Vaquero as he entered the room, and he bowed to Ray with his hands together and pressed against his forehead. Ray reciprocated the gesture then tossed *Bai* a beer. There was a knock on the door, and without waiting for a response Scumbag walked in with a broad shit-eating grin. A cigar hung from the corner of his month that was totally drenched with saliva.

"Well, it has been decided. It's time to bust your cherry…cherry," Scumbag bellowed as he rolled his eyes in a Groucho Marx imitation. "Pappy thinks you're ready so we're going to start you out a day sooner. We're going into eastern *Cambodia* tonight. You'll know more during the mission briefing." Still smiling, Scumbag looked at his watch. "You've got two hours to get your shit together. Meet me at the equipment hootch at 1700 hours. Take-off time will be at 1900 hours." Scumbag disappeared as quickly as he had arrived. Vaquero looked at his watch, it was three in the afternoon. He was as ready as he could be he thought. Vaquero laid down in his bunk for an hour to collect his thoughts. The shower could wait until later.

The flight equipment trailer was busy with activity as flight crews prepared for the evening's hunt. Scumbag was already wearing his web-gear, extremely relaxed with his feet propped up on the table, as he casually sat in the mission briefing room gnawing on his cigar and humming an old favorite tune.

"Let me help you with your shit," Scumbag smiled, and showed Vaquero how to make sure his survival radios were functioning properly and how to check out his parachute.

"Never take anything for granted my man, or your shit will be blowing in the wind."

The mission briefing was businesslike and mechanical as the pilot, Capt. Stan Buckner, went over the mission objectives. A TIC, troops in-contact mission in support of Cambodian forces under attack along Route 7 in the *Fishhook* area that bordered with *South Vietnam*. U.S. intelligence agencies had long believed that *COSVN*, the Communist Central Office for *South Vietnam*, otherwise known as the NVA's Pentagon of the South was somewhere in the *Fishhook* vicinity.

The *Fishhook* was a densely jungled stretch that pointed east into *South Vietnam*, filled with elephant grass and dense forest. A great place to hide troops and supplies from an army that wasn't allowed to pursue them into a supposedly neutral country. Massive rice paddies and rubber plantations covered both sides of Route 7, a frequently used supply line by the North, although they would never admit that they were in *Cambodia* exploiting a weaker neighbor.

Scumbag's crew relished the night stalking missions and thrived on the rush it provided. But they also took their jobs seriously. It was much more than just taking care of business; it was also at times very personal. "People's revolution my ass," pondered Scumbag as he showed Vaquero how to secure the pins that held his chest-pack parachute safely together. The *North Vietnamese* were just as corrupt as the South but in a perverse ideological way, Scumbag fumed. Driven by politically self-serving dissolute idealists that were anesthetized to the daily slaughter of their people. While the U.S. was obsessed with body counts, the North never gave the slaughter a second thought. And why should they, there were plenty of sheep that were regularly fed to the sacrificial ideological altar. This was a war of wills, not of power. Scumbag stabbed his thumb as he secured a loose pin into the safe position.

The evening lights of *Ubon* glistened as the lumbering Spectre was lifted into the night sky by the Allison T-56 four-bladed Turboprop engines. The AC-130E gunship sensors were aligned after three orbits around the city, using familiar spots on the ground as reference points, it then headed southeast toward *Phnom Penh*. Within ten minutes they would be across the Mekong River, *the fence*. A sharp, acrid odor of spent gun powder entered Ray Vaquero's nostrils as he scanned the interior of the cargo compartment while he rested on the hard cargo ramp door seat next to Scumbag. The AC-130E gunship was a flying arsenal, loaded with ninety-five 105 Howitzer rounds, six-hundred and forty 40-mm Misch-metal rounds that were highly pyrophoric on impact. The front guns were loaded with three thousand 20-mm rounds. Vaquero turned his head back around, and lit a cigarette to stay warm as Spectre 12 leveled-off at 5,000 feet while he gazed at the vast evening darkness before him. The terrain was flat and the moon light cast giant shadows on the jungle floor below them. Cambodia's central lowlands were surrounded by rolling grassy plains called savannahs. In southern *Cambodia*, the plains ran all the way to the Vietnamese border and the sprawling Delta of the *Mekong River*. But to the east, north, and west, the savannahs gave way to mountainous regions covered with dense tropical forest. Along the borders with *Laos* and central *Vietnam* was a region of high plateaus, short steep mountain ranges and thick forests. The NVA and *Viet Cong* traversed through these twisted footpaths of mountain slopes, utilizing canoes through the myriad of streams in the region towing supplies for offensives into *South Vietnam*. At one time, the region had provided uncontested sanctuary from U.S. bombings and massive military assaults against their safe havens. Still, after the U.S. and South Vietnam's incursion into *Cambodia* in 1970, *North Vietnam* would admit nothing about their operations in a supposedly neutral country. They were a back door threat, a thorn in the side of

South Vietnam's regime, and a detraction from the major offensives that were to take place in March.

Vaquero stared at the LAU-74, a four tube flare launcher that carried 24 parachute flares, bolted to the cargo compartment floor next to him. He thought about the LAU's chief drawback of flares occasionally hanging up in the tubes after being partially ejected. Vaquero thought about having to dislodge one from the tube while hanging out of the rear of the aircraft. Thoughts of accidentally being lit like a Roman Candle made him laugh for a moment. Twenty Mk-6 white flare marker-logs were stored under the LAU-74 and were used to mark ground targets. How the hell an I.O. could accurately mark a target by throwing the marker out the rear of the aircraft traveling at over 250 mph was beyond comprehension for Vaquero.

"Let's get our shit on," ordered Scumbag. "We'll be over the fence in a few minutes." Vaquero and Scotty Wilson quickly took off their flight suits and put on thermal underwear that would protect them from the harsh cold air that rushed through the open-door gun ports. Vaquero began to perspire as he labored with the additional clothing and his survival web-gear. He finally was able to maneuver himself back to his seat next to Scumbag. A few flights under his belt and he would be acclimated to wearing the added equipment, he thought. His chest-pack parachute harness felt uncomfortable. Better that it's a little too tight than fall out of his harness, he decided. Scumbag smiled from ear to ear, happy as a clam, gnawing on his cigar and truly happy with life.

Vaquero finally couldn't resist any longer. "Well, when are you going to tell me?" Vaquero asked with an inquisitive smile.

"When am I going to tell you what?" Scotty Wilson retorted with a baited smirk.

"Why do they call you Scumbag?" Vaquero asked. Wilson fiddled with his chin strap for a moment before looking back at his trainee.

"A little over a year ago I went back to the States to visit my folks. I hadn't seen them in a while. I had extended my tour for another year so

I thought it would be a good idea to get back there to see them again." The gun crew was standing around listening to Wilson. Apparently they had heard this story before, since there were smirks on their faces. "I'd been shacked up with a local, and when I told her that I'd be going back to the States to visit my parents, she got all distraught thinking that I wouldn't ever come back. She swore on all the gods in Asia that she would wait for me and would be forever faithful." Wilson occasionally giggled as he told the story.

"Lights out, we've crossed the fence," commanded the navigator Capt. Collins. The cargo compartment was in total darkness for a few seconds before the flight engineer turned on the low intensity interior red lights. "We'll be over the target area in twenty minutes."

Scumbag stood up and walked toward the edge of the ramp and stared at the dark jungle abyss below. He tugged on the restraining harness cable to assure that it was securely attached to the metal ring located in back of his parachute harness before he laid flat on his stomach, resting on a rubber cushion. The pad provided temporary comfort from the cold hard ramp floor. It was also used to absorb the shock from the bumpy ride and from the web-gear digging into his chest and ribs. Scumbag waved to Vaquero to come forward. Vaquero secured the spare restraining cable to his harness ring then slowly crept toward the edge of the ramp. Scumbag pointed out the dim orange glows of smoldering enemy camp fires burning in the outskirts of the city as they approached the periphery of *Phnom Penh*. Smoke from enemy camp fires made its way through the triple canopy and could be easily seen on the clear moonlit night.

"All bad guys, Vaquero," Scumbag said with a wide grin as they gazed at the potential threats below. "They would like nothing better than to squeeze your nuts in a vise if they had a chance to," Scumbag chuckled. "When I came back to *Ubon* after my two weeks leave, Jackie, that's what she calls herself, was ecstatic when she saw that I had returned. I guess she thought I wasn't coming back, and appeared to be a little surprised when I got out of the cab in front of our bunga-low. She was hot, Vaquero, I mean fiery." His cigar was saturated with saliva, and he would spit tobacco just about every other word. "I was-n't in my bungalow for more than ten minutes when she was taking off my clothes and dragging me into the bedroom. Boy, I didn't realize how much I had missed her, and how much she missed me until then. Jackie wasn't into foreplay, you know. She would wiggle and moan wildly while I would get her all hot and bothered. Everything was going great until Mr. Woodchuck headed down to the beaver." The gunners were busting a gut with laughter. "Suddenly, I feel this rub-bery shit in my mouth…a fucking Trojan!" Scotty Wilson, the gun crew and Vaquero roared with laughter. Scumbag just shook his head and spit a large wad of tobacco onto the ramp floor. The gunners went back to their assigned stations as Spectre 12 airspeed decelerated and began to orbit around the embattled camp, Fort Savoy.

The navigator was busy talking with the ABCCC and Savoy's com-mander, validating firing coordinates and waiting for the order to com-mence firing. Booth sensor operators were busy acquiring and storing targets into the digital fire-control computer as they waited for the clear to fire authorization, as Spectre's weapons were primed and eager to enter the fray. Fort Savoy and the surrounding jungle exploded with 60-mm mortars and Rocket Propelled Grenades. Vaquero and Scumbag watched in amazement at the explosive barrage as rockets slammed into the camp from the north eastern quadrant of the encampment. RPG rounds, which were intended to penetrate eleven inches of armor plat-ing, were now converging on the command post that housed communi-cation radios and the camp's only link to the outside world and fire support. NVA sapper mortar and RPG teams were busy providing cover fire for shadowy waves of the 66C NVA Division that slowly crept toward the triangular shaped fort. Savoy was only defended by eighty seasoned Royal Cambodian regulars, five Kit Carson Scouts, and ten U.S. Special Forces advisors that were monitoring the enemy's use of

Route 7, a major supply route that was critical to the *North Vietnamese* supply effort into the south. Savoy was about to get its teeth kicked in.

"They're in deep shit," Scumbag blurted calmly. "If we get any triple-A, let me make the call, OK?" Vaquero nodded in agreement as the fire fight around the camp intensified. The NVA and the Viet Cong had been exploiting the eastern border regions of *Cambodia* and *Laos* for some time now, and the *Fishhook* had become an important integral part of Hanoi's war. They couldn't afford to have Savoy disrupt their logistical routes. As it was, they were a bit stretched already. The camp had to fall.

"You're cleared to fire," commanded the navigator. "The camp commander takes responsibility for any short rounds." A High Explosive 105 round was loaded into the gun breach of the Howitzer in preparation to take on the mortars that were pounding the camp. Meanwhile, several platoons of VC and NVA headed toward the southwestern wall of Fort Savoy after RPG sappers had blown a huge passage through the triple row of concertina wire that strung across the berm. Shrapnel and dirt pelted the camp with hail made of steel.

All of a sudden, the shelling that had been pounding Savoy had suddenly slackened. Scared but determined the camp defenders cautiously popped their heads over the berm line. But everyone around the perimeter knew what was going to happen next, and it wasn't that the attackers were going to pull back and go home. The mortar barrage was just the appetizer as a battalion of the 66C NVA Regiment had deployed behind the jungle that surrounded Savoy, was preparing to assault the camp; they were coming to kill them...all of them.

The lull in the battle was broken by the ghostly sounds of bugles along the tree line. Whistles and shrill screams could be heard by the fort defenders as the enemy psyched themselves into a frenzy in preparation to storm the triangular fort. Sappers circled the camp along the tree line prepared to follow the initial assault team and fire a barrage of RPGs around the post's perimeter.

"Clear!" Barked the gunner after loading the 105 Howitzer and its five-pound high explosive then closing the gun breach behind it. Booth sensor operators fed the fire-control computer the locations of the mortar positions that were pounding Savoy. The high incendiary explosive had a kill radius of twenty-five yards, and one by one, Spectre drove nails into twenty mortar sites in less than ten minutes. The mortars had been silenced.

"Arm the 20's," the pilot barked impatiently, fully aware of the fort's predicament. The flight engineer engaged the toggle switch that armed the Vulcan 20-mm gatling guns.

"The 20's are armed," Replied the flight engineer, then stepped toward the pilot's window to get a good view of the 20-mm Vulcan's spew red tracer rounds as they exited the left side of the aircraft. Sounds of a buzz-saw gone mad rattled the gunship as the Vulcan gatling gun arched streams of red steel into the wood line and along the fort's perimeter.

"Give me a flare every third orbit Scotty," ordered Capt. Buckner as he tightened the Spectre into its attack orbit.

"Flare out." Scumbag launched illumination flares from the LAU-74 every five minutes, exposing the enemy's attack. The flares illuminated the base camp and the surrounding wood line in an eerie white light, as wave after wave of screaming silhouetted figures came into focus as a result of the flares. The NVA were making a full frontal assault from all three sides of the triangular camp, as swarms of them came like ghosts through a mist. Their round pith helmets and RPG weapons were highlighted by the LAU-74 flares. Savoys' triangular defense line erupted like jackhammers as the antagonists came into view. Reinforcements were pulled from the eastern wall to fight back the breach of the southwestern wall. A small reaction force of eight brave but scared Royal Cambodian loyalist troops and a U.S. advisor greeted the sappers that had penetrated the berm with a torrent stream of M-16 and M-79 grenade fire, quickly eliminating twenty NVA at the mouth of the command post entrance. Another one-hundred and fifty screaming NVA infantrymen charged out of the tree line from the southwest quadrant of the fort in a final effort to penetrate and over-run the fort defenders. They had to cross a flat, open clearing where only a one-foot berm awaited them at the end, the fort's weakest link. A volley of RPG's ripped the night air over the berm, pinning the defenders to the ground. A spooked and foolish nineteen-year-old Cambodian soldier stood up on the berm in awe of the approaching enemy when at the same moment a NVA attacker fired at the shadowy figure. The inexperienced soldier was spun around and fell backwards into a trench as an AK-47 round ripped into his head. Red bubbles slowly flowed from his forehead.

The NVA senselessly rushed across open fields and into full view of Spectre's sensors and directly into the path of the 20- mm Vulcan. The camp defenders stood up from behind the berm to shoot those that somehow made it through Spectre's wrath as they appeared out of the eerie veil of smoke and dust. NVA bodies were literally being ripped apart and strewn along the perimeter of the camp. Savoys' three 105 Howitzers were hastily adjusted to ground level to fire thousands of razor sharp flechettes into the charging force. Bright orange flashes boomed from the Howitzer barrels as the Special Forces advisors hurried the Cambodian artillery crew to reload. Wave after wave, the NVA were methodically repelled. The night sky suddenly exploded with green tracers as a quad-12.7 mm antiaircraft gun sprayed the five o'clock position of Spectre 12. Vaquero shook Scotty Wilson who had been mesmerized by the fire fight around the camp. Scumbag casually turned his head around, unaffected by quad-12.7 mm fire. It was out of their reach.

"Triple-A, five o' clock, no threat," said Scumbag coolly. Scumbag grinned at Vaquero, then threw a ground marker in the direction of the antiaircraft gun. If they had time, they'd come back after it later. The fire fight and ground assault on Fort Savoy was over. Spectre 12 calmly rolled out of its thirty-degree firing orbit, as the navigator informed the crew that the attackers had been repulsed. It had been close, Spectre 12 expended all of its ammunition as the acrid odor of spent shells permeated the gunship.

"Bingo fuel," reported the navigator. "It's time to go home."

"Well Vaquero, what do you think? How many dinks you think we got tonight?" bellowed Scotty Wilson while they both stared at the fires inside Fort Savoy.

"I have no idea, but, we sure put on a hell of a fireworks display," he responded, still coming down from the adrenaline rush. By morning the 16th SOS would be notified that Spectre 12 had killed 470 NVA in defense of Savoy. Savoy had lost thirty-nine defenders. Not bad considering that they were up against a superior force. Another Spectre was on its way to clean up as a deep sense of fulfillment and accomplishment filled the crew of Spectre 12, as they headed back to *Ubon*. The navigator grinned to himself as he played '*Riders On The Storm*,' by the Doors, blasting it over the aircraft's intercom. Vaquero was exhausted and he rested up against the right paratroop door. He lit a cigarette and inhaled deeply, attempting to digest what he had just experienced.

Scumbag smiled at Vaquero and gave him a thumbs up as he licked a fresh cigar and gnawed on it from the corner of his mouth. Scotty Wilson closed his eyes and took a deep breath, savoring the burning ammonia-like fragrance throughout the aircraft. Scumbag would sleep well, and with a clear conscience.

As the dead were stacked like cord-wood for burial outside the perimeter of Fort Savoy, a hollow-eyed shell shocked Cambodian soldier on burial detail was overcome with apprehension and dread. While dragging one of the dead NVA toward a mass grave, he had noticed a tattoo on the right arm of a young NVA sapper. There was an inscription, and it read, "*Born in the North, Died in the South.*" The Cambodian soldier's mouth was suddenly filled with a bitter copper taste, the kind you usually have when you know you are in danger…it was the taste of fear.

CHAPTER SIX

This time the dream was more profound and vivid than before. It was vibrant in hue and intensity, Vaquero would find himself and his crew running over treeless mountain ranges in full view of an unseen enemy along an impenetrable curtain-like wall. Anxiety filled them as they looked for cover. And no matter which way they turned, they couldn't get through the impenetrable barrier. They just stood there, exposed. Ray Vaqueros' eyelids quivered rapidly, absorbed in his bad dream, probing for a way out; anxiety suddenly awakened him. He calmly placed his hands behind his head as he lay motionless in his bunk reflecting on the life-like nightmare. A sudden chill ran down his back as the perspiration covering his forehead ran down the side of his face in the air-conditioned room. The dream first came to him the night he slept with Carrie Holland, he remembered, as he reached for the pack of cigarettes and lighter on the floor next to his bunk. Ray noticed that his hand quivered a little as he lit the cigarette. He stretched out his hand until the quiver subsided. Turning on his side facing the door, he tried going over the dream again, wondering whether if there was a subliminal message embedded in it. Was it meant for him or someone else? Was it a forewarning, or maybe a vision? One thing was for sure, he thought, the dream spoke in vivid pictorial and symbolic images. It couldn't be produced by an act of will nor influenced by the consciousness to tell a different story.

Vaquero lit another cigarette, turned on his back and rested his right arm across his forehead, reflecting now on the wish fulfilling dreams and fantasies with Suzanne Logan. Vaquero would relish the night, looking forward to losing himself in his fantasies of her. He willingly surrendered to the spirited dreams that spoke in a nonverbal sensual language of desire and obsession. Vaquero could still *feel* her fingers run softly down his face and mouth before she caressed and kissed him. He smiled, acknowledging how eagerly he cherished the torment and the agony the visions would bring upon his soul. But it was still, only a dream. Vaquero clutched his pillow tightly over his face and openly wept, suppressing the sounds of his anguish and misery within himself...and the passion for Suzanne Logan that consumed him.

#   #   #

"I hear from Pappy that you got your own crew," Stalls remarked, with a beach ball size grin as perspiration soaked through his flight suit on a scorching hot and humid late afternoon. "Know who your flying with?" Stalls asked. It was three-thirty in the afternoon as Vaquero headed toward the base post office with Bernie Stalls, better known as 'Sugar Bear.' At five foot five in stature, Sugar Bear was a jovial, very round, good-natured fellow from Huntsville, Alabama who had just extended for another tour with the 16th SOS.

"No, not yet Bernie, but I will tonight," Vaquero replied. "And since you brought it up, I think I'll stop by Flight Operations before I pickup my gear for pre-flight." Stalls nodded, picking up their stride, hurrying to get out of the afternoon sun into the air-conditioned mailroom. Vaquero walked slowly past hundreds of mailboxes toward his assigned, seemingly insignificant hole in the wall wondering why he even bothered to go there at all. It would only depress him more so, he thought as he tensed himself for the inevitable disappointment. Ray slowly lowered his head and stared inside the slot for several seconds to make sure his eyes or shadows were not deceiving him. There was a letter from Suzanne. He knew it right away from the appearance of the envelope, immediately recognizing the onion skin textured paper she would always use when she wrote to her parents. Exhilaration and anxiety filled him all at once. Ray couldn't decide whether to read it now or later. He desperately wanted to as he slowly brought the letter up to his nose hoping to find her scent on the envelope. He decided it would be better to read it after the mission as he quietly walked back toward Sugar Bear concealing his excitement, carefully placing the letter into the left chest pocket of his flight suit.

"Look at all this shit," Sugar Bear exclaimed, obviously excited with all the mail and several large care packages from home. "I'll see you later, Ray. By the way, can I drop this shit off in your room until I get back from my mission tonight? I need to get my ass ready for pre-flight." Stalls asked.

"Sure, go ahead." Vaquero got a kick out of Bernie's enthusiasm. He knew just how he felt. It had been over a year since he had received a letter from Suzanne Logan.

"Hmm, Lt. Colonel Dick Solomon," remarked Vaquero, slowly reading the name of his new aircraft commander. He immediately left the operations desk and headed toward his assigned aircraft for preflight. As he approached the AC-130E gunship, Vaquero could see the flight engineer was already there, busy under the left main landing gear wheel-well, inspecting the tires and looking over the landing gear strut. Maintenance crews were all around the gunship, preparing the aircraft for its night stalking mission while technicians fine-tuned the sensitive sensors located in the booth. Large spots of sweat covered the flight engineer's flight suit as he struggled out of the sweltering wheel-well.

"Hi, I'm Ray Vaquero, your new I.O.," remarked Vaquero, extending his right hand. The flight engineer grinned slightly, eyes fixed into Vaquero's, firmly grabbed his hand and introduced himself.

"I'm Doug Collier. Pleased to meet you, Vaquero," he replied in an amicable tone.

"Can I give you a hand?" Vaquero asked, anxious to help.

"Sure, check out the nose and right wheel-well, then the primary and auxiliary hydraulic pumps inside, and that should be it. I'll be up in the flight deck looking over the maintenance records for a few minutes. When you're done, come up and we'll walk back to the equipment hootch and get our web-gear." Vaquero nodded then headed toward the nose gear wheel-well to inspect the tires and check out some of the other critical subsystems of the gunship. Within twenty minutes he was finished. Vaquero decided to inspect the cargo tie-down straps that secured the upper ramp door open.

"You ready?" Collier asked, as he was completing an entry in the air-craft's maintenance log book.

"Yeah, I'm all done," He replied. Collier wiped the sweat from his forehead, then donned his Spectre cap and headed back toward the equipment room with Vaquero to collect their gear.

"Tell me something about Lt. Colonel Solomon. What kind of guy is he to fly with?" Vaquero was curious to know everything about Solomon and especially if he was anything like Major Marks.

"You'll soon find out that Solomon is an ill-bred, vulgar, crusty old-fart from Texas that has a way of getting on your nerves," retorted Collier nonchalantly. "He doesn't have much patience, and he barks at everyone when they fuck- up." Collier had a smirk on his face. "Other than that he's OK. His style is unique, to say the least. Don't look for leadership from Solomon either, he operates as a loner, won't socialize with the officers or enlisted. Treats us all the same, like shit," Collier said matter-a-factly. "We're just one of the pegs in the wheel of his machine," Collier said as they headed down the main corridor of the equipment room. Vaquero was speechless.

"Just do your job, and he'll leave you alone," Collier asserted as he turned down the aisle toward his equipment.

Vaquero unlocked the diminutive locker then stared at Suzanne's letter for several seconds. The fact that she had written to him was significant and gratifying in itself. And if for some reason beyond his control he didn't make it back, he was content with the fact that Suzanne had thought of him. Vaquero carefully leaned the letter beneath her picture that was wedged in the upper right-hand corner of the locker. He checked the lock to make sure it was secure then quickly donned his fish net like-web-gear and headed back down the aisle to sign out for his survival radios, weapon, and parachute.

His new flight crew members were friendly and laid back as they welcomed Vaquero to the crew. Vaquero took a seat in the front row of the briefing room waiting to be briefed on the evening's mission objective. Doug Collier rushed in and sat next to him. The chit-chat came to a sudden halt as the door of the briefing room slowly opened. Vaquero recognized the Lt. Colonels' insignia on the Spectre cap and shoulders of the tall, brawny aircraft commander. Solomon appeared lethargic as he headed toward the podium and glanced over in Vaqueros' direction. Solomon shuffled some papers before he found the one he wanted then launched into the mission briefing.

"Gentlemen, tonight's mission will be up in the Barrel Roll region near the city of *Ban Ban* in northern *Laos*. Alleycat, the local ABCCC has fragged us on along Route 6, which runs east to west. Our armed recce will begin near *Ban Ban*, which sits right where Routes 6 and 7 intersect." Up to this point Solomon had not looked up from his papers. The crew appeared to be accustomed to Solomon's stiff delivery. "We will then head west toward Route 13 to look for the convoys that have been spotted along the Route." Vaquero leaned forward to look at the map on the wall to see where they were going.

"*Plain of Jars*," Collier whispered into Vaquero's ear. The *Plain of Jars* was a high plateau of pasture and scrubby trees dotted with over a hundred large stone jars. They were centuries old, and no one really knew how they came to be there. Some thought that they were used in some ancient burial rite. A legend circulated throughout the area that a Prince named *Khun Chuang* used them to celebrate his victory against the Vietnamese and had jars of liquor brought to his soldiers for celebration.

"Fast FAC F-4 reconnaissance aircraft have recently picked up an increase in traffic along these routes. The *North Vietnamese* have wised-up to the blocking belts we've established over their preferred and more direct roads. It appears they have decided to go around them since they have become vulnerable to tactical air strikes that have been pounding them daily. The convoys have decided to take the longer path along route 13 instead." Solomon's delivery was dry and almost sarcastic. "Mount up. The bus leaves in fifteen minutes." Nobody moved until Solomon left the room. The crew made a final equipment check, picking up their parachutes on their way to the bus. Solomon sat alone behind the driver pensively staring out the window when Vaquero boarded the weathered bus that would transport them to the AC-130E. No one sat behind or across from Solomon. Vaquero quickly headed toward the rear where Collier was gesturing to come sit next to him.

"I hope Mr. Warmth's head is screwed on straight tonight," whispered Vaquero with a touch of sarcasm and a broad smirk.

"Ah, he's OK Vaquero" retorted Collier apologetically.

"Solomon is just doing his job the only way he knows how, you'll see." The bus lurched forward then made a U-turn toward the flight-line. Vaquero was both excited and little frightened at the thought of going out alone on his first mission and thought about how much safer he felt when DeSena or Scumbag were there next to him. Even with their occasional pranks of scaring the living shit out of him like when they picked him up one night by his arms and legs and hung him out-side the rear of the aircraft at ten-thousand feet. As Vaquero stepped off the bus, he spotted Bernie Stalls standing on the edge of the ramp of the AC-130A as the aircraft taxied toward the runway. Sugar Bear started to wave but flashed him the 'bird' instead. Vaquero just laughed and waved back.

Vaquero secured his flight bag and parachute along the fuselage in the cramped aft cargo compartment. He listened attentively in his headset as the flight crew went over their checklist items.

"Clear number three," barked Solomon to the crew chief impatiently over the intercom. He placed his right hand on the start button for number three engine on the control panel that was above his head.

"Three's clear," responded the crew chief standing in full view of Solomon's window. One after another, the Allison T-56 turboprop engines began to rotate and broadcast their familiar whine. Vaquero stood next to the flare launcher looking out the rear of the aircraft as it finally left the revetment and taxied toward the runway. He could feel the adrenaline rush through his body in anticipation of the mission. Solomon ordered the gunners and I.O. to take their seats in preparation for take-off. Vaquero strapped himself to the cargo compartment floor just three feet from the lip of the cargo door facing the rear of the aircraft. Best window seat he ever had, he thought, and doubled checked to make sure his seat belt was securely fastened.

Solomon set the parking brake after he taxied the Spectre onto the runway then moved the four throttles forward, increasing the engine's acceleration. The Spectre shuddered and lurched. It yearned to lift off as Solomon revved the Allison T-56 engines to the desired RPM's. Vaquero heard a loud metal sound as the parking brake handle was released, then a sudden surge forward that would have thrown him out the rear of the aircraft had not his seatbelt been tightly secured. Spectre 02 lifted off before dusk at around 1720 hours. The air was crisp as the gunship leveled off at three thousand feet, orbiting the city to align its sensors before heading north.

Vaquero rested up against the right paratroop door, lit a cigarette, hoping it would help him calm down. There was no doubt that he was pumped-up. That's when he realized that he was getting cold…his flight suit was covered with perspiration. Vaquero walked over to his flight bag and took out some of the extra clothing he needed to put on before they crossed the *fence*. His thermal sweatshirt and ski mask would surely come in handy tonight, as the gunners watched and laughed at Vaquero as he went through the ritual of getting undressed and dressed again. Within forty-five minutes they would cross the *fence* from northern Thailand into *Laos*.

Three Wolfpacks would rendezvous with them at *Ban Ban*. "We've crossed the fence," announced the navigator, as the flight engineer extinguished the interior lights of the cargo compartment. Vaquero gave the restraining cable connected to his harness a hard tug before he ventured to the rear of the aircraft. Spectre 02 climbed to ninety five-hundred feet as it headed toward *Ban Ban*. For centuries *Laos* had been a pathway for invaders, a passage into the lands of its neighbors, and an escape route for the defeated. It was still light out when they crossed into *Laos*. Thick forest, like an unbroken green rug, was punctuated occasionally by massive craters formed by the carpet bombing raids of B-52's. There were rugged mountains with deep narrow valleys cut by streams that flowed southeast to the *Mekong River*, which dominated the impenetrable jungle terrain below. Its trees were known to exceed 110 feet in height. A great hiding place for anyone not wanting to be found, Vaquero thought, as he gazed at the jungle floor. *Laos* had always been the centerpiece of the geopolitical jigsaw puzzle and had often found itself as the battleground in conflicts between its larger and more powerful neighbors. It was also an early casualty of the *Vietnam* War. Its future was never a serious concern to the United States, except that it wanted military access to the *Ho Chi Minh Trail* and plug its use by *North Vietnam* as an avenue of providing supplies into *South Vietnam*. The *Pathet Lao*, a communist group that formed part of Laos's coalition government were running the country now, allied with *North Vietnam*.

Booth sensor operators probed the narrow dirt trails and roads that twisted and weaved toward Route 7. Within ten minutes upon their arrival, a convoy was detected heading west with their lights off. Immediately the sensors fed the digital fire control computer with the convoy's coordinates. Solomon immediately targeted the lead truck in order to bring the convoy to a halt as the Spectre instinctively turned into its attack orbit. Solomon patiently waited for the movable and fixed target lines to superimpose in his gunsight before he gently pressed the trigger button on the control column. A 105-Howitzer round nailed the lead vehicle and it exploded disintegrating the supplies and driver into a blaze of secondary explosions. Within thirty seconds of the first shot Solomon damaged the rear truck as it came to a sudden and fiery stop. His voice over the intercom was methodical yet detached as he played the convoy's final death knell. Meanwhile Vaquero and the right scanner surveyed the darkened jungle terrain for antiaircraft fire. The convoy was caught between a *Binh Tram* and away from the protection of the antiaircraft batteries support. The trucks were sitting ducks, and in the open.

"Give me a flare every third orbit I.O.," ordered Solomon. Vaquero keyed his mike acknowledging the order. The remaining vehicles had dashed under thick jungle foliage for cover. The 20-mm Vulcan's were now armed. As Solomon tightened the Spectre back into its thirty-degree attack orbit, he fired one-thousand rounds of 20-mm high incendiary rounds into the remaining trucks and drivers. There were bright flashes of light as the Russian Zil's exploded instantaneously, igniting the fuel and ammunition into an inferno along the jungle floor. The brightness of the explosion momentarily blinded Vaquero.

"I have another mover," the Black Crow operator informed the pilot, as his sensor detected the sounds of another vehicle. Solomon leveled out the aircraft and headed five miles west further down Route 6 toward in pursuit of another kill. To Solomon's surprise, as well as to the drivers' on the ground, Spectre 02 had run into thirty stationary trucks parked along what appeared to be a truck park. A *Ho Chi Minh Trail* rest stop, if you will.

"I.O., give me another flare," ordered Solomon. Vaquero instantly fired the flare from the LAU-74. "I want the 105 on-line," Solomon commanded again, while the booth sensors fed multiple target coordinates to the fire control computer. Solomon was gloating now, daydreaming momentarily about the honors that would be bestowed upon him and for the outstanding mission that entailed the destruction of forty vehicles along with their drivers. But that accomplishment was subordinate to the attention he would receive, and how that recognition could be leveraged for his personal ambition. Solomon was ticket punching. He coveted a staff position at the Pentagon after his tour with the 16th was completed. Solomon envisioned himself standing proudly at attention as he imagined Colonel Roberts reading the citation in front of the Squadron for the Distinguished Flying Cross, then pinning the medal to his chest. That had always been Lt. Colonel Richard Caldwell Solomon the III's style. To posture, leverage, even barter was always preferable to mere obligation or duty. Anything else was too trite for his liking. There had to be a personal gain in any endeavor, or why risk his ass unless there was an opportunity somewhere to benefit, even at the expense of others; Like his crew for instance. On an intellectual level he made no differentiation between those he hunted and those that served him. Solomon never thought of the crew with the same effigy of self-esteem as he held for himself. He was the *aircraft commander*; the leader, the superior. The crew's purpose was only to serve him and him alone, he thought arrogantly. Solomon would come to despise those that shared in his moments of glory.

The flares momentarily impaired Vaquero's night vision as the blazing light cast eerie shadows along the jungle floor. Suddenly out of the darkness, a barrage of forty rounds of 37-mm triple-A reached out to touch Spectre 02 from its ten to twelve o'clock position. "Triple-A ten to twelve o'clock," called Vaquero into his headset. "No threat, hold what you got, pilot," he commanded instinctively. Bright orange air bursts erupted around the aircraft. But Solomon nervously jerked the control column to the right at the sight of the triple-A, then over corrected back to the left, as he suddenly broke into the direction of the red tracers. The triple-A harmlessly raced by above and below the aircraft.

"What the fuck was that?" thought Vaquero out loud.

Solomon impulsively ordered the Wolfpack escorts to attack the truck park and silence the antiaircraft gunners. Three F-4D escorts dived and attacked the gun emplacements and remaining vehicles. Mammoth explosions and black smoke told of the destruction levied by the fighter aircraft on the enemy emplacements. Spectre 02 cautiously circled the devastation but there was nothing left of the truck park worth shooting. The gunship broke off its orbit, leveled off, then headed west along Route 6 and found two more stationary vehicles whose drivers had abandoned them after hearing the destruction further down the road. Two more Zils for the record book.

Lt. Colonel Solomon flew the aircraft in a random search pattern heading west, no longer interested in getting into another fray. Drops of perspiration stung his eyes as thoughts of red tracers racing toward him rattled his ego. His hands shook slightly as he struggled to firmly grip the aircraft's control column. There was no need to run into any more shit if they didn't have to, Solomon reasoned to himself. He ordered the Nav to inform Alley Cat that they were getting low on fuel and would start heading south and back into *Thailand*. The sensor operators in the booth relaxed, ready for a cold beer at the Officer's Club after another worthwhile mission. Vaquero intently scanned the darkness before him.

"Instincts…just instincts," He whispered, anxious now to get back to *Ubon* and read Suzanne's letter.

CHAPTER SEVEN

Unescorted, Spectre 01 was on an armed reconnaissance mission in the Steel Tiger East region of eastern *Laos*. The night sky was dazzling as millions of stars pulsated and glittered brightly. Capt. Will Hawkins would alter his search pattern occasionally from spiral to parallel while the Black Crow, FLIR and Low Level Light TV sensors probed along the myriad number of dirt trails that darted out from under the jungle canopy in search of an elusive enemy. Apparently it was going to be one of those dull, monotonous missions where you were assured that you were going to be bored to death. The cold temperature made it even worse, as Bernie Stalls yawned and shivered in the night unable to retain body heat. His five-pound flak helmet seemed to weigh twenty-pounds as Stalls moved his neck around and from side to side attempting to work out the tightness. Not a single "mover" had been spotted as Spectre 01 continued to shadow Route 23 south into Route 911.

"This shit is getting old real fast," Stalls fumed attempting to cuddle within himself, tucking in his arms and legs closer together. The night air was crisp and cold as it rushed through the open crew entrance door and through the multiple gun ports before exiting out the rear of the aircraft. Stalls desperately fought the urge to fart but at the last moment decided not to since he was afraid it would come out cold and make things worse. He laughed to himself a little now. His ass was so tight and puckered, a sledge hammer couldn't drive a nail through it.

In his misery, he swore at the NVA, the convoys, and the antiaircraft gunners. But deep inside Stalls really admired their resilience and combativeness.

Captain Will Hawkins ordered the navigator to contact Moonbeam and request another route since they still had another hour of fuel left and were looking forward to shooting at something.

"We've been fragged up to Route 12," reported the navigator as cheers and jeers could be heard over the intercom at the change of orders from Moonbeam. Stall's crew were a leathery, exacting bunch that never shunned away from a fight. They all understood perfectly why they were there and what was expected of them. As it was, most of the Spectre crews had volunteered for gunship duty, which made them somewhat distinct from other units. The thought of finally getting into a fight stirred them as the pilot slowly turned the aircraft north toward Route 12, the *Mu Gia Pass*.

Bernie Stalls knew the *Mu Gia Pass* area as well as the back woods of home in Huntsville, Alabama. He had already flown a hundred and sixty missions, mostly in eastern *Laos*, during his first tour of duty with the 16th during the '71 campaign. Stalls chuckled, and shook his head as he wondered how the hell the AC-130's ever made it back to *Ubon* after getting their teeth kicked in after running into barrages of anti-aircraft fire. Ground crews would look on in awe as battered Spectres somehow taxied back into their revetments all shot-up and punctured with holes spewing JP-4 from the bottom of their wings. He really loved this shit, there was no doubt about that. His round face beamed with excitement at the moment by moment flirtation with death and how it was the most exciting thing he had ever done with his clothes on.

The *Mu Gia Pass* was a heavily defended narrow corridor for moving troops and supplies from *North Vietnam*. The *North Vietnamese* continually punctuated the Pass' importance by fortifying its defenses each year the war progressed. At one point in '71, Stalls knew where every gun emplacement was located and when they moved to another site. Nineteen-seventy two was not expected to be any different, except with more intense triple-A since the anti-aircraft batteries knew that Spectre would return after the rainy season was over. NVA fortifications would be dug in deeper than an Alabama tick, Stalls thought to himself excitedly.

One hundred and thirty two feet of wingspan banked into a thirty degree search pattern as it approached Route 12 which snaked its way through the *Mu Gia Pass* corridor. Stalls had all but forgotten about his stiff neck and how cold he was as he leaned out the ramp a little further than he normally would. A distinct sensation of warmth rushed through him as his instincts and senses were primed in anticipation of anti-aircraft fire he knew was coming at any moment. *The concessions of the weak are the concessions of fear,* thought Stalls as he momentarily contemplated the wisdom of Edmund Burke's maxim and how it pertained to the gutless politicians back home. The Black Crow suddenly locked in on the sounds of a sizable convoy racing down the pass toward its next *Binh Tram* way station. The FLIR and LLLTV operators quickly picked up the movement on their displays, then instantly feeding target acquisition data to the digital fire control computer, guiding the gunship closer toward the evading convoy. Capt. Will Hawkins patiently waited for the target lines to superimpose in his gunsight when suddenly the night sky was illuminated with nearly two hundred red tracer rounds racing toward the aircraft. Well fortified 37-mm batteries responded angrily to Spectre's presence with an overwhelming barrage of anti-aircraft fire that encircled the unescorted gunship. The flak exploded into bright orange glows, pelting the aircraft's tail and wings with shrapnel.

The gunship crew remained determined at the sight and touch of the imposing barrage. Will Hawkins, a farm boy from Tulsa, Oklahoma covered his mouth and yawned. He was too preoccupied with keeping the aircraft in a thirty degree firing pattern to pay any attention to what was going on outside. Like an unseen spirit in the darkness, Hawkins centered the 40-mm Bofors on its target when suddenly there was a bright flash and a muffled explosion outside the right wing of the gunship. The AC-130A violently pitched to the left as Hawkins struggled to regain control of the aircraft from its turbulent plummet toward the ground. Not knowing exactly what hit them, the navigator rushed altitude and heading data to Moonbeam and to the nearest friendly base for an emergency landing. The flight engineer, now sweating profusely as anxiety and adrenaline mixed in all at once, looked over all the aircraft's cockpit panel displays to see whether the Spectre would stay aloft.

The two forward gunners rushed to aid the right scanner who had been thrown from his position from the blast. He had a few cuts and bruises, but he was more afraid than hurt. Spectre 01 had precariously dropped 3,000 feet in a matter of minutes before Hawkins was able to regain control and stop its rapid descent. With their miniature flashlights in hand, the flight engineer, gunners, and Stalls carefully surveyed the aircraft for battle damage.

"Holy Mother of Jesus," blurted Stalls. The search party watched Stalls come to a sudden halt as he directed his beam of light outside the right scanner's station. The flight engineer walked toward Stalls, and by his facial expression the engineer knew that what he was about to see was bad. Spectre 01 had been hit by a 37-mm round, and the explosion had severed the propellers and forward halves of both number three and four engines.

"No fucking problem, Stalls," exclaimed the flight engineer attempting to calm Stalls and the gunners.

"What do you mean, no fucking problem, man! You gotta be shittin' me! We lost two fucking engines!" bellowed Stalls, astonished at the engineer's cool nerves and balls. It calmed him momentarily, helping him reach within himself to deal with the situation.

"We've got two more on the other side," remarked the engineer dryly. "And by the way, I wouldn't shit you, Bernie. You're my favorite turd." The flight engineer smiled and winked at Stalls, then headed back to the flight deck. But the thought of spiraling out of control toward the ground in a ball of flames overwhelmed Stalls like never before. His lips quivered, and his body suddenly turned cold as fear and apprehension overpowered him again. Stalls battled within himself to will the terror inside away.

"Fire in number three," reported the flight engineer calmly. The pilot and co-pilot were busy trying to keep the AC-130 stable and airborne as cross-winds tossed them around, making their task difficult to control the disabled gunship. They knew they were waist deep in shit. Landing an aircraft with limited surface control and severed fuel lines spewing JP-4 would take a minor miracle. That is, if they ever made it back before they fell out of the sky. Flames began to spread around what was once number three engine. The pilot experimented with adjusting the engine throttles, attempting to cut-off the fuel flow to the right wing.

"We're losing altitude," reported the co-pilot calmly. They would run out of air space unless they did something real fast to stay aloft. Will Hawkins calmly ordered the other crew members to jettison all the ammunition and equipment out the rear of the aircraft. Stalls' fears left him for the moment as he happily helped the gunners pitch ten thousand pounds of ammunition and the flare launcher over western *Laos*.

#   #   #

Vaquero and his crew landed forty minutes after they had crossed the fence back into Thailand. Solomon could have remained on target a while longer. He had plenty of fuel, but he didn't give a rat's ass about what anyone thought about his decision to end the mission prematurely. He had already nailed a sizeable convoy and was shot at to boot. And that fucking Vaquero, let the triple-A come too close for his liking. He would deal with him later, he fumed. No, he wasn't going to risk his ass more than he needed to. Not even Colonel Roberts could fault him or threaten him with pissing on his career plans. This mission should keep Roberts off his ass for a while. Well, yes sir, I'm sorry sir, I mean, fuck you too, sir, eat shit and die, sir, he thought sarcastically. Solomon's ego had an exaggerated sense of purpose.

Vaquero was the first to board the bus. His left knee bounced up and down in a nervous jerking motion, restless at having to wait for the others to board and was prepared to run back from the flight-line. The bus dropped off the flight crew for debriefing at the flight operations desk.

"See you back at the barracks," Vaquero said to Doug Collier, as he hastily got off the bus and ran toward the equipment trailer. After retrieving the letter from his locker, he headed toward a secluded corner of the room with Suzanne's letter in hand. His flight suit was soaked with perspiration as he slowly took off his survival web-gear and tossed it on the cold, tile-covered floor. He leaned up against the wall and slowly slid down to the floor.

Dearest Ray,

And so we both play the game…and I don't know why. Last night there was an eclipse of the moon. I wondered if you knew and thought you were too preoccupied to care. When I try to understand what it is like for you over there, my brain takes a left turn. Something, or someone, won't let me think about it.

I walked back from the Humanities building near midnight, just before the eclipse. Everything felt different. For a second, it was as if everything "clicked." I don't know why I'm telling you about this. It must seem like talking about the weather to you. I guess, it's a way to get to saying that everything has felt wrong, or somehow misaligned, from the moment you left. Papers and books fill up my days. I stopped working at the Student Union a few months ago, but I guess I never mentioned it to you. Julie is the only one who talks to me about you, but she's not spending much time in the room anymore. Stevie's parents set him up in his own apartment, and she's stuck to his side.

Judy Collins "Broken Window's" plays over and over in my head. Like you need me to depress you. What are your days like, if you want to talk about them? Can you tell me? Are you allowed to? I hope you are having fun on R&R—-then again, I hope you aren't. You must feel much older than me by now...

Hi, I'm back...my mom just called. They're all fine and are planning a trip to the Bahamas. It's great to think they can go off now that the nest is empty, but she sounded guilty telling me. I told her a little about your trip to Bangkok. I think you'd feel guilty telling her. I never know how to start or finish these letters, Ray. Does it make sense if I tell you I can't dance anymore? Saying I miss you wouldn't help...either one of us.

There was another thing I've been wanting to tell you for some time now Ray, Michael has asked me to marry him after he's completed graduate school in August. His family is pushing for a wedding sometime around the holidays in December.

I couldn't do this without letting you know.

Suzanne

He wrapped his arms around his knees, slowly rocking back and forth in silence for about twenty minutes, his eyes swollen as tears welled in them. Ray Vaquero let out a long painful wail that echoed loudly throughout the trailer, voicing his anguish and despair. Flight equipment technicians were startled by the sounds coming from the flight crew equipment room. The shift supervisor, Sgt. Hunter shook his head slowly, telling them that they should leave Vaquero alone. Hunter had witnessed the shattering of many men throughout his career, watching them as they were brought to their knees with news from home of a pending divorce or from a reluctant fiance. There are times when one needs to be left alone to grieve the loss of love. To emotionally express the gut-retching agony inside, in solitude and out loud. This was one of them, thought Sgt. Hunter pensively, as he walked back to his work bench. Vaquero used the sleeve of his flight suit to dry his face. Solomon and the rest of the crew would be back soon, he thought calmly, suddenly detached from the wave of emotions that had moments earlier engulfed him. Vaquero walked over to his locker, collected his personal belongings, never looking at Suzanne's picture which now hung slightly askew.

Pappy Duncan was working on the next day's flight schedule when Vaquero walked into his office. "Hey Ray, how's it hangin', man." Vaquero looked through him with a dead stare.

"Can you increase my flying time?" Vaquero asked in a dispassionate tone.

"Sure Ray, we always need backup." Pappy's normal rounded grin had faded slightly. "What's up?" he asked, curious about Vaquero's apparent change in mood. Vaquero stared toward the wall, pausing momentarily, avoiding eye contact.

"I'm just available, Pappy, that's all. Give me first consideration, OK?" Vaquero demanded. "I need all the experience I can get and you need the extra body." Vaquero forced himself to smile, assuring Duncan that on the surface everything was fine and that there was no ulterior motive behind his request.

Duncan nodded. "Sure, I'll give you the first shot if we need anybody, OK?" Duncan glared at Vaquero, trying to figure out what was suddenly eating him. Vaquero wouldn't talk about it. In any event, Duncan was always appreciative for volunteers versus trying to coax someone with a hang-over to fly extra missions. Everyone carries some secret torment in their baggage throughout life, Duncan pondered pensively, as he thought about the family he divorced back home to settle in with a local *Thai* half his age and his inability to adjust back in the *world*.

"Thanks Pappy," said Vaquero as he patted Duncan on the back and headed out the door.

It was still early and Vaquero planned on getting shit-faced, intending to dull all of the senses. The night air was clammy and still as he lit a cigarette outside the flight operations building. He inhaled deeply and forcibly, holding it until he could feel it burn deep inside his lungs as the sounds of fire trucks and emergency crews raced toward the runway.

#   #   #

At fifteen miles from *Ubon* the instruments on number two engine warned of possible turbine failure and imminent power loss. Capt. Hawkins made adjustments to the throttles to avoid the loss of another engine. "Unfucking believable," whispered the flight engineering as he marveled at the amazing wonderful God-bless-you-Lockheed-built air-craft. It was sphincter-tightening time, he thought as his eyes raced a mile a minute as he surveyed the instrument panels, paused, then made instantaneous adjustments carefully transferring fuel from the right wing to the left wing yet maintaining a safe balance. Fuck, they could drop out of the sky at any moment he thought. The landing gear was finally lowered manually as the aircraft hurried toward the now brightly lit nine-thousand foot long runway.

Vaquero saw Colonel Roberts and Pappy Duncan rush out of the operations office and jump into one of the Squadron's vehicles.

"Wanna come along? Spectre 01 is coming in with only number one and number two engines." Roberts said calmly.

Vaquero could only think of Sugar Bear and what might be going through his mind right about now. Spectre 01 was either going to make it or go up in a ball of flames trying.

"Yes, sir," he said, and jumped in the back seat. Fire trucks, emergency crews, and ambulances lined up along both sides of the runway.

Winds picked up momentarily, making it difficult for Will Hawkins to keep the Spectre in a proper glide path. Gently, he played with the throttles, realigning the aircraft back toward the runway. He shook his head and smiled then calmly thought this would not be a good time to lose another engine. Stalls, strapped in his seat, could see the lights of *Ubon* intensify as Spectre 01 descended rapidly toward the runway.

Spectre 01 slammed onto the runway as it came in hard and fast. Hawkins wrestled with the vibrating nose gear steering control wheel as it pulled to the left, fighting to keep the gunship on the runway. He quickly reversed number two engine, decelerating the lumbering aircraft while simultaneously depressing the brakes. The gunship had two-thousand feet to spare. Fire trucks and emergency crews escorted the crippled Spectre back toward its revetment.

Sugar Bear walked slowly over to Duncan and Vaquero while Colonel Roberts and Capt. Hawkins inspected the shrapnel covered aircraft.

"I need a fucking beer," mumbled Stalls. Duncan grinned then unzipped the right pocket of his flight suit and unveiled a bottle of *San Miguel*, popped the top off, handing it to Stalls. Vaquero and Duncan watched in amazement as he gulped it down without breathing. "I need another one," he commented, like a man who was dying of thirst, then let out a massive belch from the pit of his stomach.

Vaquero and Stalls raced to the 'Chili Pepper Night Club' after they showered and changed into civilian cloths. They had good reason to get shit-faced, and they were going to exercise that well earned American tradition. It was eight o' clock when they arrived and *Iron Butterfly's* "In the Godda Da Vida" blared in the packed, smoked-filled night club on a Tuesday night. The volume was deafening as it overloaded the senses, arousing the primal, provoking the rush of adrenaline that flight crews were addicted to. It was a nightly ritual where the insanity of the day was cleansed with alcohol and ear piercing music. Spectre crews preferred it that way, thunderous and overwhelming. Multi-colored strobe lights cast strange shadows in the over-crowded club crammed with off-duty servicemen looking for excitement with hungry hookers on the prowl looking to cash in on the multiple targets of opportunity. Vaquero and Stalls pushed and shoved their way through a mass of sweaty bodies that reeked of liquor and beer. Every night was Saturday night, Vaquero thought. It was one big huge fucking party when you stepped off-base.

They immediately downed two *Singha's*, then Stalls took off after one of his favorite hookers that was dancing with a friend on the sweltering dance floor. He wasn't much of a dancer, but it didn't matter how he looked or moved. Sugar Bear rejoiced that he was still alive.

Vaquero began to feel a little light-headed as he worked on his sixth *Singha*, hopelessly trying to erase Suzanne Logan and her letter from his mind. One of the bar girls spotted him standing by himself and forced her way toward him bent on cashing in on his despair. The prospects were good since it was the beginning of the month, which meant these guys had recently been paid. The skin-tight black silk dress clung to her skin in the damp night air. Her black spike heels made her almost six-feet tall as she cajoled and teased him, putting her hands down his pants but Vaquero wasn't interested. Frustrated and defeated she instantaneously did an about face and began her performance all over again with someone else that had just come through the door. Vaquero looked toward the dance floor to see that Stalls had already left. He downed two more *Singha's* before he staggered out onto the cluttered sidewalk. The night air was damp and foul, as he labored to light a cigarette while club patrons and hookers raced in and out of the crowded night club. Beggars and street venders were lined up along the busy avenue as Vaquero wobbled sideways along the sidewalk without any particular destination in mind. Taxi drivers parked outside the club called out to him, looking for a fare back to the base, but he just waved them away in disgust. He wandered for about an hour before he stopped to look around at his surroundings and get his bearings.

Vaquero didn't have a clue where he was, except somehow he was mysteriously misplaced from the raucous crowds of the Chili Pepper. It was around midnight as he wobbled in place to maintain his stability to read his watch. To say he was "shit-faced" would have been an understatement. And although he was inebriated, he had enough presence of mind to realize that he shouldn't be wandering around alone in *Ubon's* business district which was now deserted. There were certain elements in every city that would like nothing better than to roll stragglers for everything they had on their way back to the base. Vaquero bent over and reached for the six inch switchblade his father had given him before he left. He always carried it taped to his leg whenever he left the base. He put the knife into his left pocket with his thumb firmly pressed against the release button. A dog barked while shadows seemed to appear out of the darkness. Vaquero walked briskly away from them in desperate need of a cab and someplace to hide. As the shadows moved closer toward him, he raced around the corner to a store with its lights still illuminated.

The people inside were gathering their things and began walking out the door when Vaquero suddenly stormed inside startling them. Sweating profusely, Vaquero whispered, "*Sa- waht dee.*"

"*Sa-waht dee ka,*" responded *Toi* warmly, the proprietor of the *Thai Palace*. *Toi* turned toward the workers and spoke to them in a firm yet melodic tone. As far as he could tell, she told the workers to leave. They politely bowed then left the restaurant without making eye contact with Vaquero.

"I'm drunk, lost, and I think I'm being followed," Vaquero said calmly.

"Go back there," she ordered, pointing toward the kitchen. *Toi* quickly locked the front door and extinguished the lights in the restaurant, following him toward the back of the room. Although Vaquero could not see her immediately after she turned off the lights, he could smell her skin as she stood about a foot away from him. Their eyes focused outside the restaurant as four shadowy figures passed by the window, pausing momentarily to look inside the *Thai Palace*, then finally moving away. Vaquero could feel her eyes touch him in the darkness.

"We must go out the back way," she whispered.

"Go where?" Vaquero giggled. "It's past curfew, and all the cabs are off the street by now, unless you plan to drive me back to the base?" he replied.

"I'll shelter you tonight," she said with her large black, nearly round eyes. *Toi* gripped his hand tightly then led him out a back door through a maze of passageways. Vaquero lost count of the number of times they had turned a corner. Part of him was apprehensive; he was confiding in a stranger. *Toi* finally stopped in front of another door then quietly unlocked it. She grabbed his hand again and gently embraced it as she led him into what looked like a small apartment. Vaquero squeezed her hand in return. She finally turned on the night light that sat on a wicker stand next to her double bed. The lamp scarcely illuminated their presence in the room. Vaquero staggered, wanting to just lay down somewhere.

"You can sleep here," she said pointing to the bed. *Toi* left the room as Vaquero instinctively undressed then slid into the bed indifferent to any danger that could be lurking outside. Moments before he fell into a deep slumber *Toi* turned the night light off then slipped into the bed next to him. Ray Vaquero was stirred by her presence and the scent of feminine sensuality as she let her long jet black hair down, and gently rested her head on his chest.

Ray Vaquero fought the restlessness within him as he drew closer to *Toi*, entangled again with his visions of Suzanne. *Toi* comforted him with the warmth of her olive skin body, while she prayed to her god to chase away Vaquero's demons. And as *Toi* reached for the thin white sheet to shield him from the evening chill, she heard him mumble, "Don't leave me."

"I am with you, Ray-mond," *Toi* whispered sorrowfully.

CHAPTER EIGHT

The men of the 7th Force Recon Battalion were an uncommon breed. Daring and fearless, three to six man teams that ventured on spine tingling intelligence-gathering missions fifty to one hundred miles from the nearest friendly units with the specific intent of penetrating the enemy's back yard to provoke havoc. First to find them, then to methodically kill them without passion nor prejudice. Hidden deep in their sanctuaries in *Laos* and *Cambodia*, the NVA were constantly kept off guard by the presence of recon teams that silently shadowed their every move. Recon was a painful thorn in their side. The men of the 7th Force Recon thought they were more like...*the tip of the spear.*

Everything was vibrant and alive as the Huey raced above the thick green-velvet jungle canopy below. *Tuan* laughed with excitement as the helicopter finally dived out of the sky toward the designated landing zone. Anchored against the open door while his legs dangled out in the wind, the bony but hard *Montagnard* scanned the harsh terrain looking for potential enemy ambush sites as the jungle floor rushed up toward the four-man recon team. Weighed down with fifty 40-mm rounds in bandoleers that crossed his chest, *Tuan* firmly grasped his M-79 grenade launcher as the team was inserted by an UH-1 Huey troop carrying helicopter five miles inside the Cambodian border along a heavily used infiltration corridor. The Trail curved out of the *Fishhook* and across Highway 246, which ran east to west, then twisting toward

Saigon. Several miles away, a second Huey hovered above the ground in a different location as a diversion against NVA spotters from guessing the exact insertion point. Rodriguez squatted in the high brush, going over the maps and documents that were taken off the bodies of dead enemy couriers from previous missions that had pinpointed new NVA trails and plans along highway 246. He was eager to scout the new find while Cano Rincón and *Tuan* spied along the tree line for enemy patrols and trail watchers. The team moved quietly and skillfully through wait-a-minute vines in their tiger-stripe fatigues and bush hats. The early morning jungle heat was smothering as they patiently looked for signs of an 82-mm NVA mortar team that had been harassing a local Special Forces outpost over the last two weeks.

NVA mortar teams were usually operated by a 4-man crew that could easily harass an outpost with deadly precision from a safe distance, disassemble their weapon then quickly vanish deep into the jungle before they could be found. The 82-mm mortar was a smooth-bore, drop-fired weapon with a range of over two miles, composed of a sight, tube bipod, and a base plate that weighed over a hundred pounds. As they headed toward a nearby ridge line the four-man recon team cautiously scanned the thick jungle terrain, ever-watchful of enemy patrols and ambush. Their movement was slow and graceful, as they intentionally followed each other's footsteps. Years of fighting a slick and crafty enemy had taught recon a few tricks of their own, like replacing the cleated soles of their jungle boots with tire rubber so the prints resembled those of the enemy's *Ho Chi Minh* sandals. But what distinguished these men from other units was their underdeveloped sense of fear, and the embodiment of the battalions motto of *swift, silent, deadly.*

Each carefully returned tree branches back to their original position leaving no sign that anyone had been there while they moved in a stealth-like manner, cloaking their presence to an ever watchful adversary. A warm Southeast Asian breeze filtered through the brush while two hundred foot trees danced slowly in the morning sun light. The ridge line was covered with trails, all which seemed to have been used regularly. Rincón needed to piss badly, but he didn't dare stop for fear of ambush and concern of getting his dick shot-off while it was still in his hand. He happily relieved himself as they shadowed one of the fresh trails.

The *Ho Chi Minh Trail* was a marvel to behold, a tangle of woven and interconnected roads and footpaths. They were small dirt trails during the war against the French, but now they had grown to over two thousand miles of trail with thousands of *North Vietnamese* forces at the ready to keep the network open. *Binh Trams* were military way stations with independent organizations whose sole responsibility was to maintain their segment of the trail accessible and repair the damage inflicted by the U.S. Air Force attempts to cut the roads. With the Cambodian mainland closed to them and the coast actively patrolled by the Navy, the NVA worked feverishly to improve and expand the *Trail*. Hundreds of tons of supplies and materials were stored in bunkers and caves at each twenty mile point, then reloaded to continue their trek south. On the average it took three months for supplies to finally reach their destination. The NVA were a tenacious adversary, but also forebearing. *Tuan* was on point when they dispassionately walked by a weather beaten pith helmet and a pile of sun-bleached skeletal remains of enemy soldiers.

The 1970 Clandestine B-52 bombings had not deterred the enemy much, Manny Rodriguez thought, as he studied the now broken, crater filled landscape of the *Fishhook*. Despite the Arc Lights, battered NVA regiments continued to resupply their base camps up and down the notorious trail. Supplies would logjam after the B-52 bombings, and like ants, the NVA roadwork teams frantically cut new ones. Movement down the trail would be greatest in February and March, the peak of the dry season.

"Energetic fuckers," Rodriguez whispered to himself. While they stopped for a brief break along a well concealed jagged ridge line, *Tuan* used hand signals to draw their attention to the dust trails of an enemy patrol column filtering through the triple jungle canopy about two miles away. A *South Vietnamese* Army radioman trainee bringing up the rear was consumed with fear at the thought that NVA were in close proximity, and that they were out numbered and outgunned forced him to squat in the bush and defecate in raw terror during their brief pause. Intelligence reports had estimated that the sanctuaries in *Laos* and *Cambodia* alone had accumulated enough supplies to equip nearly a hundred battalions, and enough ammunition to provide the basic combat load for fifty-two thousand soldiers. The frightened ARVN soldier adjusted the straps to the PRC-25 radio and only link to supporting artillery units, air support, and more importantly, extraction. The long antenna of the PRC-25 would make him a marked man by any watchful NVA sniper, he thought. A feeling of dread and loneliness came upon him.

There were as many as ten recon patrols in the field at any given time. Rodriguez reported in hourly to a bank of radios manned by operators standing five-hour watches at *Phu Bai*. Hourly checks came in the form of notification when a patrol had changed its location and situation report. When the enemy had been spotted the team would report its strength, activity, and location. The findings would be plotted on a series of topographic maps covered with acetate and fixed to the walls in the stuffy operations bunker. The data would then be passed on to division intelligence, S-2, and analyzed to assess enemy activity within the teams tactical area of responsibility. Once the recon team had spotted an enemy unit, they would either have to take it under fire, ambush, shadow it, or haul ass out of there to be extracted in a hurry if it turned out that it was more than they could handle. Battalions S-2 would brief and debrief the patrols and provide them with critical information on their assigned areas of operation for the week-long missions. Usually, a patrol would know where it was going a day prior to its insertion. Rodriguez would always make it a point to go over the situation reports and enemy contacts made by other teams. Artillery and air units would be notified to make sure that there would be no unsystematic shooting or bombing where the patrol was operating, although artillery units would regularly fire harassment fire into areas likely to be used by the NVA. When the teams made contact and a fire fight ensued, the recon teams had an equalizer and priority over the network for artillery and tactical aircraft at their disposal.

While moving through the sun-dappled underbrush of light forest a sudden burst of AK-47 fire streamed in their direction from a lone NVA who had popped-out of a spider hole shattering the silence. A round went cleanly through the ARVN soldier's left arm, instantly dropping him in the thick jungle brush. Unknowingly, the team had run into a series of listening posts around a fairly large weapons cache, and the lone NVA had been one of several caretakers left behind to distract intruders from finding the supplies. Rodriguez, Rincón, and *Tuan* responded with deadly precision as the NVA was shredded by multiple impacts from the recon team's return fire, slumping what remained back into the hole.

While team Taino laid face down on the ground anticipating return fire, Rincón uncovered a communications wire hidden under the mud and brush. Covered in sweat after the brief fire-fight, Cano smiled then pulled on the wire very slowly to see where it would lead as he crawled through thick brush for about forty yards from his position. Rodriguez and *Tuan* knew that Cano was on to something and quietly turned around to follow him, while occasionally looking back in the direction of the spider hole. To their amazement, they had crawled into a two hundred cubic foot storage area of NVA rockets, and mortar rounds. They would not have found the cache had it not been for the communications line. The ordnance was stacked in square shaped holes, each carpeted with bamboo for drainage, then covered with bamboo mats, leaves and dirt for added concealment.

Suddenly, more NVA guards popped out of spider holes around the caches perimeter and began firing into the direction of the team just below the thick jungle brush. When the NVA dropped back partially into the spider holes to reload, *Tuan* fired successive M-79 grenade rounds at the attackers. The 40-mm rounds tore into the NVA's faces and above their heads. Rincón rapidly pumped his 12-gauge Remington in the direction of the spider holes, catching the NVA chest high with flechette rounds. Rodriguez entered the fray by firing his M-16 at the NVA on full automatic, stitching two NVA across their chest and head.

Rodriguez signaled *Tuan* to secure the area and see if anyone was still alive in the spider holes. The momentary silence was interrupted by the sound of 82-mm mortar exiting its tube, and could be heard not far away from the NVA storage area. Another NVA suddenly leaped out from a spider hole heading in the opposite direction running down the trail. Rodriguez and Rincón didn't pursue him right away in the event he was leading them into a trap. He disappeared into a cluster of bunkers that had not been visible earlier. They moved slowly and cautiously toward the bunker area, wanting to capture him alive if possible and question him about the NVA unit operating in the area. The insolent NVA was locked up in bunker, tight as a drum. Rodriguez motioned to *Tuan* and calmly asked him to get the NVA to surrender.

"Never happon, G.I., you numba fucking ten," responded the scared soldier. Rodriguez and Rincón couldn't help but grin. NVA soldiers feared capture and had been conditioned to believe they would be tortured and then killed. Some even feared that U.S. soldiers ate their prisoners. The defiant soldier responded to Tuan's call with a burst of AK-47 fire, so a concussion grenade was tossed into the bunker. *Tuan* went in after him and dragged him out. After about fifteen minutes, the *Montagnard* extracted the necessary information on the whereabouts of the mortar team and the NVA base camp that they operated from. To their amazement, they were nearly sitting on it, and the now talkative prisoner volunteered to show them the camp.

"Tell him to take us to it," ordered Rodriguez. They cautiously walked about two-hundred yards under a thick, double jungle canopy that hid the intricate maze of footpaths, bicycle paths and truck trails that had painstakenly been carved out of the jungle to link the various caches and base camp. The complex was enormous, perfectly hidden and out of sight from the air and nearby trails. It had over a hundred structures, mess halls, storage bunkers, training areas, and pens for livestock. The base camp had open-wall thatch-roof classrooms with chalkboards and wooden benches. Many of the hootches with trench lines lead to air raid bunkers. No one was minding the store. It had turned out to be the supply depot of the 3rd NVA Division. *Tuan* scanned through captured documents revealing that the camp had been in operation for more than four years and had even bragged that they had been untouched by U.S. bombings. Then *Tuan* heard something. He carefully put the documents into his rucksack then wandered into one of the hootches where he found an old woman squatting on the floor rocking slowly back and forth, whimpering. *Tuan* cautiously glanced around the room for any impending danger. His eyes were focused and weapon primed and ready, when his attention was drawn to an object on a table in the far corner of the room. As he got closer, he could see the feet of a small body under a black sheet and a large piece of wood on top of it. As *Tuan* moved it away slowly, concerned that it might be booby-trapped, he uncovered the body of a little girl that appeared to be no more that six years old. A string of ants was going in one of her nostrils and out the other carrying tiny flecks of flesh. *Tuan* jumped back in terror and raced out of the hootch, disguising his fear from the rest of the team.

By their best estimate, there must have been over two thousand individual weapons, plus a couple of hundred tons of munitions scattered throughout the NVA base camp. Rodriguez couldn't wait until the specialized NVA Sapper teams that were formed to hunt them down found out that Force Recon was there. Rodriguez walked over to the injured ARVN radio operator and smiled at him while Rincón assured them both that it was only a flesh wound with nothing broken. There was no need to extract the team prematurely Manny thought. They had just gotten there. *Tuan* guarded their perimeter with his daunting jungle eyes while Rodriguez sat down comfortably next to the PRC-25 to call in the grid location and coordinates of the NVA base camp back to the *Phu Bai* radio operators. An Arc Light was definitely in order, he thought as he wiped the sweat off his lean sculptured face. Arc Lights was an eye-catching name for B-52 strikes and the glow they put on the horizon at night. Hundreds of bombs detonated in a rolling chain that would last for an eternity for any NVA hiding in tunnels or bunkers. The ground shook and the horizon would burn in a flickering rainbow-like glow from one end of the strike to the other.

"Manny, I found some interesting shit here," whispered Cano. He had uncovered a detailed enemy map with a breakdown of the NVA infiltration trails from *Cambodia* through War Zone C.

"Let me take a look." Manny squatted in the shade and out of the hot sun next to Cano. "These documents and codes belong to the 101th Sapper Battalion," whispered Manny. "They're the elite enemy unit whose only purpose in life is to hunt Force Recon teams, *mano*." Manny Rodriguez shook his head and snickered snidely.

It began to rain and it was blinding and hard. The rain would provide timely cover in exiting the camp and burrow in somewhere else far away and out of sight from watchful eyes. The Arc Light strike would be delayed until the team was safely back at *Phu Bai*.

"We have another mission," whispered Rincón, while the wounded ARVN looked on, not fully cognizant of the implications of what Cano had just said. "An Air Force Forward Air Controller went down about eight miles from here." Rodriguez searched his map, pointing to their probable approach to the downed pilot.

"He went down about two hours ago right about here, but Search and Rescue has not been able to make contact by radio." Rodriguez paused momentarily to wipe the stream of water flowing off his face. "We'll try to pick up his trail in the morning. If a NVA patrol has snatched him, they're probably hunkered down for the night in this shit." Adrenaline surged through Rodriguez at the prospect of rescuing a downed OV-10 FAC pilot.

They released the scared NVA care-taker. And to make sure he wouldn't inform on their whereabouts, Rodriguez had *Tuan* tell him that they had called in for a B-52 strike. The thought of making contact with his comrades never entered his mind as he realized that he needed to get as far away from the supply depot as possible.

#   #   #

Forward Air Controller pilots never got the notoriety for their craft like their vain half-brothers, the fighter pilot. FAC's piloted ordinary looking single and dual prop-driven aircraft from the seat of their pants that would lumber dangerously above the jungle tree tops trolling for a crafty and dangerous enemy. And although they would often agree that at times they were no more than highly paid cannon fodder, their feats were dignified for the danger they voluntarily exposed themselves to willingly.

Capt. Jess Andrew Paterson had been daydreaming momentarily, reflecting on when he had volunteered for the six month tour almost a year ago under the Steve Canyon program to be a Raven and fly O-1 Bird Dogs. Paterson grinned, amazed that he had survived the wild-ass missions in the old 0-1 aircraft. Bird Dogs had no armor, no self-sealing fuel tanks, carrying only a few marking rockets. With a maximum speed of only 95 mph, the single engine 0-1 was, to say the least, an attractive target for hostile ground fire. And despite the explanations and rationale, trolling for ground fire was an unnatural act that went against a normal person's natural predisposition. But, this was not the case for the FAC. Trolling involved flying over an area suspected with NVA and deliberately taking the aircraft down to draw ground fire, tempting the AAA gunners to break fire discipline at the sight of an easy prey and give away their position.

The North American OV-10 was the Cadillac of FAC aircraft with glass canopy, rockets, bombs and machine guns. OV-10's were armed with two pods of high explosive rockets, six Willie Pete's and two thousand rounds of 7.62-mm. A FAC's job was rather uncomplicated and basic, Paterson thought as he began to roll the aircraft. They were to find the targets, order up tactical from the Airborne Command and Control Center, mark the target accurately with Willie Pete, White Phosphorous rockets, which burned and created smoke, control the operation throughout the time Tac-air remained on station, and stick around to assess BDA. In other words, they were usually busier than a one-legged man in an ass-kicking contest. All tactical fighters, gunships and bombers would be under the control of the FAC. In a large operation he'd be talking to other FAC's and to as many as five sets of fighters stacked up in layers above him awaiting their turn. Jess Paterson was addicted to the job and had developed a close bonding with the other Raven pilots, especially those supporting the Laotians fight the *North Vietnamese*. But he had taken an oath and promised his wife Donna, that after his six month tour with the Ravens was over he would complete his last six months with an outfit that had a much lower mortality rate than the Ravens. She was right, he thought, Donna was always right. Jess Paterson had not yet seen his daughter Diane, who had been conceived when they had flown to Hawaii and spent the three most wonderful weeks of their lives together before he left for Southeast Asia. Diane would be celebrating her first birthday when his tour was over in March.

Now, his biggest threat as an OV-10 Rustic FAC in *Cambodia* was boredom. He would spend hours doing stalls in his twin-propped aircraft spiraling down several thousand feet, recovering it, then doing it all over again for hours on end. He craved the death-defying excitement he was accustomed to in the *Plain of Jars* while stalking enemy convoys and trolling for antiaircraft positions. The nose of the aircraft was pointed straight up before it finally stalled. Jess Paterson intended to recover the OV-10 as close to the tree tops as possible before heading back to *Korat, Thailand*, home of the Rustics. Although he would never admit it, FAC's had a fighter pilot mentality, way down to the bone.

Two miles away, a lone NVA manned a camouflaged 12.7mm antiaircraft gun next to a well-concealed supply depot, and was amused by Paterson's aerial display. Jess Paterson was initially too far from the gunner's reach during his lengthy performance to get off a decent shot at him. The gunner thought about the recent scorching criticism he had received from his superiors and other soldiers in his unit regarding his faulty fire discipline habits, and thought better of firing prematurely. The *North Vietnamese* leaders had embraced the Chinese model of self-criticism, *Phe Binh*, and considered it to be an effective tool in manipulating their troops. The method was a simple and effective one of ridicule and peer pressure. First, they critique the soldier, detailing his positive and negative actions openly and in the presence of others. This was followed by similar observations from his comrades. The session would go on for hours and conclude with the soldier being given a chance to explain his actions and to react to what his superiors and comrades had said. It was only when Jess Paterson had decided to skim the tree tops above his position did the gunner finally take interest and set the OV-10 in his gun-sight, stitching it diagonally across the engine and wing, severing a fuel line. Rustic was now consumed with fire. Two hard lessons had been grasped.

Taino had enough rations for five days and were sure they would find the pilot and haul ass with plenty of time and ammo to spare. Besides their weapons, *Taino* carried four grenades each, a poncho for those

rainy nights, pop-up flares, two illumination grenades, a stick of camouflage grease paint, toilet paper, mosquito repellent, a P-38 can opener
for their food rations, three large compress bandages, and a tooth
brush…to clean their weapon.

The morning fog had burned off, but the sky was overcast with a low
ceiling. Air support would not be able to get under the cloud cover if it
turned out that they needed it, as Rodriguez looked up through the
thick jungle canopy to see if the weather would clear. Bad weather
always worried Rodriguez. Air support was critical to the success of
their missions at times, plus it always gave them a major edge when
confronting overwhelming numbers. As they approached the area
where the pilot might had landed, *Tuan* led them along a nearby
stream-bed to determine whether there had been any other recent visitors. NVA patrols preferred to travel along stream-beds, especially if
they were hiding a prisoner that would be heading up North. *Tuan* knelt
next to what seemed to be fresh multiple footprints. Sandals. A set of
jungle boots. *Tuan* smiled. A squad size patrol with a prisoner was in the
area. Although the enemy patrol had gotten their hands on Paterson,
recon was right behind them. And if they were close, they had the cockiness to believe they had a good chance of getting him back even if they
were outnumbered. Water from the stream was just beginning to seep
into the footprints. The recon team filled their canteens with water and
dropped Halazone tablets into each one before screwing on the lids. The
hunt was on.

Morning light had just begun to filter through the lush jungle vegetation as Rodriguez's team settled along a well concealed ridge line,
silently observing the NVA squad from about a hundred and fifty yards.
The earth was soft and damp and it gave off a foul odor of decay and
rot. Mosquitoes rose in swarms in the thick damp air as the recon team
stalked the NVA squad and formulated their plan of attack. They simultaneously spotted Capt.Paterson slumped over on his side near the
smoldering camp fire, with his arms tied behind his back. The black

pilot sat motionless staring toward the jungle floor, disheartened by his predicament and recklessness. All he could think about was his wife Donna, and the painful look on her face as she boarded the aircraft at Hickam AFB that would take her back to Durham, South Carolina, afraid that she would never see him again.

The NVA patrol was finishing their morning meal and were in the process of breaking camp. Their basic staple was usually rice, and when they got lucky it would occasionally be supplemented with some vegetables. Salt and *nuoc mam*, a sauce made from fermented fish was added for seasoning. From their distance the recon team could smell the pungent odor of the condiment. Food was usually prepared in the early morning or late evenings in underground cookers to prevent aerial detection. While the NVA squad policed the camp site, Rodriguez studied his adversary, assessing their strengths, weaknesses and singling out the leadership. Paterson's captors appeared to be well fed and wore fresh uniforms, green shirt and pants with two button-down pockets on the breast of the shirt. NVA soldiers had only one spare that they carried in their pack. Footgear was primarily ankle-high green canvas Chinese Communist made boots or sandals. Each wore sun helmets that sported a circular metal insignia with a five-point star with a gold wreath that made it look like rice stalks. Cano and *Tuan* evaluated the squad's security strength and armament, taking note that everyone in the squad wore Chicom chest pouches that were designed to accompany the AK-47 assault rifle. Made of dark tan canvas and leather, the pouch had in its center three large pockets that held one thirty-round banana-shaped magazine. Each of them were shouldering Soviet made 7.62-mm AK-47 *Kalashnikov* assault rifles, which could fire in semi or full automatic at the simple flip of a switch. But one of them was carrying a revolver, a usual sign of rank.

"Bingo," whispered Rodriguez. The holster was made of reddish brown leather with a large flap over the top that was secured by an eyelet to a brass post. Paterson's captors were members of the 77th

Straggler, Recovery and Replacement Regiment that was out patrolling their area policing stragglers and deserters when they had run into Paterson struggling to get out of his parachute. The apparent squad leader, now wielding his revolver, began to taunt Paterson, mockingly wiping his fingers slowly along Paterson's face, as if he had expected something to rub off. The others just casually looked on and laughed scornfully. Rodriguez's muscles tensed.

Paterson would not cower or show fear even as his captor made him stand while he fired his revolver around his feet. Paterson, who now towered over his captor, just stood motionless with an unassuming grin on his face, staring down at his captors. He patiently waited for the show that was intended to rattle him come to its conclusion and continue his march up north and sit out the war in isolation in a cold cell.

The squad leader paused momentarily as he lit a cigarette then slowly circled behind Paterson and gestured that he should kneel. Paterson willingly complied with the smiling, now cordial squad leader's request as he placed the cigarette between Paterson's lips. Just about when Paterson was about to inhale, the squad leader abruptly fired a round through Paterson's forehead. The rapid stream of blood abandoning Paterson's head struck the NVA instantly before he was able to get out of its way. Red bubbles now spewed from the hole in his skull as his body twitched and spasmed. The NVA patrol collected their back-packs and weapons and headed back to their base camp after not finding any stragglers during their routine patrol. Capt. Jess Paterson had provided the required dose of twisted, sadistic amusement and diversion that would usually befall most deserters that fell into their hands. The squad leader wiped his hands on his uniform as if it were a minor inconvenience. Paterson's killing was no longer viewed as a casualty of war by team *Taino*, but one of murder. Anger and disgust filled the recon team as they gazed at Paterson's motionless form as flies began to feast on him. *Taino* could deal with men maneuvering against each other, trying their best to kill each other in the fields of battle. But Paterson's fate was immoral, a cowardly act in which the NVA would pay dearly; and the retaliation would be methodical. Paterson's execution had now become personal.

Taino shadowed the noisy 12-man squad over several hours until they set-up another camp site under some thick jungle canopy. The high elephant grass provided excellent cover as they boldly crept closer to the camp, watching their every move. The NVA squad was laughing and carrying on, apparently not concerned about the level of noise they were making, assured that they were safe from harm.

"Settle in…get real comfortable," Rodriguez whispered. "You don't have much time left in this world."

Taino remained motionless in the tall grass as they watched the NVA squad go through the motions of preparing their evening meal then settling in for the night. The team no longer viewed them as human beings but more as victims, living breathing targets of opportunity that were about to be obliterated. Their stomachs now full, and tired from the long march, the NVA squad collectively sacked out for the night without posting any sentries. Their first mistake. Venomous eyes were focused on the leader as he got up during the night and headed out about thirty yards downwind from the camp into the tall grass with shovel in hand to relieve himself. In his hand, *Tuan* carried a garrote made of piano wire that was about eight inches long with wooden handles on each end. To kill someone silently, you just crossed the ends of the wire when you slipped the loop over your victims neck, tightening the loop, then twisting. But this time there would be an added feature that was in store for Paterson's executioner, and a gruesome message to the rest of the NVA squad. The North Vietnamese soldier noisily dug a six inch hole in the ground then casually squatted above it as he prepared to settle in the make-shift out house. He shuffled around in his shirt pockets looking for his cigarettes and matches, unaware of the dangerous presence that lurked just several feet behind him. *Tuan* watched him excitedly, waiting until the man was completely comfortable and settled in. The garrote had already been in position for several seconds around his neck. *Tuan* waited for the right moment. He wanted him to know that he had been careless, and was going to die. The squad leader tried to shout at the realization that something was terribly amiss as he saw the reflection of the piano wire as he lit his cigarette. But no sounds left his mouth as he helplessly tried to scream. After twisting the piano wire with all of his strength, *Tuan* lifted his victim onto his back while he pulled hard on both handles. The piano wire carved through the windpipe and neck muscles and finally between the disks in the vertebrae, severing the head. It was an act devoid of thought and conscience. *Tuan* felt no remorse for his actions but was rather pleased and honored that his American friends allowed him the satisfaction and opportunity to express his own displeasure with the *North Vietnamese* as the headless form thrashed on the ground. The dead squad leader was payback, thought *Tuan*, for the NVA massacre of his home village of *Dak Son* in *Phuoc Long province* in December of 1967. *North Vietnamese* Army soldiers had quietly entered the *Montagnard* village, then using flame throwers, incinerated two hundred and fifty *Montagnard* women and children.

Rodriguez's team silently exited the camp site to get as much distance between themselves and the squad in the event the outraged squad decided to retaliate. It probably wouldn't be until morning that they realized that their squad leader was missing. Each man took turns at watch at hourly intervals during the long tense filled sleepless night while they stopped to get a few hours rest expecting the NVA to be right behind them.

"Enemy patrol not far behind us," reported *Tuan* from high on a thick-wooded ridge line. the *Montagnard* scout had spotted two columns of NVA soldiers heading up toward their position.

"OK, we make a stand here. You know what to do," ordered Rodriguez. Cano and *Tuan* nodded affirmatively. They didn't have much time. By the time they recovered Paterson's body and located a suitable LZ for extraction the NVA squad would be on top of them.

Multiple claymores were laid into the ground and pointed toward the NVA's probable approach. Manny helped *Tuan* insert the blasting caps into the claymores and wired it to a nine-volt battery while the trip-wire was laid low to the ground. The wire was so thin it was almost invisible and less than a foot off the ground. Team *Taino* then quietly concealed themselves in the thick brush, at the ready to strike at the patrol from their prearranged cross-fire ambush positions.

As the NVA point man approached the kill zone, he anxiously looked around the thick jungle terrain, looking at every shadow and outline and any signs of ambush. He sensed danger and death all-round him as his intuition told him to stop and look toward the jungle floor. The point man spotted the scarcely exposed trip-wire. Bone rattling fear made him sweat profusely now as he slowly knelt down on one knee to study it further. And before he had a chance to stop the columns from going any further, the man behind him was puzzled by the point man's expression of horror as he nonchalantly walked right through his path setting off the claymores, tearing them apart. The initial explosion concealed the wood line with smoke and debris and the odor of seared flesh. The NVA squad had walked into the center of the kill zone of the claymores and Rodriguez's team cross-fire. *Tuan* found a survivor trying to hold his intestines in with his hands, pleaded with *Tuan* to finish him. *Tuan* gladly put him out of his misery. Another victim painstaking tried to suck air down his blood-filled throat, suddenly dying with his chest still expanded. Manny immediately thought of Angel Cruz, and if he had died in the same horrible way. The dying soldier stared into his dark eyes as he gasped his last breath. The claymores had been aimed low, and as a result, some of the NVA had their feet blown off leaving them with jagged stumps. Team *Taino* back- tracked and found another five dead NVA. The team went back and retrieved Capt. Paterson's body to take him...home.

CHAPTER NINE

Suzanne Logan's attention was drawn to the student protesters demonstrating in front of the administration building. She sat quietly in thought on a grassy knoll in front of the Business School at Columbia University while she waited for her fiancé, Michael Collins. It was March 27th, 1972, and the *Vietnam* war was at an impasse. The end was nowhere in sight, although President Nixon had brought home most of the ground troops, struggling to find a political solution to get out and save face with the American people.

Suzanne had not taken a political stance on the war until Ray Vaquero had decided to leave her and enlist. She was clearly opposed to anything that might put him in harm's way, she thought sadly now, concerned about his safety and afraid to accept the dangers that pursued him. She worried every time she watched the war on the evening news. And although she could never fully grasp why he left her, Suzanne still yearned for him, struggling with emotions that whispered to her softly that she still loved him. And there was the guilt. It was never easy to admit that Michael was no more than a substitute, a vehicle to force Ray out of her mind. She fought to contain the overwhelming panic and repressed tears that began to uncontrollably flow at the thought that Ray would be out of her life forever. She wiped the tears off her soft, tender face as she remembered his strong possessive hands. The dimple on her left cheek began to take form as she half-smiled, reminiscing and finally conceding that she could no longer live without him. *He made her feel like she belonged to him.* Suzanne moved her soft, shoulder length, chestnut- colored hair behind her ears then quickly wiped the tears away one more time and feigned a smile for Michael.

#   #   #

The monotony and boredom infuriated him as he slowly slid back inside the aircraft, convinced that the evening's mission would end as it had begun...uneventful. There was no guilt of conscience or concern over intentionally exposing the crew's back as he reached for the thick rubber pad that cushioned him against bumps and jolts during the long five hour missions. Duane Shaw carefully rolled it into a pillow and fell into a deep slumber. Spectre 09 was on its fourth hour search for an elusive truck park south of the Laotian town of *Savannakeht* along Route 13. The night was clear and vibrant as cirrus clouds brushed the evening sky at twenty-thousand feet. Major Stuart Marks cautiously glanced at the jungle below, ignoring the "moon flashes" that brightly burst across scores of ponds and river beds. They were often mistaken for muzzle flashes by inexperienced, gun shy flight crews. A single 37-mm round suddenly brightened the night sky off Spectre's nine o'clock position, five miles from their spiral search pattern. Marks, the flight engineer Bud James, and co-pilot Ryan Scott watched the bright orange air burst, aware of its significance as a warning to convoys and anti-aircraft batteries in the area that gunships were near.

"Did you catch that, Shaw? Keep your eyes open, they could open up at any time." Marks' remark stung with open distrust and suspicion. Duane Shaw had already flown ten missions with Marks but failed to display the esprit de corps Marks had expected from a member of his crew. As a result, Marks felt ill at ease and vulnerable whenever Shaw was on board his aircraft. Marks had protested vehemently, but he'd finally given in to Colonel Roberts persistence and agreed to give Shaw a chance to prove himself. Marks' contact in personnel had combed through Duane Shaw's personnel record to look for any glaring flaw that might suggest that he would put Marks' crew at risk, but there was none. No write-ups that revealed any deficiency or past reprimand for dereliction of duty. Shaw had more than fifty missions under his belt with various flight crews. That was the peculiar thing about his record, thought Marks. No one really sought after Shaw to be their I.O. Instead, Shaw had spent most of his tour filling in for other I.O.'s that were grounded with severe colds and ear blocks or away on R & R. He exuded a cold and detached demeanor from the very first day Marks and his crew had set eyes on him. And it was that air of aloofness and insubordinate cockiness that concerned Marks. It instinctively told him that Duane Shaw was bound to fuck-up one day, and he didn't want it to happen during his watch, nor on his aircraft.

The intercom was dead silent. Usually a double click on the intercom switch would have been sufficient acknowledgment of a command, especially when you were too busy looking for enemy ground fire. Troubled stares were exchanged throughout the aircraft while everyone waited for the Shaw to acknowledge Major Marks' order. Duane Shaw was in a deep slumber.

"Shaw," Marks shouted into his headset. His voice was tense but controlled. Still, the intercom was silent.

"Gramps?" Barked Marks in an imposing tone.

"Yes, sir," responded Louie Grimes sharply. The lead aft gunner was responsible for the management of the four-man gun crew. Gramps' form was barely visible as he stood quietly in the darkness between the 105-mm Howitzer and the 40-mm Bofors.

"Go wake-up that son of a bitch…he's asleep." Marks leveled off the aircraft, disengaging from the search for the truck park, while Grimes climbed up the ramp door to check on Shaw. Marks was seething yet pleased. He had Shaw by the balls now, confident that he would never fly again once they landed back at *Ubon*. He'd make sure of that. Louie Grimes tapped Shaw on the shoulder several times but got no response. He then shook him a little harder. Shaw swung his left arm around blocking Grimes third attempt to stir him.

"What the fuck do you want?" retorted Shaw, startled that he had been caught dozing.

"It's not what I want, asshole. Marks knows you were asleep." Grimes grinned sarcastically while looking at Shaw's unnerved expression then stepped back down off the ramp. Panic suddenly gripped Shaw as his ass uncontrollably puckered and began to sweat.

"Fuck," blurted Shaw while Marks banked the aircraft west toward *Ubon*.

#   #   #

"I'm going to visit a Buddhist Temple outside the city today to offer incense and prayer to my ancestors. Would you like to come along with me?" *Toi Dasananda* stared at him with her uncommon round-shaped eyes and infectious smile.

Finishing a bowl of spicy *Thai* soup with coconut milk, chicken and cabbage, Vaquero nodded in agreement.

"Sure, I'm ready whenever you are." Vaquero had planned to spend part of the day with her before catching the afternoon C-130 shuttle to *Phu Bai, South Vietnam* to visit with Manny and Cano for a couple of days. As they left her apartment, Vaquero saw that there was a *spirit house* outside of her dwelling. Spirit houses were dollhouse-like shrines where flowers and food were offered daily to the spirits. A fresh glass of wine stood at the foot of the wooden shrine.

Toi hailed a cab. After several minutes of highly intensive negotiations she finally reached agreement on the fare. She turned to Vaquero, politely smiled and said, "We will be there in about ten minutes." Her dogged stubborn facial expression transformed into one of an angel.

Ghostlike faces ringed the two saffron-robed Buddhist monks as Vaquero and *Toi Dasananda* approached. They sat cross- legged on a circle of cushions inside the temple sanctuary. The monks closed their eyes and chanted mantras as *Toi* led Ray by the hand and knelt quietly in front of them for several minutes before one of them moved. The oldest of the two appeared to be a man beyond the reach of time thought Vaquero. *Toi* whispered in Vaquero's ear and told him that he was over eighty years old. His close-cropped hair was scarcely gray, and his face was softly creased with smile lines.

"The Buddhist renounces the world to cultivate the inner spirit. To us, that is the highest type of man." Toi's faced radiated with gladness that Ray was there with her. Her voice was soft and melodic while she spoke with the older monk momentarily. The monk nodded then took hold of Vaquero's left hand and tied a cotton string around his wrist.

"*This is a Sai Sin, and it's to guard the thirty-two souls of your body, my son,*" translated *Toi* with smiling eyes.

He stared deeply into Vaqueros' hollow eyes, sensing the pain within him. "*Nothing in life is permanent, my son. We foolishly make plans, dream, and have many desires. All our wishes and desires control our lives. But it is like grasping at one's reflection in water. You must look inward for the calm....*" Mantra chants resonated throughout the temple as the monk sprinkled blessed water on both of them. But Ray Vaquero abruptly broke eye contact with him pondering his only passion thousands of miles away, and his unwillingness to let Suzanne Logan go.

Ray studied the amulet around his wrist while *Toi* knelt by another shrine and prayed.

"My ancestors are pleased that you came here today with me," *Toi* said shyly.

"Oh, so they talked with you, did they?" Ray asked, knowing that *Toi* was pulling his leg. "What did they say?" he asked jokingly.

"They wish peace and harmony in your heart, Raymond." Toi's smile suddenly turned seductive as her dark eyes revealed what she had secretly wanted to do the first moment she had set eyes on him. "And my prayer is that you come back safely after every mission." Ray stood motionless as they gazed at each other. Then *Toi* softly rubbed her cheek against Vaquero's, slowly maneuvering her open mouth with his. Ray responded to her desires, not in passion, but with mild affection. *Toi* also fought with her emotions and memory of Willie Santiago. It had been four months since Willie Santiago had died. Santiago's friends were distant and vague about the details except that he had died during an emergency landing at *Ubon*. A sense of shame flowed through her while she silently embraced Vaquero. The last two days with Vaquero made her realize how hardened and detached she had become after Santiago's death. The *Buddhists* were right, she thought, her eyes closed as she rested her head on his chest. You must live your life abundantly, each and every moment as if it were your last.

"I need to get back to the base, *Toi*," Vaquero smiled at her warmly, concealing his deep-seated devotion to Suzanne Logan.

"Will you come see me right away when you get back?" *Toi* asked as the cab parked within ten feet of the base main gate.

"I'll come by the *Thai Palace* as soon as I get back, *Toi*," Ray assured, pressing her hand. "Thanks again for everything. I'll be back in three days." *Toi* leaned over and kissed him gently on his forehead. Ray could see the cab driver's hardened stare through the rear view mirror, resentful of the affection *Toi* shared with the foreigner. Ray stood on the curb as street vendors engulfed him. Ray waved good-bye and gazed at her beaming smile as the cab steered back onto the main road. Toi's faced glowed with joy as she gazed back at him from the rear window until Vaquero's form was lost in the crowd. It was a stare he would never forget.

\#   \#   \#

The elite NVA mortar sapper team was two days ahead of schedule. After crossing the *Mekong River* a week earlier, a very young and determined jungle fighter quietly went over the plan of attack with the four-man team. The sappers listened carefully as *Le Thanh* reviewed the plan for the twentieth time. Huddled in a tight circle in an abandoned wooden hut on stilts three miles outside *Ubon* RTAFB they schemed to demolish the Spectre gunships of the 16th Special Operations Squadron. Information obtained by communist sympathizers and informants that worked on the base had been invaluable. Inconspicuous barrack housekeepers, gardeners, and bar maids that worked at the Officer's and NCO clubs had easily acquired a wealth of information from intoxicated and the generally talkative Americans. When the orders were finally authorized by *COSVN, North Vietnam's* southern command, to strike at the American airfield, it was only a short period of time before inside sources had meticulously mapped the airfield and the weak security defenses and routines. *Le Thanh* opened an eight and a half by eleven color-coded drawing that detailed the exact location of fourteen gunships in their revetments identified by model and tail number. *Thanh* snickered. It was all too easy. Americans weren't very good at preparing for the unexpected, he thought confidently.

Thanh was in excellent physical condition and fit to go on the mission despite the battalion's political officers' objections and insistence that his place was with his anti-aircraft battery in preparation for the spring offensive. *Thanh* had trained with sapper units and had gone through nearly twelve months of training at *Son Tay, North Vietnam* where they learned to penetrate enemy defenses and master the use of various types of weapons and explosives. As a member of the *Lao Dong Party, Thanh* had cleverly manipulated his influence and status as a distinguished and highly decorated anti-aircraft gunner to get himself assigned to the sapper team through his contacts in *Hanoi*. Political officers didn't know shit about executing military objectives, *Thanh* thought sarcastically as he tightened the straps of his rucksack. They were only efficient at extolling the virtues of the *Party* and its revolution, and how the political objective took priority over military operational goals. He stood motionless in thought, surprised at the realization that his adversary most likely grappled with the same dilemma, and assholes. *Thanh* slammed a fresh magazine into his AK-47 as he walked outside the hut, turning the selector switch to armed. The team was sanguine as they prepared to march the two and a half mile trek toward the air base armed with an 82-mm mortar. And they were driven with the knowledge that their side was ready to sacrifice more of themselves over the long haul than the Americans were prepared to bleed for the South.

#   #   #

Toi Dasananda smiled incessantly as she hurriedly dried herself off after a hot shower, unable to get Ray Vaquero out of her mind. She frantically stumbled around her small apartment looking for something to wear before heading out toward a remote part of *Ubon*. *Toi* stood frozen in front of the mirror, suddenly remembering that Willie Santiago would often take her there to watch the roaring aircraft fly overhead at dusk. She zig-zagged in and out of traffic as she raced toward a deserted road a mile outside the base in her Honda two-seater motor-scooter to get a glimpse of the C-130 that would carry Ray Vaquero to *Phu Bai*. *Toi* parked the motor-scooter under a very old, well-shaded hundred foot Teak tree. Heat waves rose slowly off the ground as she wiped the sweat off her brow. It was two-thirty; *Toi* looked in the direction of the airfield. She knew she had arrived in time to observe the imposing olive-colored camouflaged transport climb above her position. The surrounding jungle was unusually quiet with a dead stillness in the air. Birds nestled in the trees abruptly raced in flight as two pair of F-4D's suddenly appeared, soaring overhead and frightening her momentarily.

The roar of the aircraft was deafening as the pilots kicked in the after-burners, then slowly banked to the left on a course that would lead them east across the *fence*. *Toi* then heard the familiar whine of Allison T-56 turbo-prop engines as they slashed their way into the dense tropical air propelling the aircraft down the runway. She stood on her toes on top of her motor-scooter as she watched the fully loaded transport utilize most of the nine thousand foot runway to get airborne. She waved fran-tically hoping that Vaquero could somehow see her as it flew directly over her position stirring the trees and brush around her. *Toi* stared at the lumbering aircraft until it was just a dark spot in the fiery afternoon sky.

The black pajama-clad sapper team reached the thick bamboo sanc-tuary below a grassy knoll that would hide them from view long enough to fire nearly fifty 82-mm mortar rounds that had been hidden in a tun-nel under some shrubbery. One of the sappers immediately headed toward higher ground with his Soviet *Dragunov* sniper rifle slung over his shoulder to hold off any assault from the airfield defenders or any-one else unlucky enough to wander into his kill zone. Two other sappers quickly assembled the bipod, base plate, tube and sight of the 82-mm mortar while *Le Thanh* laid several U.S. claymores along the dirt road path. As expected, the airfield was buzzing with activity as maintenance and munition crews prepared the aircraft for the evening missions. *Thanh* counted fourteen black tails jutting out from the top of their revetments as he privately admired their destructive force through high-powered binoculars. The Spectres' were in the nest.

A flimsy wooden guard tower stood out in the open fifty yards out-side the west end of the air field's weak defensive perimeter. The after-noon sun was bright orange and extraordinary as it hung motionless in the western sky. A lone *Thai* sentry desperately looked for shade in the cramped wooden tower leaned up against one of the posts that faced the airfield. He looked at his watch then cursed out loud at the thought of another two hours of guard-duty before being relieved.

The sniper had a perfect panoramic view of the watch tower and dirt road. It was the most probable approach that would be used by the base security forces he theorized. He scanned the kill zones through the telescopic scope of his weapon. He came back to the tower again, made some minor adjustments on the focusing ring, then centered the crosshairs of the scope on the back of the young sentry's head. His peripheral vision suddenly detected movement to his far right. *Toi Dasananda's* form appeared unexpectedly from behind the giant tree, catching the sniper by surprise. She was walking beside her motor-scooter slowly back down the trail. Slightly out of range, the sniper was unable to adjust his position without compromising his primary target on the tower. While she was out of his firing range, she could certainly hear his gun fire and alert the base security to the location of the mortar crew. But it was already too late. The *Thai* guard was hurriedly awakened by the hollow metal whooshing sounds overhead and the immense terrifying explosions as 82-mm mortars struck the airfield, showering shrapnel across several F-4D's. Maintenance crews instinctively scurried for cover in anticipation of additional volleys as the sapper team walked the deadly rounds between the airfield and the Spectre's. Curled up in a fetal-like position, the sentry screamed into his radio for backup, disclosing the direction of the incoming mortar fire. The guard threw the radio on the floor as he frantically attempted to become one with the tower. In his uncertainty and preoccupation with *Toi*, the sniper now realized that his blunder cost the team precious seconds to inflict maximum destruction to the gunships and the airfield before the base security forces had located them. He failed to execute the objective instantly without hesitation or thought, neutralizing the sentry immediately and preventing him from disclosing their firing position.

Toi, overcome with fear, instinctively dived into the elephant grass and rolled into a ball, covering her head from the thunderous explosions. With cold indifference the sniper efficiently squeezed-off two rounds from his *Dragunov* rifle striking the Thai guard in the right

thigh shattering his leg. The impact of the round elevated the guard off
the ground providing the sniper a better view of his quarry. Another
round ripped through his lower spine exiting through his chest. The
sentry gasped for a brief moment before the next round shattered his
skull.

Toi Dasananda cried out in terror as the mortar fire multiplied in
intensity. The impact violently shook the ground, spraying dirt and
shrapnel everywhere. An AC-130A was pelted with razor-sharp metal
fragments across the left side of the aircraft's fuselage and wheel-well,
imbedding itself into the protective four-inch thick armor plating. Tires
of another aircraft caught fire and exploded as a 82-mm mortar found
its mark inside the protective shield of the revetments.

Le Thanh spotted the racing convoy of security personnel headed
east in their direction. The base security response had been faster than
he had expected, he thought. He took a deep breath, openly disappointed that his focus was now forced elsewhere. *Thanh* adjusted the
firing coordinates to fend off the enemy forces to buy time for a speedy
departure. From his vantage point *Thanh* could see the airfield was
severely cratered in several places. The damage was significant enough
to keep the U.S. aircraft on the ground for a few days. But more importantly it would keep the Spectres grounded long enough to sit out the
battle that was brewing across the *fence.* Two F-4's and three gunships
were severely damaged, ripped and torn, spewing JP-4 fuel from under
their wings.

A barrage of mortar fire halted the U.S.-Thai assault in their tracks as
thirty base defenders bolted for cover around the surrounding trees and
brush. Burning red tracer lines from two fifty caliber machine guns
mounted on jeeps blindly showered the distant slopes and tree-line
attempting to locate and silence the attackers, pelting *Toi* with dirt and
rock as bullets from the base security forces impacted all-round her.
Anything was better than just staying put, she thought, consumed with
fear. The tall elephant grass to her left was scythed by a ferocious volley

as the soldiers continued to blindly probe the thick brush-covered fields. She stood up and ran for safety toward the bases barb-wired fence that encircled *Ubon* RTAFB. Her heart raced uncontrollably as the deadly rounds zipped close to her head.

The sniper invisibly crept back toward the mortar location, picking off several of the security force along the way when they foolishly exposed themselves. *Le Thanh* continued to walk the mortars back and forth keeping the base security forces pinned close to the ground as they prepared to exit the area. A final barrage intensified again as one of the sappers stayed behind to fire the 82-mm mortar, showering his enemy with sheets of hot shrapnel while the rest of the sapper team faded into the jungle.

Toi Dasananda was suddenly hurled into the air by the force of multiple explosions. In shock now, she helplessly staggered aimlessly along the dirt road while thick streams of blood flowed down her forehead, nose and ears. Hobbling, struggling to stay conscious, telling herself that she could escape through the barbwire fence several feet away. But Toi Dasananda's life was abruptly extinguished after setting off multiple claymores. An innocent victim, entangled in a conflict not of her choosing.

#   #   #

The stench in the air overwhelmed Vaquero as he stepped off the C-130 transport. A forklift operator patiently waited in the shade off the right wing in full view of the off-loading passengers to stack dozens of caskets into the stomach of the aircraft. A scorching afternoon heat, reeked with rotting flesh and burning shit combined with gasoline, forced Vaquero to cover his nose and mouth with his hand. *Phu Bai* was a confined area, laid out in neat orderly rows of tents that seemed to go on forever. The *Montagnard* compound was built close to the safety of the base as well. But the constant pounding of rockets and mortar fire forced the *Jeh* villagers to sleep in bunkers and tunnels that honey-combed throughout the compound.

"Fuck me…" Vaquero blurted. After getting directions to Rodriguez and Rincón's unit, Vaquero could hear *Jimi Hendrick's* "Voodoo Child," blaring from their tent. He quietly entered the tent, noting an old wooden trunk at the foot of their cots and a large flag of Puerto Rico hanging on the wall. Their cots were each covered with a thin mattress and a worn-out mosquito net. A small table and four straight-back wooden chairs were in the middle of the dusty tent, serving as a place to play cards and writing letters, he thought. Claymore mines, grenades, weapons, and ammunition were haphazardly stored throughout the hooch, and it made Vaquero a little uncomfortable. Beer cans were scattered throughout the confined tent. But Rodriguez and Rincón had just returned from a long and arduous trail watching mission and were catching up on some much needed sleep. Sound rest was something fugitive for Manny and Cano.

Vaquero threw his soft overnight bag on Rodriguez's head, then he jumped onto Rincón's back as he slept.

"What the hell…" Rodriguez shouted.

"Wake-up you bean-fartin, banana-eatin' faggots." Vaquero razzed them while he held Cano in a headlock. "You guys ain't so tough," Vaquero teased. Rodriguez laughed at Vaquero's heckling and Cano's predicament.

"Watch out for him, Ray, he'll think you're *Hanghe* and he'll poke you." Vaquero leaped from the bed and ran over to Rodriguez for protection.

"Who the hell is *Hanghe*?" Vaquero asked, out of breath from the horse-play.

"*Hanghe* is Tuan's sister, our *Montagnard* scout I told you about in my letters." Vaquero nodded.

"She wears him out more often than Lupo's sister ever did. *Hanghe* wants his Latin seed real bad man." Manny and Ray broke into uproarious laughter. Cano sat up slowly, impervious to their badgering, scratched his nuts for a moment then ran over and leaped on Ray and Manny.

"*Hanghe* wants to have my baby; is that so wrong?" Cano replied innocently.

"Yeah, she's got this thing about blondes." Manny countered. "She wants her baby to have his skin, Ray. Hanghe's got this thing about Cano's skin."

Vaquero caressed Cano's face. "Yeah, it's because it is so sensitive," he goaded in an effeminate tone. Cano pounced on them again.

Three very close friends got shit-faced while they sat on a dusty, red, clay-filled floor half a world away from home. They laughed so hard at Cano's spirited tales with *Hanghe* that tears ran down their cheeks as they rolled on the floor. The war seemed distant and illusory now as three despondent hearts were warmed by the bonds of brotherhood, yearning for that time of innocence that had long past. Manny and Cano looked thin and ashen, and their skin was taut and colorless. It was the jungle. The jungle was devouring them, Ray mused sorrowfully.

"Well, it's that time to visit *Hanghe*," Cano announced happily. Rodriguez shook his head and grinned.

"Let's go, Ray. I'll introduce you to *Tuan* and look for someone's sister," he said jokingly with an exaggerated Spanish accent. "The *Montagnard* village chief is usually hitting the brew right about now." Rodriguez was slightly wasted himself. "You ain't lived until you've had *Jeh* brew." His words slurred.

"Yeah, that shit will definitely give you a brain spasm," chuckled Cano as he scratched his head. Manny led Ray into the *marao*, the *Jeh* communal house for guests. He greeted *Tuan* and his family, and introduced Ray. The three Americans sat in a circle with other *Jeh* members while the village chief prepared his concoction near the center of the room.

"*Tuan Bang Ong* is a member of the *Jeh* tribe. His people have occupied the mountain highlands of Southeast Asia for centuries," commented Rodriguez while Vaquero watched nervously. "*Montagnards* are thirty different primitive tribes, and they account for fifteen percent of the population in *Vietnam*. They've always lived in these mountains, Ray," pausing momentarily as he offered cigarettes to the group. "They're good-natured, loving people, *Montagnards* feel no compulsion to become involved in the shit happening around them. It's not their nature." *Hanghe* walked in casually and bare-breasted into the *marao*, taking her place behind Cano. Vaquero watched Cano and *Hanghe* exchange lover's glances, while Cano contemplated the right moment when he could slip away with *Hanghe* and fill her with his seed.

"They only want autonomy, and the ability to direct their lives the way they see fit. I'm sure you can see that they have been victimized by the circumstances of this war, but it doesn't matter to them which side wins, Ray, the *Jeh* just want to go on living." Vaquero cautiously stared at the draft of rice wine that was rigged to flow through a plastic gasoline siphon. Rice husks floated atop the beverage.

"I was looking forward to an ice cold beer. In fact, I'll even settle for a warm bottle of beer," whispered Vaquero hoping that their host didn't understand English.

"If you refuse to drink the rice wine, Ray, you will insult the chief, and he will think he'll die." Rodriguez said firmly. The village chief was about forty five-and wore only a black loincloth. "*Jeh* life is governed by spirits and superstition. The *Jeh* believe in the *Yang* and the *Kanam*. The *Yang* are the rulers of the mountains, the earth and sky, and river. Are you with me Ray?" Rodriguez asked, not wanting to go over it again. "The *Yang* is considered to be a good spirit since it is able to control *Kanam*, the evil ancestor of spirits that roams the forests. The *Kanam* torments the lives of men and requires appeasement. To control the evil spirits, the *Jeh* sacrifice buffaloes, chickens and pigs to the *Yang* so they will help control the *Kanam*."

The drinking continued through the night as the village chief spoke of life's destiny and the mysteries of the jungle. Then they listened to *Tuan* tell of his team's exploits and the failed rescue attempt of the downed Air Force pilot. Smiles rounded the *Jeh* member's faces in the *marao* when *Tuan* described in gruesome detail the fate of the NVA squad leader. The wine took over Vaquero's senses as the flickering camp fire cast eerie moving shadows everywhere. *Hanghe* and three of the *Jeh* tribesmen danced around the mesmerizing fire, chanting ancient songs of the *Jeh*. As Vaquero fell asleep, Cano helped Manny remove Ray's flight suit, laying him slowly down onto the ground. The *Jeh* village chief carefully studied the strange symbols on the piece of paper that Rodriguez had handed to him. He prepared to tattoo Vaquero's left arm the symbols that Manny and Cano both carried. When they were through, they carried him back to their tent and gently laid him down on Rodriguez's cot for the night. Cano slipped out to finally meet with *Hanghe* prepared to do his best to impregnate her. Rodriguez listened to Vaquero's moans as he hallucinated again with shadowy images, struggling in his nightmares to live beyond his fears. Curled up like a ball, Rodriguez slept soundly on the dirt floor next to his best friend, assured that Vaquero would come to his aid when he most needed him.

#   #   #

Spectre 07 was operating southwest of *Hue* in search of a sizable convoy that had been spotted by a *South Vietnamese* FAC. The FAC had mysteriously disappeared off the ABCCC radar screens. Russian Zils had been spotted with their lights on through a hole in the thick jungle carpet, racing down on a narrow path through a mountainous terrain and deep in a valley of hills that reached nearly four thousand feet. Spectre 07 attempted to contact the FAC to no avail. It had simply vanished.

Mike Walters cupped his hands and blew hard on his finger tips for warmth. They tingled from the freezing temperature at twelve-thousand feet. His nose started to run and drip into his bubble shield, occasionally obstructing his view. "This sucks big time, man," he blurted. Walters hadn't planned on wearing his thermal underwear since their original mission was planned at seven thousand feet. It was usually pretty warm and comfortable at that altitude. But the thin flight gloves were no match for the frosty air that blasted through the open aircraft port holes. Walters wished they'd hurry and shoot something so the aft gunners could hand him a hot shell to warm up with. Suddenly, the bitter cold left him as he recognized the tell-tale glow of a SA-7 that was fired at the AC-130A from the top of the mountain.

"Strela at six o'clock, hold what you got," commanded Walters, calmly tracking the missile as it arched smoothly in the darkness toward the aircraft. The SA-7's motor burned with a spooky blue light porpoising back and forth the way the shoulder-fired weapon was supposed to as it honed-in on the heat exhaust of the Allison T-56 engines. Time appeared to stand still, and seconds were an eternity as Walters stared at the missile as it drew closer to the aircraft. When it was within three seconds of striking the gunship, Walters fired multiple decoy flares that hung under the gunship's wings. He then directed the pilot to make a tight sixty degree left hand turn, attempting to conceal the heat of the exhaust from the missile, but the path of the SA-7 didn't change as it surprisingly exploded into number three engine. The explosion jarred the aircraft, causing a bright flash then fire as the missile found its target in the darkness. Number three engine violently separated from the right wing.

The aircraft shuddered violently and it began to lose altitude rapidly. Frantically, the navigator radioed over the UHF frequency that Spectre 07 had lost an engine and needed to make an emergency landing. Walters instinctively came back inside the aircraft, disconnected the restraining hook from his harness and reached for his chest-pack parachute in the darkness. He had practiced hooking the rings to his body harness thousands of times in the past with his eyes closed, but now he was nervous as the aircraft bounced violently in all directions. Just when he finally hooked one of the rings to his chest-pack, the right wing violently came off the doomed gunship. It went into an uncontrollable cartwheel roll. The adrenaline surge affected his ability to stay calm under such circumstances. Walters had hooked only one side of his chest-pack to his body-harness when multiple explosions tossed him and two aft gunners out into the darkness.

Chapter Ten

Smoke from his French *Gauloises Caporals* hung in the damp morning air. The senior Politburo member exhaled deliberately as he watched the rain squall slowly inch its way south from the east wing window of the Central Committee's headquarters in downtown *Hanoi*. He grinned, pleased with the inclement weather and the role it would play as the invasion got under way across the Demilitarized Zone. Fourteen NVA divisions and twenty-five separate regiments were about to force their way south in a conventional attack from three fronts, leaving only one division to protect their rear. Over one hundred and fifty thousand fresh troops supported with Russia's finest T-54 and T-34 tanks along with long-range artillery pieces would lead the way. American air strikes would have little impact in thwarting the initial onslaught, he contemplated. An impenetrable cloud cover still blanketed most of the country.

The senior, much older member of the *Lao Dong Party*, had hungered for such an invasion. The 1968 *Tet* offensive had wiped out over ninety-percent of his forces after all the dust and smoke had cleared. Undoubtedly it was only a minor setback, he thought coldly, reaching into his pants pocket for the crumbling blue package and another unfiltered cigarette. He was untouched by the enormous losses they had sustained over the last ten years that would have resulted in instant capitulation for any other army. They were accustomed to such slaughter, he rationalized. It was the price he exacted from the people of *North Vietnam*. First and foremost for the *Party*, then for the so-called revolution.

General *Vo Nguyen Giap*, Defense Minister of the Democratic Republic of *Vietnam*, was a pompous little man with forceful manipulative skills who prided himself in his ability to influence the other members of the *19th Plenum* to attack in 1972 after the *Tet* miscarriage. The timing and the opening could not have been more perfect, mused *Giap* with his customary measure of insolence as the torrid rainstorm intensified. It was March 30th, 1972, and President Nixon had withdrawn most of the American combat units from *South Vietnam*. Less than one hundred thousand soldiers remained in-country from more than five times that number only three years earlier. The puppet *South Vietnamese* Army and the U.S. Air Force were now left to bear the brunt of the fighting, while the U.S. ground combat position reflected a discernible indecisiveness commonly associated with a defeated ally no longer committed to the war. The Central Committee members could scarcely miss the implications and trends *Giap* had pointed out so eloquently. They clearly saw through Nixon's Vietnam policy for what it really was, a reflection of a hasty blueprint to retreat from their obligations to the South. America's Achilles heel had always been public opinion, *Giap* had argued for years. It finally became North Vietnam's political as well as military battle cry to bleed the Americans often and repeatedly in 1972 until they were gone. *Giap* and the Politburo were not about to settle for another half-ass settlement like they had with the French, without a decisive military victory against the South and especially against their arch enemy Richard M. Nixon. *Giap* had personally code-named the offensive *Nguyen Hue,* in honor of a nationally well known Vietnamese emperor who in 1789 had maneuvered his troops hundreds of miles to attack another great power, the Chinese army. They too were defeated, sneered the seasoned bureaucrat.

#   #   #

Mike Walter's heart raced uncontrollably as the barking dogs drew closer. NVA patrols with flashlights searched the moonlit forested terrain around him firing several rounds into the air attempting to flush him out.

"Stay cool blood, don't go try and be the Lone Ranger and do something stupid like shoot your way out this shit. Uncle Sam will be coming to get your black ass out of this fucking jungle real soon now, you hear," he whispered to himself confidently as sweat from his forehead rolled into his eyes. Walters nervously peered through the thick bamboo brush he had jumped into for cover. His hands trembled as he anxiously opened several packets of pepper he carried in the pants leg of his flight suit. He then sprinkled them around his perimeter in case the dogs got too close to his position. Although he was well hidden, squatting quietly in the center of a bamboo thicket, Mike Walters had no intention of moving since the NVA were still in the area looking for him. He thought of drawing his .38 revolver again but decided against it. Walters knew he could take down two or three of them if he had to, but what chance would he have against dozens of automatic weapons? All that would accomplish was hasten pissing them off and getting himself killed.

Walters quickly downed one of his water bottles as fear and adrenaline flooded his senses. Walters' ears tuned in again for the sounds of approaching footsteps. When he thought it was safe, he cautiously switched on the beeper to his survival radio broadcasting on emergency frequencies to aircraft in the area that one of 'their own' was alive. He turned off the radio then listened again to see if anyone was prowling around his position. It was quiet, and the barking dogs now appeared to have gone searching in another direction. In a low raspy voice, Walters spoke into his radio.

"Mayday, Mayday, this is Spectre 07, over." The radio crackled loudly with static. Walters accidently dropped the radio then struggled to locate the volume control in the darkness. A surge of panic passed through him at the thought that the NVA patrol would surely find him. He sat there for thirty minutes cautiously scanning the jungle around him, employing the well-honed night vision he had developed after having flown well over a hundred missions over the *fence*. He turned on the radio beeper for five minutes then switched over to the assigned communication frequency to transmit one more time. It occurred to him that the NVA could be monitoring his transmission. The NVA were known to have captured U.S. radios and were competent at utilizing the equipment in locating downed flyers and ambushing the search and rescue teams when they had the opportunity. But it was worth the risk, he thought nervously, anxious to get the hell out of there.

"Mayday, Mayday, this is Spectre 07 over," Walters repeated again in a tone that was barely audible. The cheerful soothing voice of the OV-10 FAC code-named Nail out of NKP Thailand, was barely a whisper when it came over his radio.

"Spectre 07, this is Nail One-Three, I read you five-by-five, over." Walter's smile stretched from one side of his face to the other.

"Roger Nail One-Three, I copy you loud and clear, over. Nail, standby-one." Walters listened carefully again for sounds that seemed unnatural. "I'm back Nail, just checking my perimeter for unwanted visitors, over." Walters was calmer now, knowing that he had been found, enjoying the comfort of talking to a friendly voice.

"Spectre 07, are you wounded, over?" inquired the FAC, determining if a night SAR operation was required.

"No, I'm all right," Walters paused momentarily. "Just scared shitless man."

"Stand-by one Zero-Seven," interrupted Nail abruptly.

"I've got your exact location pinpointed buddy, just stay put for the night. A SAR team will be back at first light to pull you out of there, over." Nail's precision Loran navigation equipment was able to pinpoint

Walters exact position by using a series of radio bearings off Walters' survival radio. Walters was relieved. "Hey, you OK?" Queried Nail.

"Yeah, I'm all right, Nail. I just don't know how to thank you man, that's all." The FAC pilot smiled as he quickly banked the aircraft into a tight sixty degree turn, heading west toward *Nakon Phanom, Thailand*.

"You can buy me a beer at *Tippy's* tomorrow night at *Ubon*, just keep your ass put for the night, OK? responded the FAC, assuring Walters that he would be safe until morning.

"You got a deal, Nail. I'll see you in the morning."

"Goodnight Spectre." Walters turned off the survival radio, placing it back into the web gear vest pocket. Exhausted, Walters curled into a ball and instantly fell asleep.

#   #   #

The loadmaster rolled up his communications cord and locked the crew entrance door of the olive-colored C-130 cargo transport work-horse. Ray Vaquero was the only passenger onboard and was fast asleep. He lay stretched across the red canvas jump seats next to the right para-troop door, undisturbed by the noise and vibration of the aircraft. The cargo bay was full of crates and supplies that were headed for the PX at *Tan Son Nhut* Air Base in *Saigon*, its first stop before it continued on toward *Ubon*. The loadmaster carefully rechecked the tie-down straps to assure that the heavy loads wouldn't shift in flight as the aircraft pre-pared for take-off. He looked at Vaquero for a moment, saw his Spectre cap and figured that he must have a hell of a hang over as his arms and legs nearly reached the cargo floor.

"Hey buddy, ya need to strap-in," the loadmaster said, shaking Vaquero's left arm. Vaquero winced at the sudden pain. His left arm was still tender from the needles that punctured him the night before. His bloodshot eyes could hardly open as he sat up in the seat falling back into a deep slumber again. The loadmaster fastened Vaquero in, then himself, sitting next to his fatigued passenger. After the aircraft was airborne, Vaquero was awakened by the strong smell of black coffee. The loadmaster stood in front of Vaquero grinning, holding two paper cups.

"Hey, I'm Vinny Ascoli, how ya doin'?" Ascoli's smile exposed his perfectly capped teeth as he leaned forward handing Vaquero a cup of black coffee. "Man, you look like you've been kicked in the head by country mule," Ascoli laughed as he brushed back his jetblack hair with his right hand. Vaquero slowly nodded in agreement, unable to find the energy to utter a word.

"You fly on Spectres?" asked Ascoli inquisitively. Vaquero nodded again as he slowly sipped the scalding brew. "That's a bad-ass motherfucker of an airplane man," Vinny Ascoli remarked, attempting to engage Vaquero into conversation. Vaquero only nodded wishing the loadmaster would go away. His arm and head were throbbing terribly.

"Did you hear about the attack on *Ubon* yesterday and the Spectre that went down outside of *Hue* last night?" commented Ascoli, casually assuming that Vaquero had gotten word of the bad news. Ray's eyes widened.

"What happened?" Vaquero asked, barely getting the words out.

"Pretty simple man, some VC or NVA sappers snuck up on the base and fired a bunch of mortar rounds into the air base in broad daylight. Do you believe that shit?" Ascoli shook his head and laughed in disbelief. "Those yellow little fuckers have a serious set of big balls," he remarked.

"Anybody hurt?" Vaquero queried intensely.

"Yeah," Ascoli hesitated for a moment. "Some *Ubon* security forces got zapped by a sniper. I, uh, think there was one civilian casualty. Something's goin' down man. Rumor has it that the North is going to try another Tet like offensive." Ascoli stood up and walked back toward the flight deck.

"Hey, you didn't finish telling me about the gunship that went down. What happened?" Vaquero shouted over the engine noise and vibrations.

"All I heard was that it took a missile. They never knew what hit them man," responded the loadmaster coldly as he climbed up the flight deck for another cup of coffee. Vaquero stood up and stared out the port hole of the paratroop door. The lush jungle terrain appeared strangely different to him now in daylight. Roadways and the landscape were covered with craters from daily bombings. Sober now from the jolt of the news, Vaquero wondered what it all meant, though his instincts told him that it was not good. Something was up. Why would the North go out of their way to attack *Ubon* when there were much bigger air bases much closer to the fighting. *Da Nang, Tan Son Nhut, and Ben Hoa* were all in-country and much more accessible, with the exception that those bases didn't have any AC-130 gunships. That was it, wasn't it, Vaquero finally concluded. His arm began to ache again so he removed the left sleeve of his flight suit to check if the tattoo looked infected.

"Fuck, where the hell did you get that?" asked Ascoli spilling his coffee. Vaquero's tattoo went completely around his bicep. Shaded blue and red, it portrayed a chain with small links that interconnected with no ending and no beginning. It was a symbol of the life-long bond between three friends that had pledged among themselves since elementary school that they would always look after one another.

Ascoli raced back up to the flight deck and returned with a damp cloth for Vaquero's swollen arm. Blood still oozed from the fresh wound, staining his flight suit. "What does it mean?" the loadmaster queried with a puzzled look on his face.

"A promise," whispered Vaquero as he turned and gazed back toward the jungle.

#   #   #

The SAR mission was executed flawlessly. A Search and Rescue force of two HH-53 Jolly Green helicopters escorted by a flight of four armed prop-driven Douglas A-1E Skyraiders code named 'Sandy' raced toward Walters under a thick cloud cover at five hundred feet. Once Walters had popped smoke, one of HH-53's swiftly dropped out of the sky and plucked Walters from his hideout while hovering above the triple jungle canopy with its forest penetrator. As the rescue unfolded, two Sandy's circled above the recovery point trolling for enemy ground fire loaded with eight 500-pounders. The rescue mission multiplied in nail biting suspense and drama in anticipation that a hidden enemy would open up on them at any moment.

Skyraiders were heavy, and slow as shit, but you could stuff them with everything but the kitchen sink under the wings because it could loiter over a target for hours. If the NVA were there, they thought better to keep their heads low than fuck with Sandy's four 20-mm cannons. It was all over in fifteen minutes. The force regrouped and headed west back across the *fence.*

"The drinks are on me! Anybody got a cigarette?" Mike Walters chattered nervously, wondering out loud if he would make back in time for happy hour. He laughed and talked a mile a minute with the Jolly Green flight crew on his ride back to *Ubon.*

#   #   #

The C-130 finally landed at *Ubon* a little after four in the afternoon. There was an air of tension and heightened security as patrol guards in machine gun toting jeeps could be seen patrolling the base perimeter and in increased numbers as Vaquero walked toward the 16th Special Operations Squadron building. Forty F-4E's were stacked on the taxiway waiting to take off. Exhaust fumes saturated the flight line while maintenance and flight crews busily prepared twelve Spectres for early evening missions. Something big was going on, he thought, excited now that he was going to be part of something grand and momentous. Flight operations desk was mobbed as Vaquero pushed his way through the crowd of flight crews to get to Pappy's office. Checking the board for assigned aircraft tail numbers, Vaquero noticed that he was scheduled to fly the following night…with Stuart Marks. Vaquero exchanged high-fives with Scumbag and Bob DeSena as they headed toward the equipment trailer for the mission briefing.

"What the fuck, over," blurted Duncan with his familiar rounded grin. Duncan stuck out his hand and gave Vaquero a strong and fervent handshake. "Welcome back. Ray, I hope you're well rested and ready to kick-ass after your mini-vacation. We need you." Duncan was pumped.

"I'm ready, Pappy, just tell me when and where," replied Vaquero. "What's all the excitement about around here?" Vaquero leaned up against Duncan's desk. Pappy sat down in his chair, propping his legs up on the desk, flicking his cigarette ashes on the floor. "I heard on my way back that the base was mortared yesterday and that we lost an aircraft last night near *Hue*. Who was on the aircraft?" asked Vaquero solemnly, having assumed that everyone on-the gunship had been lost.

"Three got out." Duncan said calmly as he lit another cigarette. "Mike Walters and two gunners were blown out when the fuel in the cargo bay ignited. Took a Strela in number three engine. They're down at Tippy's right now celebrating with the SAR crew that pulled them out of the jungle." Duncan chuckled. Laughter was the avenue to lessen the tension and fear that every man in combat secretly concealed, as well as denying that each night you crossed the *fence* you could end up as bug shit.

Pappy gently rubbed his tired, weathered face. His eyes were bloodshot, and he hadn't slept much since the attack on *Ubon* and the downing of the Spectre. There was never a time when you didn't find him at the squadron office or just hanging out playing cards and drinking beer with the I.O.'s in the barracks when there was nothing else to do, especially during the long rainy season. He would always be there in the shadows, believing that he was personally responsible for each of them.

"A couple of our birds will be down for a week, took a shit-load of shrapnel. We're lucky no one got their heads blown off." Duncan's chest heaved as he coughed. "Two F-4's had some minor damage, but nothing serious," Duncan grinned. "The sappers were after us, you know." Vaquero nodded in agreement. "Unfortunately, there was a civilian casualty, got caught in the middle of this shit." Pappy stood up and made a change to the monthly planner, then looked back at Vaquero with his rounded grin.

"The G-2 weenies believe the NVA have launched a major offensive in all three military regions in *South Vietnam* as we speak. The photo recon boys can't see jack-shit because the whole country is blanketed with a thick cloud cover. But some of the Fire Support bases and out-posts near the DMZ have radioed in that they're about to fall.

Don't know what it all means, but I can assure you, we'll be in the middle of it." Duncan's smile was tired now.

"I've got some good news for you, Ray. You've been reassigned to Major Stuart Marks' flight crew. Duncan pulled another drag from his cigarette.

"Yeah, I saw the board when I came in. Why me?" Vaquero had a good hunch that it might have something to do with pissing Solomon off during his last flight. He still couldn't figure why Marks would settle for him over a seasoned I.O. Always the quintessential diplomat, Duncan rationalized the change by saying that Marks needed someone who was going to be around for a while and could integrate with the rest of the crew. Duane Shaw only had four months left before he rotated back to the states, so it seemed to make sense.

"You're damn lucky, Ray. Most other guys around here would cut off their left nut to fly with Marks." The phone rang, and Duncan asked the person on the other end of the line to hold on for a minute. "Another thing, Ray, Marks wants you to run down to Tippy's to get acquainted with the rest of the crew before you fly tomorrow night. And do me a favor, keep an eye on your roommate Walters. See if he's doing OK, all right? Let me know if there's a problem."

Three airmen staggered out of Tippy's laughing hysterically, draped over their female companions as Vaquero's cab pulled in front of the infamous flight crew hang-out. They immediately stumbled into the cab and quickly headed toward another popular club in *Ubon*. As Vaquero pushed through the double doors, he debated whether he should have stopped by Toi's as he had promised her. He was greeted by a shower of beer and foam as he entered the packed club. Four officers with large beer bottles saluted Vaquero and proceeded to douse him from head to toe. "What's the password, sergeant!" screamed the lieutenant above the blaring music from the Filipino band. The club was crowded with Spectre crews, Wolfpack fighter jocks, and SAR rescue teams collectively celebrating another day of survival and the wonderful gift of life. Every inch of Tippy's was decorated with some form of Air Force memorabilia representing every squadron at *Ubon* RTAFB. Scores of airplane models twisted slowly from the crowded ceiling and aged photographs of pilots and crews posing with their aircraft covered Tippy's walls. Air Medals and Distinguished Flying Crosses were nailed on a large beam next to the bar.

"Uh, how many guesses do I have?" responded Vaquero sheepishly, acknowledging that it was the wrong answer. The four sadly shook their heads and doused him again.

"Ghostriders!" they shouted loudly, then handed Vaquero a *San Miguel*. The foursome staggered toward the dance floor and danced among themselves. The Filipino band began to play "Ghostriders in the Sky," to the delight of the raucous crowd. Vaquero swore the building was going to collapse from all the jumping and shaking by the patrons. He then spotted Mike Walters at the end of the bar buying drinks for the SAR team and the Nail FAC that had saved his ass from the NVA.

"How's it going, Mike?" Vaquero greeted Walters with a warm pat on his back, staring at him intently. He was glad to see his roommate had come through the incident unscathed.

"Vaquero!" shouted Walters, pulling him closer to the bar to meet the SAR team and Nail FAC from NKP.

"You're one lucky S.O.B. Mike," Vaquero said, toasting the survivor with his *San Miguel*.

"I survived and I'm alive!" howled Walters. "That's all that really matters in this messed up war, isn't it?" Vaquero grinned, nodding his head in agreement.

"Yeah, that's all that really matters Mike," repeated Vaquero assuringly. Getting back to the 'world' in one piece was what everyone openly thought about these days. Walters was sweating profusely, excited and running purely on adrenaline now. The reality of what happened to him was beginning to sink in as he wiped the dripping sweat from his forehead. The loss of his crew. Guilt. The uncontrollable panic and fear when it all came crashing together. Pappy Duncan would give him a few days off before deciding if Walters was ready to fly again. By then he would know if Walters had suffered any psychological trauma and was ready to deal with getting back on an airplane. But they didn't come more hard-nosed than Mike Walters. He'd be begging Pappy to let him back over the *fence* to hang his ass over the Trail after only a week.

"Hey Mike, have you seen Major Marks around here?" Vaquero asked as he looked around the crowded club.

"Yeah, I just saw him a minute ago." Walters stood on top of his stool scanning across a sea of bodies pressed tightly against each other. "There he is," shouted Walters as he pointed toward the far end of the bar.

"I see him," Vaquero replied as he headed toward his new aircraft commander. "I'll see you later, Mike, let me know if you need a ride back to the base."

"I ain't goin' anywhere my man. You're gonna have to use a can opener to pry my black ass off this stool," retorted Walters as he downed another beer.

Major Stuart Marks was busy talking with two of his crew members when Vaquero approached them. "Major Marks?" asked Vaquero as he stretched out his hand. Marks nodded and firmly shook Vaquero's hand. "I'm Ray Vaquero, your new I.O., sir," Vaquero remarked sharply. Marks' image and reputation was bigger than life, thought Vaquero, trying not to appear nervous.

"Welcome aboard, Ray. Glad to have you." Marks' smile was broad and sociable. "I want you to meet a couple of guys you'll be flying with. This is Capt. Eric Castillo, the best Black Crow operator in the squadron. And over here is Bud James, B.J. for short, our Flight Engineer." Castillo and B.J. greeted Vaquero warmly as they made room for Vaquero to squeeze into the tight circle.

"Excuse me a second, Ray, I'm going to try and find some of the other guys that are here so you can meet them." B.J.'s form quickly disappeared in the throng.

"Want another beer?" asked Castillo. Castillo reached behind the bar when the bartender wasn't looking and snatched two beers from behind the counter, handing one to Vaquero. "I'm running a tab," Vaquero and Castillo stared momentarily at each other before bursting out in laughter. "Where are you from Vaquero?" Castillo asked.

"New York," responded Ray. "How about you?"

"I am pure bred, blue blood *muy macho* Cuban Latin lover from Miami," Castillo laughed. Eric Castillo was raised on the south side of Miami after his parents had fled Cuba on a small boat in the late fifties while Fidel Castro was busy eliminating his enemies. Naturally tanned and good looking, Eric Castillo was about five foot nine with light brown eyes and thick wavy hair. A stocky build from lifting weights, Castillo was usually found at the base gym pumping iron when he wasn't flying.

Bud James reappeared with some of the other crew members and they immediately proceeded to introduce themselves to Ray Vaquero. There was Ryan Scott, the co-pilot; Chris Andrews, the navigator; Charles Watson the LLLTV operator, Nick Bristle, the FLIR sensor operator; and Tom Lettieri, the Fire Control Officer. "I couldn't find any of the gunners, Gramps must have made them go back to the barracks early to get a good night's sleep for tomorrow's mission," remarked Bud James jokingly. During all the introductions and hand shaking, Marks' flight crew had slowly encircled their newest crew member. Vaquero suddenly realized that something was about to happen and he was the center of attention.

"Drink it. If you truly want to be part of this crew you have to prove how far you're willing to go," remarked Bud James, handing Vaquero a beer mug made out of a 105 Howitzer shell casing, with a 20-mm shell as its handle. The brightly polished silver mug was engraved with the Spectre logo and the names of all that had ever served under Marks. It was his personal stein.

Vaquero looked confused as he looked inside the empty stein. "Sure, I'll drink it," he said jokingly wanting to play along. Suddenly everyone in the circle began filling the massive mug with beer, Jack Daniels, Bloody Mary's, Scotch, and Rum. To top it off someone had tossed in a couple of cigarette butts. Marks crew began chanting loudly. "Do it!" Others in the club joined in and watched Vaquero to see if he had the balls to drink the mixed drink from hell. He took a deep breath then slowly closed his eyes never daring to look at what was inside the huge mug that was filled to the rim. Ray Vaquero's face turned beet-red as he chugged the grotesque looking concoction, occasionally chewing on some foreign matter that had been tossed in. Foam ran down the side of his mouth and into his flight suit as onlookers cringed with amazement at Vaquero's performance. Marks stepped in and pulled the stein away from him.

"That's enough," Marks laughed. "You did an outstanding job there son." His new flight crew patted Vaquero on the back and welcomed him aboard. Marks pulled up a stool next to Vaquero. He smiled rue-fully as he watched the crowd dance into a frenzy. "What would you be doing back in the world if you weren't here, Ray?" The question startled Vaquero. He hadn't given much thought to life back in the *world*. It was too much of a distraction and he had a while to go before his tour was over.

"I'd probably be back in college sir," Vaquero answered firmly as he suddenly sensed a buzz beginning to kick in.

"Well, you keep planning for that day son, this war will be over as soon as our fearless leaders in Washington pull their heads out of their ass and get us out of this royal cluster-fuck of a war." Marks emptied his glass of Jack Daniels. "You know, superior weapons are not always the decisive factor in war; it's the will." Marks paused momentarily. "It is the will and the inner strength of the man and his leadership that really decides the issue." Marks staggered slightly as he headed toward the restroom. Within a half hour Vaquero had passed-out on the stool and had to be carried back to the base by Eric Castillo and Bud James.

#   #   #

Vaquero jumped into the waiting cab and quickly gave the driver directions to the *Thai Palace*. Ubon's streets were crowded with ped-dlers and pedicabs all seemingly impervious to the war that was waging not far from their border. The War had been good for *Ubon*'s economy, he pondered. Between the black market and the influx of American dol-lars, the rural agricultural town had prospered over the last ten years. Ray was anxious to see *Toi* again, he thought, as the cab raced around one of its many laneless traffic circles. *Toi* was genuine and sincere, and it was her natural unselfish openness that constantly reminded him of Suzanne. Two elderly women packing boxes were startled as he entered the *Thai Palace*, strangely devoid now of its accustomed aroma. Ray walked toward them with his infectious smile and asked them where he could find *Toi*. One of them started to cry uncontrollably and ran into the kitchen while the other told him. Ray stood motionless while he listened in shock and disbelief. Suddenly he was overcome with nausea and uncontrollably vomited out on the sidewalk. Toi was buried in her home town in *Chiang Mai*, in northwestern Thailand.

Walters listened attentively while Vaquero told him what had happened to *Toi Dasananda*. He spoke in a hushed tone as he sat on the edge of his bunk with his hands folded. Ray paused often between sentences, forcing himself to control his anger and sorrow. How could something like this happen to someone so perfect and innocent. Walters placed his hand on Vaquero's right shoulder to console him. Vaquero's tears quickly transformed into rage and hatred, he began kicking and smashing his metal locker.

"I'm sorry, Ray. I really am, man," remarked Walters. "But you have to find a way to let it go. You can't let this shit get to you, man." Walters' words were soft and from the heart. "You owe it to yourself and to your crew. That's all that really matters, Ray. *Toi* would want it that way, too. She wouldn't want this shit to eat at you and affect you in a way where you would fuck up over the Trail. You have to let it go.." Mike Walters left the room, closing the door quietly.

Vaquero sat motionless for over an hour in thought. Suddenly he stood up and slowly walked toward his desk in the far corner of the room and quietly pulled two sheets of paper from the top drawer. Ray Vaquero wiped the tears away and began composing a letter to Suzanne. He needed to let her know, one more time, how much he loved her.

Suzanne,

I wish you could have seen the look on my face when I received your letter. I couldn't decide if I should read it right away or wait until after I got my feet back safely on the ground. Keeping my head focused and clear from distractions is critical in what I do, though it's never been difficult thinking about you in the midst of all the chaos over here…I've always sensed you close by.

I mentally psych myself into the mission right when the aircraft is rushing down the runway like a run away freight train. Everything is loud and deafening. It's really wild in its own sort of way. There's no turning back at that point as Ubon's glimmering city lights have faded in the distance when we've finally crossed the fence. If I concentrate real hard, I can still see glimmers of light through the thick jungle foliage. I guess that's what hope looks like; all you need is just a glimmer…

After the mission I went to a quiet spot in the equipment room and read your letter. I go there a lot to think or when something is bothering me like we used to in our private cloak room at Columbia. The scent of your perfume still lingers in the envelope and the paper you wrote on. I read it often. Sometimes I close my eyes and run my fingers over your words, hoping to somehow touch you, feel you. Mike Walters and Sugar Bear tease me when they catch me sniffing the pages looking for your scent; they jokingly try to take it away from me. I can't tell you enough that it means everything to me to hear from you, Suzanne. You should also be glad to know that I stopped feeling sorry for myself a long time ago. Over time, I've come to realize how you were just as much of a casualty of my decision to leave as I was. I wish, somehow, I could take that pain away from you…

You said in your letter that you were getting married soon. But why do I continue to sense that you still love me? Tell me that I'm mistaken so I'll stop pretending, please? Tell me there is nothing left between us and that we could never have again what we thought was there. Say that it wasn't real, or that it's just my imagination. Explain why I dream about you every night, and why you tell me that you still love me.

You will always be my first, and last breath.

I need you desperately,
Ray

#   #   #

It was an unbelievably dazzling night as Vaquero hung outside the ramp door. The words "Hell Fire" were clearly visible across the barrel of the 105 Howitzer while half his body was literally suspended outside the Spectre. The evening sky pulsated with stars as if in tune to the battle that was about to unfold beneath. Three F-4's from Wolfpack had arrived and were on station, trailing the gunship, poised and eager to kill. Gramps slowly crawled up to the lip of the ramp and laid next to Vaquero, feeling a sense of security that wasn't there before as the seasoned lead gunner intently eyed Vaquero at his assigned post. Vaquero detected his presence and quickly turned around and smiled at Louie Grimes, flashing him a thumbs up. It was the way he carried himself, thought Gramps confidently. Vaquero's movements were calculated and deliberate as he methodically probed the darkness for danger. Ray purposefully scanned through his field of vision, an unobstructed three hundred and sixty degree sweeping view of the aircraft, and mentally prepared himself to shield his crew from harm's way. He leaned out a bit further making sure that the flight deck was clearly in his line of sight. NVA gunners would intentionally lead the aircraft with their deadly ground fire in an attempt to kill those in the cockpit first, thus simultaneously sealing the fate for the rest of the flight crew.

Vaquero grinned menacingly as he caught a glimpse of the ominous dual 20-mm cannons that protruded from the left side of the Spectre. He was seething now and full of hatred toward his unseen adversary and determined to avenge Toi's death with someone. Anyone. Once airborne with sensors aligned, Moonbeam fragged Spectre 12 into Steel Tiger East toward the heavily defended town of *Tchepone* in eastern *Laos*. A *South Vietnamese* OV-10 FAC out of *Da Nang* had spotted a large column of headlights lined up along what appeared to be a major refueling station. It was quickly chased away by a fusillade of antiaircraft fire that ringed the perimeter of *Tchepone* and its critical refueling depot. Marks slowly banked the aircraft to the left and into its familiar search pattern while its sensors hunted for the convoy.

The U.S. military had always referred to *Tchepone* as Base Area 604. Though the old Laotian village was deserted and bombed out now, *Tchepone* was strategically valuable and important to the *North Vietnamese*. Many other road segments of the Trail passed through *Tchepone*. Close *Tchepone*, and you would significantly damage the North's ability to fight the war in the South. River channels from the western tip of the DMZ that flowed into *Tchepone* were also used to transport weapons and supplies. The North was well aware of the importance of maintaining *Tchepone* open. Ringed around the jungle mountains of *Tchepone* were hundreds of anti- aircraft positions that were fortified during the rainy season in 1971 in preparation for the spring offensive. Unknown to U.S. intelligence agencies, surface to air missiles would soon become operational around Base Area 604.

Spectre 22 immediately began taking inaccurate 37-mm and 57-mm fire between its nine to twelve o'clock position.

"Triple-A, no threat," called Vaquero instantly over the intercom as bright massive air bursts detonated near the gunship.

"I've got them." Capt. Eric Castillo's Black Crow soon detected a large convoy three miles away in the heart of *Tchepone*. Castillo quickly fed the target data to the other sensors and the digital fire control computer. Fifty-eight trucks with their engines running were filling their fuel tanks at a major pumping station. The triple-A multiplied in intensity now as the gunship drew closer toward the convoy that was vulnerable and in the open. Anti-aircraft gunners fired wildly as hundreds of rounds illuminated the gunship, pelting it occasionally with jagged pieces of shrapnel. The Wolfpack flight leader asked permission to silence the guns, but Marks held back the escorts only until the triple-A became a serious threat to his aircraft and crew.

"Gramps, load the 105," ordered Marks almost causally.

"The 105 is ready sir," barked Gramps. His biceps bulged while he slammed and locked a round into the breach of the Howitzer that recoiled forty-eight inches when discharged. Marks fired the massive weapon as soon as the cross-hairs were lined up on his Heads Up Display. The lead Russian Zil incinerated as it exploded with a full load of fuel and ammunition, setting ablaze nearby trees and sage brush.

"Man, they're running all over the fucking place," blurted the FLIR operator Nick Bristle. The NVA appeared as white hot spots on his infrared display as they frantically searched for places to hide from Spectre's deadly accuracy as they abandoned their cargo.

"Let's get the one in the rear," ordered Marks calmly again, cutting off any avenue of escape for the convoy.

"Triple-A nine, twelve, two-o'clock, no threat," interjected Vaquero forcefully as forty glowing red tracers soared harmlessly above the aircraft.

"Roger I.O.," responded Marks assuredly, confident now that his crew and back were not exposed.

"The buck stops here," whispered Marks as he systematically worked his way up and down the road decimating another NVA convoy loaded with much needed weapons and supplies.

"I think I've found another radar site, Major," remarked Charlie Watson, the LLLTV sensor operator. Nick Bristle immediately swung his FLIR sensor to validate the new find. Spectre's sensors detected another radar site and the presence of more vans slightly north from where they had found the supply convoy. This time Marks ordered the F-4's to destroy the radar site and gun emplacement before it had a chance to lock-in on them and open fire.

"Can't figure why they didn't open up on us," thought Eric Castillo out loud. Unknown to Spectre 22, they had run into a SAM site that wasn't fully operational. The SAM site crew had no intent of drawing any attention to themselves. But as fate would have it, they had been found. Almost silently three Wolfpack swooped down and surgically obliterated the radar vans and the adjoining batteries after Marks had marked the location with a 105-mm round. Marks banked the aircraft into a tight left hand turn, heading south again and dogged on finding the pumping station to put it out of commission.

"B.J., arm the 40's," ordered the Major. The flight engineer instantly moved the toggle switch to the armed position. Gramps then manually loaded a four-round clip into the converted antiaircraft gun that could fire up to 120 rounds per minute. Marks methodically probed the surrounding tree line with an endless stream of 40-mm White Phosperous rounds in search of the hidden fuel lines. Better known as Willie Pete's, it was a perfect ordnance for making things ignite and burn. Conrad Hill and Kevin Collins continually fed Gramps 40-mm four-round clips to feed into the weapons' breach. Suddenly, there was a mammoth explosion. The detonation of the fuel lines turned night into day as flames soared and spread for miles, causing secondary explosions. Two hidden fuel tankers parked next to the pumping station disintegrated when Marks drilled four Willie Pete's into a fuel storage area adjacent to the pumping station, turning the depot into an inferno. Thick black acrid smoke from the blazing petroleum climbed above a thousand feet, blinding the FLIR and LLLTV operator displays. Vaquero watched in astonishment as secondary explosions intensified the flames as tons of stored ammunition supplies cooked-off around the fuel station depot.

"We've done all we can do here," remarked Marks calmly, satisfied with a good night's work. Chris Andrews contacted Moonbeam and reported the Battle Damage Assessment. Moonbeam would later frag F-4 recon flights the following morning to validate and assess the BDA and determine if the NVA convoys continued to approach *Tchepone* despite the pummeling they were taking.

"Which way home, Chris?" inquired Marks happily as he broke off from the attack orbit. The aircraft surged as Marks pushed the throttles forward, banking west after the navigator put him on a course that shadowed the *Se Bang Hieng River* as they headed back toward *Ubon*.

The silhouette of the black bird of prey crawled across a night sky illuminated by the blasts of multiple detonations rolling in succession across the jungle floor. Vaquero was transfixed by the destruction while he continued to search for targets as the aircraft slowly distanced itself from *Tchepone*. Eric Castillo, Nick Bristle, and Charlie Watson casually moved away from their display screens, no longer interested in probing the dense jungle terrain for other targets. As the aircraft initially crossed the *Se Bang Hieng River*, Vaquero detected a v-shaped stir in the river that had been illuminated for only an instant by the moonlit night. It was a sizable wake, he thought, which could only have been made by large wooden junk carrying supplies.

"Pilot, I.O., I think I've spotted a rather large boat in the river." The sensor operators nearly jumped out of their seat as they reached for their sensor hand controllers.

"Shit-hot Vaquero, where is it?" asked Marks enthusiastically.

"It's was off to our nine o'clock position heading to our six, sir." Vaquero no longer had a visual sighting. "Take a hard left sir. I think he's heading toward the shoreline.

"Shit, he's right," exclaimed Castillo. "He heard us and he's on the run. It's a big mother, too, sir. I'd say roughly about a forty footer, and she appears to be weighted down."

Spectres sensors honed-in on the doomed junk as it desperately tried to elude the gunship. Only seconds passed from when the cross-hairs of his display were aligned and the 105-mm round was out of the barrel of the Howitzer and into the belly of the supply vessel. The ship never exploded. It just split in half and vanished beneath the flow of the *Se Bang Hieng River*.

Revenge indeed is sweeter…Vaquero reveled in the thought as he thirsted for more.

CHAPTER ELEVEN

Thin streams of sunlight filtered through a lush green triple jungle canopy while ancient three-hundred foot trees groaned in a sultry Asian breeze. *Le Thanh's* four-man sapper team slowly trudged through a narrow supply corridor on their way toward Base Area 353 in the *Fishhook: North Vietnam's* southern theater command: *Communist Operations, South Vietnam.* The midday air was sweltering; perspiration dripped off their clothes and faces. A sudden hand signal from *Le Thanh* brought them to a halt while an OV-10 Nail FAC flew overhead as it trolled for antiaircraft fire along Route 13. *Le Thanh* and his sappers were on the last leg of their journey toward the Cambodian town of *Snuol* that bordered with *South Vietnam.* It had been two weeks since they had boarded a small wooden craft in the river town of *Pakse, Laos* after crossing the *Mekong River* from *Thailand.* The twenty-foot Sampan cautiously navigated south along the mighty *Mekong* toward the Cambodian river town of *Kratie,* their final destination before heading on foot toward *Snuol.* On two occasions they had narrowly avoided being blown out of the water by U.S. helicopter gunships that patrolled the river. *Thanh* signaled all clear as the OV-10 banked right and headed north. An hour had passed before the team was finally met by a three-man, trail-watching security force from *COSVN.*

The *Fishhook* terrain was a startling array of mountains and valleys protected by a natural triple canopy. Impenetrable and dense, the vegetation above the trail had been ingeniously intertwined by NVA road teams that hid them from aerial reconnaissance. It covered an intricate maze of footpaths and trails had been carved out to link the enormous supply caches throughout the NVA sanctuary. As the team turned onto a wider trail, *Le Thanh* noticed that every twenty yards or so, roadside trees had shallow cups carved into their trunk. At night, the cups were filled with kerosene to serve as guide-lights for troops and convoys that raced down the *Ho Chi Minh Trail*. For years, NVA troops and supplies would assemble in the *Fishhook* before heading South. A myriad of freshly excavated trails led in and out of *COSVN*, despite U.S. Air Force attempts to crater the main roads with MK-82 500-pound and Mk-83 750-pound bombs. Direct hits on the roads would cause landslides and craters, hampering road crew repairs, but at best for only a week. Road and trail repair teams had also laid scores of logs along the major roads leading toward their hideout, hampering entry for any would-be enemy. *COSVNs* fanatical security worker bees had cut back hundreds of trees and vegetation to one side, giving them good fields of fire and kill zones. No one was ever going to get very close to them from the ground, and if they did, they would surely die. Protected by two companies of the 7th NVA, and 5th *Viet Cong*, three-hundred and fifty hard core, suicidal diehard fanatical maniacs were prepared to fight to the death.

Le Thanh and his team was ready to drop from exhaustion when they suddenly entered the massive base camp. *Communist Operations, South Vietnam*, was bustling with activity. *Thanh* had never seen anything like it, he thought, as he marveled at the shear size of it. Base Area 353 was the size of a small town, populated with over seven thousand troops. Surprisingly, the camp had not been detected after so many years of fighting, though it was extremely well camouflaged by a thick, umbrella-like jungle canopy. The camp spread out for over two square miles with hundreds of hootches, classrooms, manufacturing facilities, and training areas. Well-constructed trench lines also led to fortified underground air raid shelters, and their supply storage bunkers were well protected in bunkers and carved out karst caves. Two hundred tons of munitions were stored throughout the camp. *Le Thanh* was amazed by it all. There was even a sunken clay swimming pool and beach-like chairs made out of bamboo. The team was escorted to a bamboo- barrack on stilts with adjoining quarters, constructed for *Le Thanh's* sappers and their families.

#   #   #

You could have cut the tension in the air with a knife as the Joint Chiefs of Staff briefed the President and his Cabinet on *North Vietnam's* latest aggression. "This is complete total bullshit!" blurted the President when advised by the JCS that a dozen outposts across the DMZ had already fallen to the *North Vietnamese* Army. Seasoned NVA troops were rapidly gaining ground from three fronts in a conventional attack with tanks and heavy artillery while the *South Vietnamese* Army's 3rd Division was retreating, and in disarray.

"What the fuck have we've gotten back in return for all the damn money and equipment we've sunk into that country." The President's voice shook the room. His face turned crimson in anger as he nervously ran his fingers through his thinning wavy hair. "Don't those people know any other maneuver besides retreat?" he shouted sarcastically. The NVA attack had kicked-off with an immense artillery barrage on three fronts. From the North, two NVA divisions and three infantry regiments supported by two hundred T-54 tanks marched across the DMZ toward the provincial capital of *Quang Tri*. Another division raced toward the old imperial capital of *Hue*. A second offensive struck from the central part of *South Vietnam*. Two divisions supported again by a tank regiment would head toward *Kontum* and *Pleiku*, both important communication centers in the Central Highlands. The third assault in the southern front was led by three divisions along with three hundred

Russian T-54 tanks that were quickly driving toward *Loc Ninh* and *An Loc*. The President glared coldly at those in the room that had falsely advised him over the last three years that *North Vietnam* could not continue to take the pounding for much longer.

"Gradual Escalation Theory my ass!" he fumed. "We're trying to pull out of this shit and *Hanoi* launches an offensive while I'm trying to win a reelection. And the assholes on the Hill and on the street want a piece of my ass if I attempt to do anything to stop them." He was nobody's fool. The President of the United States clearly understood his adversary's motives. *North Vietnam*'s leadership also knew he was under a tremendous amount of pressure from the Congress and the people to continue the withdrawal without regard to the tactical situation in *South Vietnam*. The JCS officer's hand quivered slightly, unsure if he should continue with the briefing.

"Well…fuck em all." The President slowly stood up and walked over to the window with his arms crossed. There was a long painful pause. "Somebody in this room better have a fucking plan."

The Secretary of Defense sat stiffly in his chair.

"General, please continue." The Secretary of Defense hung on every word. It was his briefing and his ass that was on the line now. He knew all too well that no one there would come to his aid if the President were to turn on him. He sensed beads of sweat rolling off the top of his head, and quickly wiped his brow and forehead with his stiffly starched white handkerchief. He too was perplexed and alarmed by Hanoi's ferocity and impervious attitude toward the tens of thousands of their soldiers marched to the slaughter like sheep. Years of gradual escalation of U.S. military pressure should have convinced them by now that the United States would continue to punish them whenever they launched a major offensive, or so he thought. His right eyelid nervously twitched while his mind computed what might have gone wrong with their analysis. Thousands of exhausting hours calculating all the possible *"what if"* scenarios with his inner circle of civilian analysts that rarely sought counsel from the military. They were usually the last ones informed of policy or changes in the tactical approach toward prosecuting the war. In his limited, finite wisdom, the Secretary of Defense and his staff had concluded that *Hanoi* was ready to parlay and negotiate seriously for a settlement. But that was before the current offensive. North Vietnam's behavior and ruthlessness never did quite compute.

The President had a penchant for missions labeled with aggressive, forceful, designations. And in many ways it was a reflection of his personality and how he usually dealt with his adversaries when cornered with overwhelming power. "Mr. President, the military plan is to push back the *North Vietnamese* advance with massive retaliatory airstrikes and interdiction of their logistical lines of communication. This action will buy time to complete our troop withdrawal on schedule, as well as punish *Hanoi* for its actions."

Wrecking *North Vietnam*'s transportation system in the heartland was the first objective of the U.S. plan. *North Vietnam*'s reliance on its harbors, highways and railroads to transport war material was critical to their war effort. Once the bridges were down and the railroads and highways interdicted, the Air Force and Navy would turn to other lucrative targets that had been off-limits for years because of political sensitivity and concerns over world opinion. But no longer, the President was about to turn the screws slowly on *Hanoi*. He ordered the military to go after the petroleum storage facilities, power generating plants, military barracks, training areas…and *COSVN* headquarters.

U.S. air strikes in the North would have little impact on the war in the South. *North Vietnam* had stored enough supplies to last them for over a year. But it would clearly send a message to *North Vietnam*'s leadership that the U.S. President was about to raise the stakes to get them to the negotiation table.

"What's the operation called, General?" asked the President placidly.

"*Linebacker*, Mr. President." The President was much calmer now, and at the same time excited at the prospect of dishing out some payback of his own. With U.S. air supremacy, *North Vietnam*'s conventional attack would leave them open and vulnerable to air attacks. And who knows, he thought optimistically, with a little luck they'll weather the storm and hopefully win some concessions from those bastards at the negotiations table. *"Squeeze them by the balls and the rest will follow,"* the President whispered contemptuously.

On April 1st, 1972 the President of the United States authorized massive air attacks on hundreds of military targets inside *North Vietnam, Laos, Cambodia,* as well as mining *Haiphong Harbor* in *Hanoi.* For the first few days of the offensive torrential rain and a thick cloud cover grounded most of the U.S. fire power. Though there were over two hundred jet fighters and bombers still in Thailand, more planes were desperately needed to thwart the swift NVA advance. Additional tactical fighter units were rushed in from Japan, South Korea, and the States. And another sixty B-52s were sent to Anderson Air Force Base Guam, augmenting the total number of B-52s between Guam and *U- Tapao Thailand* to two hundred and fifteen. Navy attack carriers, the *Kitty Hawk* and the *Constellation* were quickly deployed off the coast of *Vietnam* in the *South China Sea.* The *Midway* and the *Saratoga* were also deployed shortly after. Within a month, tactical air would be at full strength. All the *South Vietnamese* Army had to do was just hold the advance.

The United States Presidents' bold move perplexed the collective minds of the *Politburo* leadership. But some of them privately admired him for his tenacity and forcefulness. War was a violent chess game of deception and control, usually exploited by heartless men dispassionately detached from the masses they so eloquently claimed to serve. Despite his lack of control over the masses and protesters, this American president did not cower under pressure like his predecessor. It was his *will* to prevail and not in his power to unleash the massive destruction they most feared.

Victory on the battlefield was never the primary objective of the *North Vietnamese Politburo*. Political maneuvering was far more consequential than mere battlefield victories or defeats. Thousands of *North Vietnamese* soldiers would become the sacrificial pawns thrown to the slaughter for the sole purpose of posturing at the negotiations table, and executing the primary directive; *The political task is the primary task, and the only mission…*

#   #   #

Capt. Glenn Thompson had precariously dodged and weaved in and out of twenty barrages of 37 mm triple-A fire as the gunship devastated a supply convoy racing out of the *Ban Raving Pass* in eastern *Laos*.

"Marker out," reported Bob DeSena, tossing out his last marker log after carefully directing it over a triple-A site for the Wolfpack. DeSena caught a glimpse of the F-4 as it dived through Spectre's orbit to attack the triple-A site with a laser guided MK-84 2000-pound bomb. The explosion and shockwave was spectacular as night turned into day, obliterating the gun-site and its crew. Forty enemy trucks lay dead on the darkened trail now ablaze as secondary explosions of ammunition and fuel cooked-off.

"I've got a lock on hot barrels Captain," reported the sensor operators.

Captain Thompson banked Spectre 12 left again as the FLIR and LLLTV operators locked-in on the hot barrel of another 37-mm gun site, centering its own 40-mm weapon on the attackers when it suddenly flew into a steel wall of 57-mm and 37-mm antiaircraft fire. A 57-mm round slammed into the right wing while a tracerless 37-mm ripped into the right side of the aircraft's fuselage. Shrapnel tore a massive hole into the pylon tank, bursting it into flames enveloping the right wing.

"Mayday, Mayday, this is Spectre 12. We've been hit by triple-A." The navigator broadcasted their condition to Moonbeam and to nearby aircraft. Captain Thompson labored to keep the wounded Spectre airborne long enough to plan their next move. Flames quickly spread as the ruptured tanks fueled the spreading fire. There was no way they were going to put out the blaze, the Captain realized.

"Get everybody ready to get out Bob," calmly ordering DeSena to prepare the crew to bail out. Thompson finally stabilized the wounded Spectre, but he didn't have a clue how long it would hold.

"Is everybody ready back there, Bob?" Thompson asked, anxious to get the crew and himself the hell out of there. Bob DeSena checked to make sure that everyone had their chute on properly. He patted them reassuringly on the back as thirteen crew members paced nervously on the aft cargo door staring out into the darkness.

"Yes, sir. Just give the word."

"Let em' out!" ordered Thompson. Within two minutes DeSena got everyone out safely as he watched every parachute safely open.

"They're out, sir, Let's go!" DeSena looked over his chest-pack one last time. Glenn Thompson let out a nervous sigh as he slowly engaged the autopilot and positioned Spectre 12 on a slight turn to insure a crash landing away from friendlies. The few seconds it took Thompson to walk in the darkness from the flight deck to the rear of the aircraft felt like an eternity. When he got to the aft cargo door, DeSena checked his parachute and gave him a thumbs up. Thompson then signaled DeSena to jump. Five seconds later, Thompson exited the crippled aircraft. Within minutes the blazing fire devoured the aircraft and munitions turning the Spectre into a plummeting fireball.

Bob DeSena was in the proper position when he pulled the T-handle on his chest-pack. But as the chute unraveled, it entangled itself on the bubble shield of his flak helmet snapping his neck violently backward fracturing a vertebrae in his neck. DeSena's limp form drifted silently toward the ground crashing abruptly through the jungle canopy then slamming into an area covered with elephant grass. DeSena's shaking hand struggled to unzip the pocket to his URC-11 survival radio as the pain in his neck overwhelmed him. After finally activating the emergency beeper, DeSena passed out.

#   #   #

Multicolored strobe lights exploded wildly across the clubs patrons casting surrealistic shadows on the walls. "Hey, needle-dick," shouted Eric Castillo, filling Vaquero's glass with *Jim Beam* as he sat stoically and shit- faced on a bar stool. "That was shit-hot what you did tonight in spotting that Sampan," Castillo said proudly.

"Piece of cake Captain," Vaquero saluted, nearly falling off the stool. "Why don't you come out one night and hang out there with me?" Castillo frowned in terror.

"No can do, G.I.! I might be a little crazy *mano*, but you need to have a sizable pair of *Cojones* for that shit." Vaquero laughed as Castillo clutched his balls with his right hand.

"How the hell did you get involved in this shit, Ray," asked Castillo, filling his glass one more time. Vaquero paused for an eternity as he pondered the question which had haunted him over the last two years. He gazed into his drink for a moment before glancing back at Castillo.

"I really don't know, Eric, I just did," he said, smiling weakly. "I've been trying to figure that out myself. The only thing I know is that we come into this world with two lives. There's the life we're supposed to live, and there's one that's steered by events and circumstances we have no control over." Vaquero shrugged his shoulders. "Call it fate or poor judgment, I'm not sure anymore, man. I can't tell if I'm in control, or if I'm just along for the fucking ride." Vaquero emptied the drink, placing it slowly on the counter. "Sounds like a bunch of horseshit, doesn't it?"

"No. No, it doesn't," confided Castillo. Eric Castillo gazed at Vaquero pensively, as he thought about his own life. Few in life get a second chance to amend their past and navigate across personal *fences* and uncover who they really are. Eric Castillo was immersed in this war because of his family and their collective hatred toward Fidel Castro, and communists in general. It was expected of him. And along the way, Eric Castillo had never given much thought that there existed another, significantly different person hidden underneath the flight suit. Life had to be more than just a chain of a seemingly endless succession of events, he thought introspectively, as he sipped a drink slowly from his bottle digesting Vaquero's words.

Three female dancers in bikinis and high heels suddenly climbed on top of the bar and began to dance to Jimi Hendricks tune, "*Foxy Lady.*" One of them stood directly above Castillo and Vaquero. She was long and slender with olive colored skin and thick jet black hair that reached down to her waist. Her brightly painted red lips and dark eye shadow electrified Castillo as he lustfully undressed her as she slowly twisted her hips provocatively in his face, pushing Castillo's organ forward to full throttle.

Aroused to say the least, Castillo climbed on top of the bar counter and began dancing wildly with the entertainer. She incited him as she slowly opened the center zipper to his flight suit placing her hands gently on Castillo's hips, pursing her lips while she toyed with him. Castillo's expression was fiendish. His right eyebrow was raised and his eyes peered through narrow slits as he lewdly gazed at her sultry movements. Vaquero instinctively knew what Castillo was going to do next as he comically gyrated and thrashed his body and arms wildly around her.

"You ain't got a hair on your balls…" Vaquero shouted as the dancer's firm breasts trembled in his face, compelling Castillo's groin to throb even more. Whoever said that the hand was quicker than the eye must have been Puerto Rican, thought Vaquero. Like the swift strike of a King Cobra, Castillo had untied and removed the top to her bathing suit, throwing it into the raucous crowd before she had a chance to cover herself up, exposing her ample breasts. The dancer went ape-shit. She jumped on Castillo's back rabbit-punching the shit out of him on the back of his head. Ray quickly jumped up and grabbed her around the waist, pulling her off Eric Castillo. Her arms and legs thrashed wildly as she continued to lunge toward Castillo. Mike Walters pushed through the crowd, grinning from ear to ear.

"What are you going to do now, Tonto?" he said, laughing hysterically at Vaquero.

"Well, don't just stand there," Vaquero said. "Give me a hand!" At the right moment Walters lunged forward and grabbed her legs. The club owner and a Second Lieutenant from Wolfpack helped carry the girl to the rear of the club to calm her down and get her away from Castillo.

"Let's get out of here before they call the M.P.'s," suggested Vaquero. They bolted out the door, laughing uproariously. Pappy Duncan pulled in front of *Tippy's* driving one of the squadron jeeps when the three stumbled onto the sidewalk.

"You boys look like you could use a ride," Duncan said calmly with his usual unassuming grin.

"No shit, Sherlock. Like, step on it, Pappy, there's going to be a hanging in a few minutes if we don't get our collective asses out of here," chuckled Walters. Duncan burned rubber as he sped away from the scene of the misdeed and headed back toward the base.

"I'm thirsty, how about you guys?" Castillo and Walters nodded their approval. Vaquero's grin was silly. He was totally shit-faced. "I'll buy, Pappy. How about it?"

"Bernie Stalls got his orders today. He'll be going home in ten days, so we decided to have his champagne party tonight," replied Duncan. Walters found the case of champagne that was under his seat. He ripped the box open and passed out three bottles. On Walters' signal, Castillo and Vaquero blasted the two guards at the gate with the plastic corks as Duncan sped toward the flight line. Two fire trucks trailed Spectre 10 as it lumbered toward the revetment after a successful mission in northern *Laos*. Flashing red lights and blaring sirens, the fire trucks broadcasted that another lucky son of a bitch had flown their last mission and was going back to the *world*.

Vaquero could see Sugar Bear waving something wildly from the back of the ramp door as the gunship pulled into its parking space. After lowering the ramp door Stalls was blasted by a shower of champagne and water as he stepped off the back door. The force of the water cannons knocked Stalls down. But the mood suddenly shifted from joy to sheer terror. In his effort to avoid the water cannons, Sugar Bear ran in the direction of number three engine with its propeller slowly windmilling. You could hear a collective gasp from the spectators as they watched in horror, unable to stop Stalls in time before he ran into the path of the propeller. Call it luck or divine intervention, Bernie Stalls had miraculously run between the Hamilton-Standard blades avoiding decapitation. It took a minute before Bernie Stalls realized what had happened. Then, with his familiar beachball size grin and throaty chuckle, he calmly walked around the right wing toward the rear of the aircraft waving a pair of his girlfriends beige-colored lace panties.

"You're one lucky…" Duncan was not one to show emotion, but he couldn't hold back. He hugged Sugar Bear like a father would embrace a son after narrowly avoiding a tragic accident. Pappy Duncan struggled to regain his composure. He cleared his throat and rubbed his face with his right hand for a moment before he finally looked up at Stalls.

"What the heck is this shit all about?" Duncan asked, pointing to the underwear that was wrapped around Sugar Bear's neck. Stalls always paused for an eternity before he spoke.

"Well, I figure if I got shot down and captured on my last mission, the NVA would set me free once they got a whiff of Patty Lee," he said in his Alabama drawl. Duncan just shook his head in disbelief while Castillo, Vaquero and Walters hung on each other laughing hysterically.

"I need to stop by the squadron office for a minute before we go have that drink you guys promised," Duncan said. Vaquero, Walters, and Castillo quickly climbed back on board the jeep.

"Where are you guys goin'?" Sugar Bear cringed while his crew mates continued to douse him with champagne down his flight suit. As if on cue, everyone in the jeep shouted, 'Chili Pepper!'

"Meet you there!" Stalls Squealed as the water cannons found their target one more time.

Solemn expressions were written on the faces of everyone standing around the Operations Center as Duncan and the others walked toward the duty officer. Pappy Duncan knew at once that another Spectre had gone down "Who went down?" he asked.

"Spectre 12, about thirty minutes ago. As far as we know, everyone got out OK," said the visibly shaken Ops duty officer, Captain Rogers. "SAR will be out to pick them up at first light." he said, shuffling papers, trying to look efficient. Duncan's eyes shot up toward the mission flight board to check which I.O. was on Spectre 12. DeSena.

"It's OK, Pappy," assured Walters, cutting the tension in the room. "Did you hear what he said? Search and Rescue will have them all back here by morning." Pappy never heard Walters, he just stared blankly at the board. He had been one of the first to arrive at *Ubon* RTAFB in 1968. His ulcer bled a little more whenever a Spectre came back from a mission all shot-up, spewing JP-4 or when one of his boys got seriously hurt. Duncan winced slightly as the ghosts and guilt from the past began to torment him again. Steve Debenek had just turned nineteen years old when Pappy Duncan flew with him on his final check-ride before assigning Debenek to his own flight crew. Everything had gone smoothly during Debenek's last training mission. Triple-A fire had been moderate over the *Parrots Beak* in *Cambodia*, and Debenek seemed to have it well under control while Spectre bloodied another convoy. Debenek was ready. Duncan was going to split the ramp time, but Steve begged Pappy to let him complete the mission on his own. Pappy looked into Debenek's eyes. It was a look of trust and self-confidence, full of fire and intensity commonly found with youth and innocence that willingly responds to the call of duty.

"OK, but let me know if you need a break." Duncan felt like a proud father whose son was about to venture out on his own. Duncan lit a cigarette as he walked down the ramp intending on curling up in a corner and somehow stay warm on the cold, hard metal floor.

"Thanks, Pappy." Duncan could see Debenek's broad smile through his plastic bubble shield as Steve connected the restraining cable to his harness and leaned out the ramp door. Pappy had cozied up against the right paratroop door when suddenly there was an explosion and a bright flash of light as the Spectre was suddenly rocked by a tracerless 37-mm round below the ramp, hurling Debenek against the secured upper ramp door. His head was cleanly sheared off by the shrapnel showering Duncan with blood and bits of bone and flesh. Tears welled in his eyes as Pappy remembered the warm smell of Debenek's blood and seared flesh covering his plastic face shield.

Duncan sighed deeply, focusing his attention back on the flight board, accepting the fact that he could never get accustomed to the gut-wrenching stress of waiting each night until all of his boy's were safely back from across the *fence*. Bob DeSena was the finest I.O. he ever had, and he got nailed.

"I think we should call it a night, guys." They all knew it was an order and not a request. "I'll drop you guys back at the barracks. You're going to need all the rest you can get." Vaquero, Walters, and Castillo quietly exited the Operations Center.

All fifteen crewmen of Spectre 12 were recovered the next morning without incident. It was the largest mass crew rescue ever in Air Force history. Bob DeSena was air-evaced to the states wearing a halo-brace screwed into his head. Pappy Duncan held DeSena's hand firmly as he walked beside the stretcher as a medical team loaded DeSena onto the C-141 Starlifter. Duncan patiently waited on the flight line until the Starlifter was a faint spot in the distance.

#   #   #

Combat missions at the 16th Special Operations Squadron doubled to three hundred fifty during the month of April. Fourteen aircraft and their flight crews were pushed to the edge with double missions and fifteen-hour days. A stifling humidity and sweltering heat caused havoc with the gunships' sensitive electronic sensors and avionics, failing at times during the middle of a mission. Like frenzied ants, Spectre maintenance crews worked feverishly around the clock patching up the shrapnel holes, reloading the aircraft to send them back over the *fence*. Triple-A barrages during the offensive was nothing like Spectre crews had ever confronted before. Many of the Spectre flight crews began wearing Buddha pendants as talismans.

#   #   #

The *North Vietnamese* Army went after the *Ben Het* ARVN Rangers with a vengeance. The camp was a small listening outpost manned by one hundred *South Vietnamese* Army Rangers and ten U.S. Special Forces advisors that kept a close watch on the NVA activities across the borders. ARVN Rangers and U.S. advisors had never expected to take on a regiment of *North Vietnamese* regulars supported with twenty-five PT-76 and T-34 Russian tanks. Three days and seventy-five tactical air strikes had failed to break the communist's attack on the Special Forces listening outpost. Massive black plumes of smoke from tactical air strikes encircled the outpost, turning night into day. A sudden warm breeze swept the stench of rotting corpses mixed with BLU-27 napalm across the camp. The exploding napalm collapsed the lungs of the fearless attackers caught in the open. Those that survived the air strike, burned to death.

Spectre 07 had just come on station and was quickly briefed on the camp's situation by an OV-10 Covey FAC out of *Da Nang, South Vietnam.* A U.S. Special Forces radioman, huddled in the command post, calmly came over the radio as three NVA tanks breached the western defensive perimeter.

"Spectre 07, there's a T-34 tank trying to crush the command bunker with us in it, over." The T-34 was a medium size tank that weighed 35-tons when combat loaded and armed with an 85-mm main gun. Eric Castillo immediately picked up the roaring electronic impulses as the tank driver slowly spun the tank above the command post. Capt. Nick Bristle, the FLIR operator, locked-on the T-34, feeding target data to the fire control computer.

"Load the 40's," ordered Marks as he quickly lined up his target on his headsup display.

"The 40's are clear to fire sir," barked Gramps. Marks scored four direct hits on the T-34, stunning the tank crew inside the well-armored vehicle.

"Uh, you stopped it sir, but I think all they got is a bad headache. Looks like the 40's just splashed on the tank, sir," reported Charles Watson, the LLLTV operator. The T-34's engine was still running but it wasn't moving any longer.

"Get the 105 on line," demanded Marks. Within seconds of the command, Conrad Hill quickly loaded the breach of the 105 Howitzer. Marks rocked the T-34, severing the turret off the tank with a direct hit. He surgically placed another round directly were the turret had been. The T-34 lifted into the air by the tremendous explosion, landing on its side and off the command bunker.

"Good shootin' Spectre, got any more of those?" the radio operator asked, impressed by Spectre's accuracy. "Got more tanks coming our way along Route 512. Could use some illumination, too." The radio operator's voice was almost casual.

"That's affirmative," radioed the navigator Chris Andrews. Spectre's electronic sensors targeted fifteen more tanks into the fire control computer's memory.

"I.O., launch flares every third orbit," commanded Marks. Ray Vaquero acknowledged the order by pressing his mike switch twice. From the north, a mix of T-34 and PT-76 tanks approached the embattled camp. The PT-76 was a lighter, much older amphibious tank that weighed 15-tons, armed with a 7.62 mm machine gun, mounted coaxially with its main gun. Two quad fifty-caliber machine guns saturated the night sky with hundreds of spiraling red and green tracers, blindly probing the darkness for Spectre. It was a brilliant light display, but Spectre was well outside the envelop of the antiaircraft fire. The FLIR and LLLTV sensors locked in on the quad's hot barrels. Spectre responded with its own Vulcan 20-mm Gatling gun, showering a deadly steel curtain of armor piercing rounds on their adversary, annihilating the gun crew and weapons.

"Spectre 07, this is Covey. We've got three Wolfpack F-4's inbound with LGB's. Can you play the music for them? Their LRD is down."

"Roger Covey, we can play the music. Just say when," responded Andrews. Laser Guided Bombs were a new weapons delivery system introduced during the spring offensive. Two aircraft were needed to deliver the LGBs, one to laser the target and the other to drop the bomb. Its accuracy was lethal. F-4D's, equipped with a laser ranging device dubbed Pave Knife, irradiated the target while the other F-4 dropped the LGB. Spectres had been equipped with a Laser Ranger Designators but hadn't been combat tested until now.

"Spectre 07, this is Jasper flight leader. Start the music anytime, over."

"Roger Jasper. We're playing your song," responded Chris Andrews.

The LGB weapon consisted of a two or three-thousand pound bomb equipped with a laser guidance package. The LGB sensor would lock on the reflected laser energy, silently gliding itself toward the target. One by one, Spectre 07 irradiated the column of approaching tanks with its Laser Range Designator for the Wolfpack, leaving a thick trail of black smoke and twisted metal along Route 512. Within thirty minutes the hunter-killer team had destroyed another fifteen tanks. With all of their munitions expended, Spectre 07 raced toward *Pleiku* to rearm and head back to *Ben Het*. The camp continued to be pummeled by a relentless and determined adversary that would not capitulate.

CHAPTER TWELVE

What made Ray Vaquero's adrenaline flow in combat was the finality of the act; death was near, and if it reached out to take him it would be swift and overpowering. He'd fly as often as he could, rushing toward another Spectre gunship that was about to depart on another combat mission after just landing minutes earlier himself. Venturing over *the fence* was a far better fate than smoldering in solitude in his room, he thought. He thirsted for combat; Vaquero would sweat in anticipation for the heart-stopping, panic-stricken missions in which he would emerge shaken and scared to death at times, but rising to feel invincible. In the midst of battle he would go into a trance, shielded from fear or concern, for his well-being.

#   #   #

Army Colonel Haywood Keene had spent the last two weeks directing tactical air strikes and gunship fire keeping the NVA at bay around *An Loc*. He could have left when the choppers came to take out the U.S. Army advisors leaving the ARVN soldiers to fend for themselves. But Haywood Keenes' conscience refused to leave them their without his help. They needed him. He knew it and so did they, but the ARVN commander wasn't going to beg, it was not Keenes' fight.

Marks turned the Spectre slowly into a wide orbit around the embattled town of *An Loc*. The fighting was fierce as the battle raged from building to building. Hundreds of red and green tracer rounds lit the night, making it difficult to identify friend from foe because of the close fighting positions on the ground. Marks then came up with an idea. He relayed to the navigator to contact the friendlies on a nonsecure radio channel to identify their position with green flares, knowing that the NVA would be listening. Within seconds green flares immediately lit-up from dozens of locations in the town. Then he called for red flares. Several red flares appeared.

Haywood Keene called out over the radio. " This is Mustang, I've got no fucking red flares, hit them all!"

"Roger that, Mustang, we're happy to comply," retorted Lettieri, the fire control officer. "Keep your heads down."

"We got the bastards," exclaimed the FLIR operator.

"You see that red tile covered structure on the northwest side of the main street?" Keene asked, dejected, thinking that it was impossible for Spectre to fire its weapon precisely where he wanted it.

"Where do you want it?" asked Lettieri.

Keene was puzzled by the question. "What do you mean, Spec'?" Keene asked.

"First floor window or second?" Letterei asked with a grin.

"Yeah, sure," replied Keene in disbelief. Marks fired two bursts through the front door, then ten rapid 40-mm bursts through the first and second floor windows killing everyone inside.

"Out-fucking-standing, Spec," cheered Keene along with the ARVN at Spectres' awesome fire power. An expert at directing TAC-air, Colonel Haywood Keene continued to skillfully direct Spectres and fighter aircraft against the advancing NVA battalion, forcing them to retreat and regroup. Once again, Spectre was cleared from *An Loc* while another Arc

Light rained destruction on the NVA that were mulling over their plan of attack in the adjoining forest. The assault was abruptly canceled. That night, 37-mm and SA-7 fire intensified around *An Loc*. Two birds, a OV-10 FAC and a gunship were damaged by SA-7's but were able to make it back to *Ubon* safely. Spectre flight crews were reporting up to ten SA-7 firings per mission. High threat sectors were avoided whenever possible, but the SA-7's and missiles would always show up somewhere else as *North Vietnam* raised the stakes. Scotty Wilson's crew took a Strela in number one engine, but managed an emergency landing at *Tan Son Nhut* Air Base in Saigon.

Colonel Haywood Keene narrowly escaped *An Loc*, before the next wave of Arc Lights obliterated the NVA that were strolling down the street in the open as if they owned the fucking place.

#   #   #

He was perfect, the representative from *Hanoi* thought. They prepared to promote *Le Thanh* as *COSVN's* Political Officer during a brief ceremony, deep inside a carved out karst hillside in the *Fishhook*. *Le Thanh* came from a poor background and the *Party* viewed that as advantageous over those that were more educated, and were generally not trusted. So what if Thanh's background was propagandized for their benefit. His lower-class background was viewed as an asset to continuously rally the masses. When they were losing men by the thousands every month the *Party* needed to look for positives where there were none. When there were minor victories, they were quick to remind the populace that "We are winning, but prepare for a long struggle."

#   #   #

Drenched in sweat Vaquero tossed and turned in his bunk as he dreamed. He had been shot down by anti-aircraft fire as his crew looked for a way out of a thick bamboo thicket grappling to get back over the *fence.* With his .38 caliber revolver drawn, Major Stuart Marks led his crew through a dense fog in the darkness. Suddenly the colors in the dream were bright and vibrant as Suzanne Logan stood no more than a couple of feet away from Ray Vaquero. Her smile was radiant as she silently gazed at him for a long while. He couldn't explain how she could be there, but it didn't matter, He wanted to embrace her for an eternity. Her voice was the sound of a thousand voices when she suddenly took a step forward and whispered softly, "I'm always there for you." Then she was gone. Vaquero lay motionless in his bunk, realizing what it was, where he had just been. He jumped out of bed and raced to his desk and started to write her a letter. But as the self-doubt began to set in, he quickly reminded himself that it was only a dream. Vaquero tossed the paper into the waste basket. He silently donned his flight suite and Spectre cap, and headed back toward the flight line.

\#   \#   \#

The pace of the Spring Offensive began to wain as the NVA body count reached over one hundred thousand dead. *North Vietnam's* conventional infantry approach to the offensive left them defenseless against the massive air strikes. More than four thousand B-52 strikes were flown between May and June against the vulnerable NVA positions, breaking *General Vo Nguyen Giap's* back and sending the *Politburo* back to the drawing board and *Giap* into retirement.

The monsoon season arrived earlier than expected. Over the next few months, Spectre missions decreased significantly due to the weather, concentrating their efforts instead against the *Khmer* insurgents in *Cambodia* and their supply lines. cover.

\#   \#   \#

It was about 7:30 am when a strange hooting sound awakened everyone bringing them out of their rooms in their underwear to see what the excitement was all about. A hairy ape-like creature ran down the hall with its arms in the air frightening everyone back into their rooms. Scumbag got a good laugh as he teased them for running away.

"We knew you'd have a son someday asshole," someone blurted from the end of the barracks. "That's what you get for screwing around with those apes you sleep with." Laughter echoed throughout the barracks.

"Fuck you, and the horse you rode on, Duane. If you really have to know, it looks like you! I just brought him by to meet his father!"

Vaquero came in through the back door after spending five hours on stand-by. He walked over to the refrigerator behind the bar and grabbed a beer. He wasn't ready for bed yet.

"Where'd you get that thing?" he asked as he sat on the lounge chair in front of the black and white TV.

"I traded a case of Jack Daniels for it. Not a bad trade." The Gibbon was wrapped around Wilson like he was its mother. It stood about two feet high, and its brown coat was dense and shaggy. Mike Walters walked back down the hall toward Vaquero and Scumbag.

"Why's it making that noise?" Walters asked, scratching his head.

Scumbag grinned as he bit into his cigar. "He's marking his territory Mike, I think he wants you!" Walters quickly went back into his room and locked the door.

"Keep it away from me man, I ain't messin' with no fuckin' monkey. You hear me Scumbag? Just keep it away from me!" Vaquero and Scotty Wilson got a good laugh from Walters' reaction.

The sky finally opened with a torrential downpour that was loud and impressive, instantly flooding the base and the town of *Ubon*. It rained unceasingly for two hours, and it looked like it would never stop. Vaquero walked over to the open barbecue hootch about thirty yards from the barracks with a six-pack in his hand. He enjoyed listening to the roar of the rain on the metal roof on the hootch. The rhythmic sound of the rain would help him sleep well, he thought.

"Hey, Vaquero, catch." Pappy Duncan spiraled a football into Vaquero's gut, spilling his beer. Ray walked out into the rain and threw a deep pass to Duncan who was down field about forty yards. Vaquero bent over from laughter as Duncan ran through some deep puddles that covered the field. Finally making the catch, Duncan fell and slid across the ground.

"Fuck it man. It's only water, right?" Duncan said with a throaty chuckle. "Come on, you go out now." Duncan dropped back quickly to pass as Vaquero attempted a post pattern over the middle. As he tried to make his cut, he slipped and slid for about ten yards, completely covering his face with mud. Two more I.O.'s came out from the barracks and joined them. Then four flight engineers joined in and they started a touch football game in the torrential cloudburst. After an hour, it was nine on nine in what was now a very serious game of touch football, in a mud bowl. Mike Walters blitzed up the middle, nailing the halfback behind the line of scrimmage, driving him backwards with a ferocious hit into the ball carrier's stomach.

"Shit Walters, this isn't tackle, man." Duane Shaw was out of wind from Walter's hit. "What are the rules, man? We need some rules," complained Shaw.

"Jungle rules, Shaw. Anything goes," retorted B.J., who was bruised up pretty bad but was holding his own.

"Fine. Let's play, I think I got it now." Shaw found a hole off the left side and ran down the field for a touchdown. Duane Shaw called out to Mike Walters, mocking him as he danced in the end zone. Vaquero caught the ball on the ensuing kickoff, carefully lining up behind his blockers. Out of no where Duane Shaw suddenly steam rolls over one of the blockers nailing Vaquero in the chest with his head.

Shaw stood over Vaquero enjoying himself, then bellowed, "Jungle rules right?" Vaquero jumped up quickly, covered in mud, and sneered at Shaw as he headed back to the huddle. Shaw knocked the breath out of him but he wasn't going to give Shaw the satisfaction of knowing that the hit hurt him.

"OK, this is where we put Shaw on injured reserve," said Scumbag, coming in for Duncan, who needed a breather.

"Is he scheduled to fly tonight?" Scumbag asked. Nobody knew for sure so Scumbag took a time out to consult with Duncan.

"Go easy on him, Scotty. I need him on the schedule," Pappy cautioned.

"No problem, Pappy," beamed Scumbag as he headed back to the huddle with his cap on backwards, gnawing on what was left of his cigar. "Sweep right to Walters. Vaquero, you're the lead block for Mike." Walters and Vaquero smiled as they exchanged low-fives. "I want the center and guards to pull, too. Let's run over that honky! On three. Ready, break." The team quickly lined up along the line of scrimmage, looking for Duane Shaw who happened to be playing outside line-backer, right where they wanted him.

"Hut-one, hut-two, hut-three!" shouted Scumbag, as he turned quickly to his left flipping the football to Walters. The guards and center led the charge, knocking defenders down that stood in their way. As they rumbled toward Duane Shaw, who now quickly back peddled, wanting to get out of the way of the Mack truck that was about to run over him. But it was too late. Vaquero cut his legs from under him, tossing Shaw in the air. When he reached the end zone Mike Walters did his James Brown rendition, while everybody watched and laughed their ass off, including Shaw.

#   #   #

Just before the start of another hunting season, rumor spread around the 16th SOS that *COSVN* had put a bounty on Spectres' head. A pig and two cartons of cigarettes for any antiaircraft crew that nailed a Spectre. Rumor or not, Pappy Duncan was going to turn it around to get his men pumped after a long monsoon season. Though Colonel

Roberts couldn't finger the culprits, he knew for sure that there were many involved in the conspiracy, including several of his pilots. And that Sergeant Hunter's technicians secretly and ingeniously rigged a parachute and harness for a fifty-pound pig that was hidden in the equipment room right before the mission along the Cambodian border. Following Duncan's dimensions, a local *Ubon* tailor made an olive green Spectre jump-suit with a squadron patch stitched along the sleeves and chest. The fact that they did it during Lt. Solomons' watch made it even sweeter. Solomon's crew had hidden the pig in the booth as his aircraft flew along the *Fishhook* during one of the later missions one night, delighted everyone, including the squadron commander, Colonel Roberts. Pappy Duncan was on board, just to make sure that nothing went wrong or that Solomon didn't lay into the I.O. Right before the drop the gunners strapped two cartoons of Kools, on the back of a pig. NVA loved menthols. The sensor operators gathered outside the booth as the swine willingly walked off the edge of the ramp. He truly had no idea where he was going.

#   #   #

The SA-2 missiles in *Tchepone* were fully operational now. NVA missile crews worked feverishly during the rainy season to get them ready. For most of the war, surface to air missiles were primarily a threat in *North Vietnam* and *Laos*. Toward the end of the Spring Offensive, the North hid hundreds of SAM missiles south of the DMZ and along their strategic routes in *Laos* to protect their supply lines and critical junctures during the upcoming dry season. Air crews called them flying telephone poles. With a length of 35 feet, the SA-2 was a two-stage surface to air land based guided missile. The entire weapon system consisted of a missile, radar van and generator. Transported on semi-trailer transporter/erector vehicle, the missile could be detonated by contact, proximity fuse, or on command from a radio signal. Using nitric acid and hydrocarbon fuel as propellent, the SA-2 could reach speeds up to Mach 3.5 before burnout. It had a slant range of twenty-five miles and an effective ceiling of 60,000 feet. Aircraft were tracked by radar which fed the signals to a computer from which radio signals were sent to the missile.

"We received new orders' Colonel," interrupted the navigator.

"What are they," blurted Solomon, annoyed that he was cut off in mid-sentence.

"Orders from Moonbeam sir. They want us to take a peek into *Tchepone*. See if we pick up any movement in the area, sir." Spectres' Black Crow and Moving Target Indicator could easily detect a vehicle from five miles away, even at slow speeds.

"Anything else," muttered Solomon sarcastically.

"Yes, sir. They said to keep a safe distance from the center of town."

Solomon was one to push everything to the periphery, irregardless of his men's welfare. He was always preoccupied with personal rewards and saw this mission as only another opportunity, a step up the military ladder if he could score another big kill. Higher altitudes supposedly increased survivability for Spectres. Statistically, you had a greater chance of being shot down by antiaircraft fire than by a SAM. But so what, he thought. Going up against big guns and getting away unscathed was always a matter of chance, Solomon rationalized. He was cocky and willing to tempt fate one more time. The self-destruct range of the 37-mm was fourteen-thousand feet. Fifty-seven's was even higher, so Solomon didn't give much concern to distance or altitude from the target as he slowly drifted Spectre 05 closer into *Tchepone*.

"Triple-A, three, six, nine O'clock," shouted Duane Shaw. A hundred rounds of 37-mm suddenly streaked toward them despite a thick cloud cover below, suggesting the presence of radar controlled antiaircraft weapons.

"Break left," shouted Shaw again as another barrage streaked toward its left wing. The gunship was now in range of the SA-2 radar.

"I have a radar lock," the Black Crow operator frantically notified Solomon that his sensor was picking up the rattle snake-like sound in his headset, signaling that a SAM had been launched toward them. Duane Shaw's eyes bulged out of his head as he searched for the missile out the ramp door as Solomon shoved the control column forward, heading down toward the deck.

"We have multiple radar locks coming from our six sir," call came from the booth. Spectres' ECM pods labored to jam the SA-2 radar signature of the gunship. Duane Shaw saw the first missile from his six o' clock position, quickly launching chaff from tubes that hung from under the aircraft's wings.

"Triple-A nine and six O'clock. Hold what you got." Shaw braced himself for the impact. Solomon ignored Shaw's warning, nervously zigzagged along the contour of earth when he was greeted by a barrage of triple-A, taking shrapnel from ten rounds of 37's in its wing and tail. Sixty seconds later Solomon is diving toward the deck again as they narrowly avoided another SA-2 that had locked onto the chaff. Another missile fired. More chaff, as rivets began to pop from the wings from the stress and strain on the aircraft. G-forces from the tight turns pinned Duane Shaw and the gunners to the ramp door.

"SAM fired and he's locked on!" shouted the electronics warfare officer from the booth. "Do you have a visual Shaw?" Shaw scanned his complete field of view but he could not see the SAM until it was too late. This time it came directly from beneath the gunship. The Black Crow heard it but never saw it as it slammed into the belly of Spectre 05, disintegrating the aircraft into a giant fireball.

After the downing of Spectre 05, a flight of F-105G Wild Weasels equipped with antiradiation missiles went back to *Tchepone* to take out the missile sites. Armed with AGM-78 and Shrike missiles, the antiradiation missiles honed in on the enemy radar and took most of them out. But NVA missile crews were clever as well. SAM operators often turned off their radar or used their guidance radar only for brief periods of time. If they knew that they were being pursued, SAM units would move to another area and hide.

When the JCS reported the downing of the Spectre to the White House, the President and his staff agreed on a retaliatory strike. In less than thirty minutes the National Security Council and the JCS agreed on *COSVN*. *Hanoi* never acknowledged that they were operating sanctuaries in *Cambodia*. They were confident that the United States would not launch air strikes against them because the enormous outcry of American public opinion would not permit it. Conversely, if the camps were struck, *Hanoi* could not acknowledge their existence.

Operational command and control of B-52's fell under the Strategic Air Command. A B-52 cell formation consisted of three aircraft in a two-mile trail. The second and third bombers were stacked to provide a five-hundred foot vertical altitude separation. Each "cell" was identified by an assigned call sign. If a particular target required greater fire power than three "buffs," a "wave" or a "compression" strike was formed by adding more cells to get the desired effect. Six waves were fragged to strike *COSVN*.

CHAPTER THIRTEEN

He inhaled his cigarette until it burned the tip of his finger. Manny Rodriguez sat quietly on an empty ammo crate in the Ops Center tent. Nicotine stains from smoking two packs a day over the last year had permanently stained the side of his middle finger an orange-yellow. Rodriguez nervously ran his fingers through his hair, sipping a warm can of beer while the mission Ops officer briefed him that his team would be sent on a routine bomb damage assessment mission into the *Fishhook*, in eastern *Cambodia*.

Routine. What the fuck was ever routine in *Vietnam*? Rodriguez sarcastically thought to himself, slowly crushing the empty beer can with both hands. He had seen a lot of *dead* reasons to make them cautious whenever they crossed the *fence* into NVA territory. Why the fuck now? The war was over and he and Cano were short-timers looking forward to laying low for another two weeks before catching the 'freedom bird' home to bask in the sun at Dorado Beach. Who gives a flying fuck about what's left of anything after a B-52 strike? For the first time since he had been in-country, Manny Rodriguez had a bad feeling about going out on a mission.

"Why us, sir? I mean, what's the point now? Who gives a rat's ass for what's left of the camp after a B-52 strike? Why can't they send in the fast FAC recon birds instead?" Rodriguez felt uncomfortable. He was never one to shy away from his responsibilities, nor was he afraid of any man. This time, somehow, it was different. He wanted out of this mission.

"Orders Rodriguez. Somebody 'upstairs' wants to make sure that base camp has been destroyed. Plus, your group is the best team we have for the mission. You're familiar with the area. Get your team ready, you're going out in the morning at 0500 hours." The mission Ops officer turned his back to Rodriguez, scanning a map of the *Fishhook* area.

"There's nothing for you to worry about, Manny. Nothing could have survived the pounding they got, it'll be like a walk in the park."

Tuan waited outside the tent as he always did right before a mission. He could tell that something was bothering Rodriguez. Manny squatted down next to him. "I'm OK, *Tuan*. I'm just tired of this shit. This, none of this seems make sense anymore." Rodriguez smiled at *Tuan*, looking into his eyes then handing him a warm beer. *Tuan* loved American beer far better than the *Jeh* brew back at the village. He smiled broadly then devoured the *San Miguel*. Manny worried about *Tuan* and his family and what would happen to them once they pulled out. *Tuan* never could quite understand the political niceties of negotiations and settlement, or that he was about to be abandoned despite his loyalty to the United States. Rodriguez suddenly felt ill.

"I need to find a way to get you out of here *Tuan*. Let's go find Cano and get our gear ready." Rodriguez erased all thoughts of home and Dorado. It was time for another mission.

Three days earlier six waves of B-52 compression strikes shit all over COSVN's forested headquarters. Six bombers per wave, the B-52's had flown in their standard three-ship cells with a three-minute spacing between cells. The Arc Lights were grouped into three waves each night, with about five hours between waves to provide the psychological impact of a sustained and unrelenting bombardment. If the NVA was actually there during the bombing, the poor bastards never knew what hit them. Heat waves slowly rose from the jungle floor blending with the stench of rotting vegetation. Cano Rincón waved to the Vietnamese radioman to keep up with the team. The scared soldier's eyes were opened wide as he reluctantly brought up the rear. The foliage along the trail that led to the base camp had been intertwined by NVA road teams which provided excellent cover from aerial reconnaissance. Residents of the 3rd NVA Division didn't know what hit them when the B-52's silently rained death over the hidden encampment. The forest of War Zone C was the exclusive property of the 3rd, or so they believed. They were tough, hardcore banana-farting little bastards that would fight to the death, thought Rincón as he stopped to put a stick of gum in his mouth. Team *Taino* cautiously walked down a narrow trail that led to the camp, covering their movement with their weapons. The 3rd NVA Division had considered their area so secure that the camp's political officer allowed the residents to bring their wives and children from *North Vietnam* to live with them in the camp. *COSVN* had been in operation and undisturbed for six years, but all that had changed when maps and documents were recovered from the bodies of enemy couriers by another Recon team, pinpointing the exact location of the elusive base camp.

Sunlight streamed through the foliage overhead as a red dust clung to their sweaty faces and arms. The smell of death suddenly reached them three miles out from the base camp as it carried through the swaying trees. Rodriguez and Rincón stopped to tie sweat towels over their noses and mouth to obstruct the stench, *Tuan* was not at all fazed by the fetor. There were no sounds and nothing moved when the team entered the camp. Manny and Cano were awed by the devastation as the earth around the camp had been blown to shit and turned upside down. Massive craters had split the earth as if it had been gouged by some massive piece of jagged metal. NVA living quarters had literally vaporized. Clothing and rucksacks were sprawled around the base as *Taino* cautiously surveyed the destruction wrought by the B- 52 Arc Light. Cano gagged as he moved through the destroyed campgrounds. There were countless bodies everywhere. Stiff and bloated, their tongues hung out as flies celebrated on the discolored corpses. Maggots feasted in the mouth of one charred NVA soldier that looked to be no more than fifteen years old. The force of the Arc Light had hurled many of the NVA soldiers into the air and into the trees, decorating them like a Christmas ornament with intestines and other human parts draped across the branches. Manny and Cano retched, on the verge of vomiting.

Nothing usually fazed Manny, except the time when he helplessly watched the killing of the young black Captain during a failed rescue attempt. When they recovered the body, flies were gorging themselves on the strips of flesh that were torn from Paterson's head, flung along the jungle floor. It was more than he could take. From then on, if a fly ever landed on him, he'd tear its wings off. "Motherfucker, I hate this shit." Manny whispered. But, orders were orders. They had to search the bodies for documents for the G-2 assholes in the rear. He tried to slip off the rucksack of the first NVA he found, but the body was too swollen, the straps were cutting into the soldier's bloated form. *Tuan* stepped forward, and with his hunting knife, cut the straps from the dead soldier. Cano was sure the body would burst and shower them with rotting gore. Cano took a step back, expecting the corpse to explode. *Tuan* threw the rucksacks into a pile to go through them later after they completed surveying the camp. He then strolled into the camp's medical center, and to his surprise he found several NVA inside and alive, bleeding from the nose and ears, suffering from concussions as a result of the bombing. As he came out the rear of the building, *Tuan* stared at a flagpole still standing with a tattered NVA flag hanging from it. He felt a sudden chill and the hairs on the back of his neck stood on end. The camp grounds were honeycombed with slit trenches and bunkers. In the center of the camp was a large life-size black and white picture of *Ho Chi Minh*. *Tuan* was spooked that it wasn't destroyed during the bombing raid. NVA unit crests hung from several of the hootches that were somehow untouched by the destructive force of the air strike. The earth here had been ripped open, and massive craters yawned toward heaven.

Manny Rodriguez felt an uneasiness, a feeling that they were in danger. Paranoid that there were still more of those tough little motherfuckers in hiding and would appear at any moment, his instincts told him to get the team out of there. As they slowly paced deeper into the camp, Rodriguez found other parts of the base camp had somehow escaped destruction. They also found exposed trails that interconnected to bivouacs and underground bunkers full of supplies. Many of the hootches were unscathed. "Fuck me," blurted Rodriguez uncontrollably. *Taino* hastily sifted through some of the NVA rucksacks.

"Call for the chopper," whispered Rodriguez, as Rincón walked quickly toward the ARVN radio operator. As *Tuan* took point to lead the team out, he saw a rainbow in the distance. It was a bad omen, thought *Tuan*. Rainbows were a bad sign to the *Jeh*. He believed in an evil phantom called *Yang Griang* that lived at the end of the rainbow. The *Yang Griang* would suck up the water from rivers and give it to the spirits of those who had died unnaturally, then wander the forests bringing hardship to the living. As *Tuan* led the team toward a pre-arranged extraction point, they began to take sniper fire from their left and right flanks. One hundred yards to their right, darting shadows suddenly came into focus as twelve NVA sappers wearing green fatigues and sandals rose from the elephant grass. One was toting an RPG launcher while the others brandished heavy weapons and satchel charges. *Taino* squatted low to the ground with their backs toward each other scanning the trees and brush for the snipers. *Tuan* led the team slowly up to a small rise in the jungle overlooking a section with thick bamboo. They could see three NVA in shorts with AK's and RPGs in hand, moving slowly towards them. Suddenly, RPGs sped past the recon team with trails of smoke and a horrific whoosh as they exploded against the trees. The stillness in the jungle was disturbed by the sudden crack of automatic weapons. *Taino* instinctively returned fire with a ferocious barrage of their own. Four determined NVA soldiers charged out of the brush toward the four man recon ream. Rodriguez saw them first and instantly discharged his M-16 on full automatic, dropping them in their tracks while green tracers snapped passed over his head. *Taino* had run into a *North Vietnamese* Army RPG sapper team and a security battalion that was on its way back to *COSVN*. *Tuan* lobbed several grenades from his M-79 toward a sapper that was about to fire another RPG toward *Taino*. Cano's peripheral vision nailed two sappers that were shadowing the team with two rapid bursts from his 12-gauge Remington. There is no firearm more versatile and lethal than the shotgun. The single purpose of the shotgun was to hit moving targets with large quantities of deadly lead pellets, or worse, flechettes. The 12-gauge was preferred by U.S. recon teams. Cano favored the pump-action version with an autoloader that automatically ejected spent shells upon firing, feeding new ones into the chamber. He preferred the single-barrel, single-trigger gun which fired three to five shells without reloading. The loading and ejection mechanism of the pump-gun was only partly automatic, since the action was operated by a slide on the forearm that had to be pumped manually. But in the hands of an expert like Cano, it could discharge rounds faster than the autoloader.

Taino frantically raced toward a slit trench that zigzagged toward what looked like a cave. Rodriguez cautiously led them into a well-fortified, concrete reinforced L-shaped bunker cut into a limestone karst hillside. The hunters were now the hunted. NVA automatic rifle fire poured over the sandbagged bunker so heavily, that it showered chunks of wood and rock all over the four-man team. Rodriguez grabbed the radio from the *South Vietnamese* soldier and went inside the fortified cave that was full of supplies and weapons. The rest of the team spread out along the L-shaped bunker, defiantly returning the NVA fire.

"Nest, this is *Taino*, over." Static crackled over the PRC-25 radio.

"*Taino*, this is Nest. What's your situation, over?" Music and loud screams disrupted the communication between *Taino* and *Phu Bai* as the NVA attempted to interfere with Taino's transmission. A NVA radioman could be heard shouting political slogans and curses in broken English.

"We need arty and air support, like right now. Stand-by one." Rodriguez calmly plotted azimuth and coordinates for the nearest fire support base. When a fire fight ensued, recon always got priority for artillery and tactical aircraft. He quickly changed frequencies on his PRC-25, making contact with a FSB base a few miles away.

Fire Support Base Defiance sat on a poorly defended hillside just nine miles away from the *Fishhook*. With five 105-mm Howitzers at his disposal with a twelve mile range, Captain Clayton Buck would do everything in his power to even the odds a little for over-matched recon team. He spit a large wad of tobacco juice on the ground before barking orders to the artillery gun crews. Buck despised the NVA leadership that all too often would march their troops into inevitable slaughter. We're not like them, he thought scornfully. *We don't eat our young.*

"Shot out!" barked Buck into his radio handset as a 105-mm marker round raced toward the team's location. In a matter of seconds, it exploded about a hundred yards in front of the bunker. White smoke swirled lazily, rising above the thick jungle canopy. Rodriguez made minor coordinate adjustments that would bring the artillery closer to their bunker.

"That's kinda' tight, *Taino*, you're sure you want them that close?" Buck asked, worried that they might get caught in the barrage.

"So are they, Defiance. Spread it around," responded Rodriguez, grinning confidently. He had won the battalion's contest for directing accurate artillery.

"Keep your head down son, they're on their way," replied Buck.

"Roger that, Defiance, let er' rip." Rodriguez informed the team to take cover below the sandbag line, arty was about to shit all over the sappers. The 105-mm artillery barrage rained down like freight trains along the team's perimeter as flashes boomed from the barrels of the

Howitzers. Captain Buck had ordered the FSB team to fire 'nails,' which had a wide bursting radius. The flechettes showered the surrounding jungle with dart like rounds, literally nailing some of the NVA to trees and into the ground. The barrage from hell lasted for almost an hour. *Taino* could hear the screams of the soldiers that became victims of FSB Defiance artillery barrage. But when the smoked cleared, NVA sappers continued to fire their AK-47s and RPG's toward the bunker as they retreated into the jungle for cover. Manny and Cano smiled at the thought they had them on the run, at least for now. A FAC out of *Da Nang* flew overhead and was attempting to make contact them. Rodriguez crept over to the radio once he heard the Fac's voice crackling over the PRC-25.

"*Taino*, this is Covey 11, over." The OV-10 circled above the thick jungle canopy.

"Covey 11, this is *Taino*, over. What's up?" Rodriguez was upbeat. Despite the odds, he knew that his team would have priority for tactical air and fire base support. The NVA sappers couldn't get near them as long as they had clear weather and air support.

"I've got Cobras inbound in two minutes, *Taino*, where do you want them?" Covey was a calm and cool operator. Covey 11 was already orchestrating his tactical attack plan in support of the surrounded four-man recon team.

"We'll mark with Willie Pete, Covey. Look for our smoke, over." Rodriguez ordered *Tuan* to fire eight M-79 grenade Willie Pete rounds into the area where the NVA were hiding. The trees and brush caught fire, spewing dark smoke above the jungle canopy. Cobras had a cruise speed of 171 mph. Affectionately referred to as Snake, the Cobra was a ferocious piece of weaponry with a bad attitude. It carried a minigun and an M-129 40-mm grenade launcher, a machine gun with a cyclic rate of fire of 450 rounds per minute. The Cobras' rockets pods carried seventy-six 2.75 inch rockets at a time. Snake was a lean, mean, kick-ass machine that would snap through the jungle above and below tree top level. And if an antiaircraft gunner pissed the pilot off by shooting at him, it would swiftly rotate on its own axis heading 180 degrees back in the direction where the ground fire came from to shit on the gunner's day. Three Snakes from the 1st Air Cavalry arrived on station. After going over their attack plan, Covey fired a marker rocket to pinpoint the point of attack for the Cobras.

The Snakes lined up the tree line and began their methodical sweep and deadly attack with their miniguns and 40-mm rockets. Dirt and flesh exploded all over the landscape as the Cobras spewed hot steel into the heart of the sapper positions. The sappers answered back with mortar rounds that landed close to the L-shaped bunker, raining shrapnel and dirt around the bunker's perimeter. As the mortars inched closer, the recon team could hear the dull hollow thump coming out of the 82-mm mortar tube. The Cobras were ready for another run.

"Flight leader, make your first pass from the northwest to southeast. I'll fire a Willie Pete to mark, over," Rodriguez instructed. *Tuan* fired a M-79 white phosphorous grenade into the general direction in which they wanted the Cobras to lay down their rockets. The Cobras rolled in and punched off eight rockets into the advancing NVA. One of the rockets nailed the mortar team as it attempted to move its location closer to the bunker. But despite the destructive, air power, the sappers just kept coming. Covey 11 relayed the situation to Cricket, the daytime Airborne Command and Control Center. Taino needed something with longer staying power, Covey 11 thought, then quickly putting in a request for Spectre.

Another AH1G Cobra gunship came on station and began strafing around the fire that had been started by the burning Willie Pete. The jungle shook from the buzzing sounds of the 7.62-mm mini-guns screaming two thousand rounds per minute into the jungle floor, then the roar of 2.75-inch flechette rockets shredding everything standing along the perimeter of the Taino's bunker.

While Rodriguez, *Tuan*, and the ARVN radioman were returning fire, Cano had crept into the cave to look around. The karst cave was loaded with enough food and supplies to last a battalion six months. Most of the cache were U.S. weapons and ammunition. Cano returned to the mouth of the bunker draped with bandoliers and hundreds of rounds for two M60 machine guns that he had found.

"Hey Manny, I found a couple of pigs." he said gleefully. "Give me a hand." M60's were referred to as pigs because they loved to eat lots of ammunition. They positioned two M60 machine guns on its tripod at each end of the L-shaped bunker to cover their kill zones. Rodriguez and Rincón now manned both machine guns, establishing perfect cross-fire positions. Manny instructed Cano to direct his fire at ground level, forcing the NVA to crawl through a wall of steel. With two M60s on-line, Rodriguez ordered *Tuan* back into the cave to see what else they could use. Several minutes later *Tuan* came back with boxes of grenades and ten LAW rocket launchers, a lightweight shoulder fired-weapon that was originally designed to kill tanks. But now LAWs were used against everything from bunkers to individuals.

"*Taino*, this is Covey 11. Keep your heads down, two Wolfpacks inbound with nape." Covey had stacked the sky with Phantoms, Cobras, and Skyraiders, anxiously waiting their turn to enter the fray.

"Roger Covey, we copy. Heads down, over." Rodriguez replied, then signaled to the team to duck. The ground shook violently as the F-4's splashed Napalm across their perimeter. The team felt the heat on their faces as the flames rolled across their bunker. Misty rain clouds rolled in over the battle site, providing a ceiling of less than one thousand feet. Bullets occasionally scythed the brush as the NVA continued to probe the recon team's defenses. When it got dark, *Tuan* and Cano silently slipped out of the bunker to set trip-flares and claymores along their perimeter. Fortunately for *Taino*, the sappers had pulled back for the evening to lick their wounds and prepare for another assault in the morning. Rodriguez called for harassment artillery bombardment from

FSB Defiance on two NVA mortars just west from their bunker that continued to pester them. One round exploded close enough to pelt shrapnel into the sandbags. "Assholes!" shouted Rodriguez.

#   #   #

Early the next morning, Blue Chip notified the 16th SOS that an American recon team was trapped by a large NVA force in the *Fishhook*. The word spread throughout the squadron like wild fire. Blue Chip was the Seventh Air Force command and control for combat units outside of *South Vietnam*, and it was about to task Spectre to provide around clock air support coverage until the team could be rescued. It was 11:00 a.m. when Mike Walters raced back to the barracks to tell Ray Vaquero the news. It was Vaqueros' first day off in more than three weeks. He was dead asleep after having flown nine consecutive double missions with different flight crews. They'd fly for five hours then refuel and rearm at *Tan Son Nhut* Air Base in *Saigon* then take off again and fly another five hour mission.

"Vaquero, wake-up." Walters shook him several times without getting a response. Vaquero was in a deep dreamless slumber physically fatigued from the rush of adrenaline, stressed by too many combat missions. His eyes were wide open but he could not see Walters; he looked through him with a haunting dead stare. "Something big is going down, man. I just heard there's a four-man recon team that's surrounded by a battalion of NVA in the *Fishhook*. The word around the squadron is that we're going in there tonight to provide air support." Walters was beside himself with excitement.

"Who are they?" whispered Vaquero with a raspy voice as he slowly sat up on the edge of his bunk still wearing his flight suit.

"They're out of *Phu Bai*. They went in on a routine BDA when they ran into a battalion of sappers. The Captain at the Ops desk told me confidentially that Moonbeam has diverted a shit-load of TAC-air to the *Fishhook*. *Taino* is putting up a good fight while they're holed up in a NVA bunker.

"What did you say?" Vaquero asked, looking at Walters intently.

"*Taino*, the recon team, is holding their own, why?"

"I know them," Vaquero replied. He hastily put on his boots and ran to the squadron mission Ops to check which Spectre was fragged to the *Fishhook*.

"Where do you think you're goin', man?" Walters asked with a puzzled look on his face.

"On a mission," Vaquero responded firmly. Ray Vaquero grabbed his flight gear and ran at full stride toward Spectre 01. The flight crew was boarding the aircraft when Vaquero ran up beside Pappy Duncan.

"I'm going with you." Vaquero's voice was firm, as he donned his headset and gloves. Pappy could see the rage within Vaquero's eyes.

"Sure." Pappy calmly said, displaying a warm smile meant to calm Vaquero down. He cupped the blue flame from his Spectre lighter and lit Vaquero's cigarette. Ten minutes later, they grabbed their gear and boarded the aircraft.

Captain Will Hawkins bypassed the sensor alignment over *Ubon* after takeoff, pushing the aircraft throttles forward as the fourteen man crew raced toward the besieged recon team. By the second day of the siege the NVA began moving heavy weapons toward the *Fishhook* area with the intent of encircling the recon team and closing the door on any chance of rescue. *Hanoi* saw the siege as an opportunity to propagandize the U.S. violation of the *Cambodia's* neutrality as a sovereign nation. They were going to make an example of *Taino*.

A ferocious barrage of AK-47 fire began to crack through Taino's bunker as the determined NVA were relentless in their attack and obsession in reaching the cave. *Tuan* rapidly fired five more 40-mm rounds from his M-79 grenade in a scattered direction, anticipating the sappers' approach to their position. Manny and Cano's interlocking fire with their M60s continued to maintain hundreds of NVA sappers at bay. Suddenly, at the far side of the bunker, the *South Vietnamese* soldier's leg disappeared after taking a direct hit from an RPG. It barely bled, cauterized from the heat of the rocket. His other leg was in shreds as white jagged bone protruded from his pants leg. He died moments later. Manny and Cano's eardrums burst from the explosion. All they saw was black smoke. Cano was knocked out momentarily, pelted with shrapnel from head to toe.

Dark towering plumes of mushroom-like clouds rose above the triple jungle canopy as Spectre 01 arrived on the scene. Ray Vaquero caught a glimpse of three F-4's as they soared skyward after their bombing run on the lush green carpet. Looking directly under the belly of the gunship, Vaquero spotted red tracers spewing from the mouths of two Cobra gunships on an NVA position, showering them with a red curtain of machine gun fire.

Tracer anti-aircraft fire was literally impossible to detect in daylight hours. It was only when a barrage of black puffs of smoke exploded all around the aircraft like an old 'Twelve o' Clock High' movie did the flight crew realize that antiaircraft gunners were gaining on them. At this point, the NVA had not moved in any of their big guns into the area. But it didn't matter, Vaquero didn't give a shit. He was impervious to the dangers seven thousand feet below, and determined to save his friends.

"They lost their radioman," the navigator reported over the intercom to the Spectre crew. Vaqueros' body tensed. After several minutes the navigator made contact with *Taino*, receiving firing coordinates along a zigzagging trench line where the NVA were hiding from the artillery and tactical airstrikes. Spectre 01 peppered the trench line with fifty Willie Petes from its 40-mm Bofor, spraying the NVA with the burning white phosphorus.

"Good shooting, Spec; you got them on the run," Rodriguez shouted over the radio. The NVA scrambled out of the trench into the thick jungle forest.

"Recon team leader Rodriguez says good shootin', Hawk. He wants you to walk some 105 rounds north of the trench line." Vaquero signaled to Duncan to spot him on the ramp. A 105-mm round instantly killed twenty NVA, landing in their midst as they frantically ran toward the forest. Hawkins slowly walked another twenty rounds toward the petrified adversary, backing them away from the recon team. Shawn Woods saw Vaquero come up the stairs to the flight deck.

"Listen, Shawn, I know this sounds unusual, but I know those guys down there. I grew up with them. And, I was wondering if I could talk with them for a minute. Let them know that we're going to get them out of there." Shawn talked it over with Hawkins for a moment. Vaquero saw the pilot nod his head in approval.

"What are their names?" Woods asked as he connected Vaquero's headset into another communications line.

"Manny and Cano. Their scout's name is *Tuan*."

"*Taino*, this is Spectre 01, over." Loud static crackled over the headset.

"Spectre 01, this is *Taino*, come in, over." Manny's voice sounded the same when they ran from the Lords in Brooklyn, thought Vaquero.

"Stand-by one Taino." Shawn Woods gave Vaquero a thumbs up.

"Manny, it's Ray. How are you doin' man? How's Cano, is he OK?, over." The NVA worked feverishly to disrupt the radio transmission.

"Ray, is that you?" Cano crawled over to Rodriguez.

"Yeah, it's me. You guys OK?"

"Where the hell have you been *mano*! The NVA were about to cut us a new asshole," Rodriguez said calmly.

"You came when it counted man, remember? That's all that really matters." All of a sudden Vaquero was anxious.

"Don't worry, Manny, we're going to get you out of there real soon. Spectres will be overhead all night, so just hang in there," Vaquero said, assuring Rodriguez that they wouldn't fall into the hands of the NVA.

"Roger Spectre. Look forward to seeing you again, Ray." Rodriguez replied affectionately. There was a long pause then static. "Gotta go Spec', hope to talk with you soon, over."

"We'll be back tomorrow *Taino*, over," Vaquero responded. Vaquero disconnected his communications cord and silently left the flight deck. After three hours on station, Spectre 01 headed back across the fence as another Spectre arrived to shield Rodriguez, Rincón, and *Tuan*. Another 82-mm mortar began to find its range as the defenders hunkered down in the bunker, sprayed by dirt and rocks.

"I've had enough of that shit. Mark the motherfucker, *Tuan*," blurted Rodriguez. *Tuan* lobbed a Willie Pete in the direction of the pesky 82-mm mortar.

"Covey, get somebody to hit my smoke! That mortar is bearing down on us, over!"

"Roger *Taino*. Sandy is on its way." Covey cleared the A-1E Skyraider that had been patiently loitering over the defenders for more than an hour. The A-1E Skyraider dived straight into the target releasing napalm canisters on top of the 82-mm mortar team, instantly cremating them. Screams and shouts were heard as the napalm flew everywhere. The entire jungle was consumed in flames and smoke. Sandy came back around and opened up with his gatling gun, literally chewing up the ground, ripping the NVA that were in the open into shreds. Out of nowhere an NVA quad barrel 23-mm antiaircraft gun suddenly nailed the Skyraider in its left wing. The pilot barely made it out before the wounded A-1 crashed in the thick forest three miles away. As he hovered above the battle scene, an AH-1G Snake pilot saw the gunner stitch the Skyraider across its wing.

"This is Snake 22, I've got the bastard." Snake 22 made a 180 degree turn toward the gun site. The last thing the gunner saw was the AH-1G Cobra barreling straight at him at 160 knots. There was no time for him to do anything except kiss his ass goodbye, as the pilot centered the cross hairs on his heads-up display directly on the gunner.

Manny, Cano and *Tuan* were hunkered close together inside the bunker. The sun beat down on them at a hundred and ten degrees during a momentary lull in the fighting. Their jungle fatigues were torn from crawling through the bunker hauling ammo boxes firing back the NVA, then frantically diving for cover, all which seemed to occur all at once. Their elbows and knees were rubbed raw, but they weren't feeling a thing at the moment. The adrenaline somehow took away the pain and anxiety of their predicament. Suddenly, the attackers were on the air.

"We're not afraid of your fire power, *Taino*. You are outgunned, surrender now or you will be obliterated," remarked the self-assured NVA political officer.

Cano leaned toward the top of the bunker. "Oh yeah? Have you checked the score lately, *comrade*? I'd say recon 250, Uncle *Ho* zero! Well? Come get some *pendejo*," Cano shouted back sarcastically.

"We're in deep shit Cano," said Manny in a matter a fact tone as streams of brown sweat dripped down from their faces.

"Yeah, but, they don't know we know that yet." Cano grinned. How they could smile at a moment like this was truly remarkable, Manny thought. But close friends found comfort being next to one another, especially at a time like this. Rodriguez let out a soft inaudible sigh. They were exhausted, and they slept with a dead stare listening for enemy movement. His arm ached as he reached into his right pocket and lit a cigarette. And for the first time in his life, he silently cried as it all seemed to come together, and perfectly clear.

Manny looked into Cano's blue eyes. "What you thinking about Bro?"

"I was just thinking how things might have been different if they hadn't sent us on this mission. What good did it do and for whom?" Manny was silent. Rodriguez didn't want to die and rot in the fucking jungle. Not here. He drew heavily into the cigarette exhaling ever so slowly as if surrendering his last breath, but wishing he would live till morning to talk with Ray Vaquero again.

"Hey, Ray will get us out of here," he assured Cano, with a sense of relief as the ambers from his cigarette extinguished. The bunker and surrounding jungle, was as quiet as a tomb.

CHAPTER FOURTEEN

The coded message from the Joint Chief of Staff to *MACV* was direct; proceed with the rescue. Military Assistance Command *Vietnam*, head-quartered in *Saigon*, was the nerve center of the American war effort in Southeast Asia since the early 1960's. Deep within the *MACV* operations center staff officers quickly formulated a daring plan to rescue the embattled Force Recon team. It was a three-pronged strategy that called for insertion of twenty elite ARVN Black Panther snipers to distract the NVA away from *Taino*. While the snipers were busy baiting the NVA into the open, two Spectre gunships would fly in ahead of the SAR team at tree top level and saturate the wood line with a massive barrage of 20-mm Vulcan gatling gun fire. *MACV's* first order was to create a lot of confusion and bedlam on the battle scene. And if everything proceeded according to plan, a SAR rescue force from Detachment Fourteen, Thirty-Eighth Aerospace Rescue and Recovery Squadron, *Tan Son Nhut* Airfield, would swoop down quickly to extract the team.

MACV planners had surmised that NVA trail watchers would more than likely monitor all of the existing landing points close to *Taino*. A new landing zone in a thickly wooded area where the NVA could not foresee, would have to be created. Over time, the U.S. military had developed a bomb for every conceivable application in *Vietnam*; one that instantly created a landing zone for helicopters was no exception. They called it Commando Vault. It was a huge bomb, weighing in at fifteen thousand pounds, and it was dropped by parachute out of the back of a C-130 Hercules. Three C-130's flew at eight thousand feet to three designated drop zones eight miles from *Taino*. Two were decoys. Called BLU- 82, the ordnance was fuse-extended to detonate three feet above ground level. The tremendous blast cleared enough of the jungle canopy to permit the landing of three helicopters that carried twenty brave and determined ARVN snipers.

#   #   #

It was 11:00 a.m. when Major Marks finally found Vaquero sleeping across several chairs in the squadron's briefing room adjacent to the Ops desk.

"Hey, Vaquero, let's go son. We're scheduled to fly in three hours." His I.O. was exhausted, but the Major wasn't going to stop him from flying his fourth consecutive mission to the *Fishhook*. Marks understood the deep rooted faithfulness and loyalty Vaquero had for his friends. Ray rubbed his eyes as he slowly got up. He had slept less than four hours after getting back from his last mission earlier that morning.

"What's going on, sir?" he asked, as he yawned and stretched his arms.

"We're leading an assault and rescue attempt of the recon team in four hours. Get your gear, and meet me at the briefing room. I'll fill you in once we get the crew together." Marks headed out the door toward the equipment trailer. He had anticipated that someone up the chain of command would eventually give the 16th SOS the go ahead on a rescue. Marks wanted it as much as Vaquero. The squadron commander was eager to get Marks out of his office when the support mission finally filtered down from *MACV* to Blue Chip. As it was, Roberts wanted Marks on the mission anyway. There were a lot of good pilots that flew for Roberts, but there was a big difference in how Marks and the others handled their aircraft. Others knew how to fly, but Major Stuart Marks wore his aircraft like a glove.

"OK gentlemen, lets get started. We don't have much time," ordered Marks. The flight crew moved quickly into their seats.

"Here's the game plan. Two AC-130E Spectre's will fly in low toward the *Fishhook* at five hundred feet. Once we're there we will lay a suppressing fire over the target with our 20-mm Gatling guns on the NVA. Sappers are hunkered down in slit-trenches all around *Tainos'* position. In tandem, the two Spectres will walk a wall of steel toward the sappers, pushing them away from the bunker. Any questions?" The room was silent but Marks' sensed the intensity and desire in his crew.

"Two HH-53 Sikorsky Jolly Greens will trail fifteen minutes behind us. Once we've pushed the sappers back, the HH-53's will pluck recon from the midst of the *North Vietnamese* battalion. Crown, a rescue command and control HC-130P from the Thirty-Ninth, Aerospace Rescue and Recovery Group out of *Korat Thailand* will orbit above the battle scene at fifteen thousand feet as the rescue mission unfolds." Crown would be responsible for controlling the two Jolly Greens and six A-1 Sandys that made up the rescue task force. It was a daring plan. But, for it to succeed the Black Panther snipers and Spectres had to create enough confusion and diversion to give the SAR team just ten minutes to hover over Taino and get them out.

"Let's get it done gentlemen," Marks directed, donning his flight gear as he raced toward the crew bus. Ten precious minutes; it seemed like an eternity. The plan had been judiciously reviewed by *MACV* down to the smallest detail. Though the Generals in *Saigon* thought the plan would work, there was no way they could factor in advance the unexpected, or what the NVA was preparing for the rescue attempt they knew would eventually come. Search and Rescue forces were trained and prepared to overcome enemy resistance that varied in magnitude and intensity. After decades of war, the NVA were masterful at setting up flak traps, using the survivors as bait to lure the Sikorsky's into ferocious walls of ground fire. Throughout the war, SAR flight crews were not constrained by strict rules of engagement that determined how they flew their rescue missions. Nor were there any formal written directives that determined how much effort should be expended on a rescue mission. Their mission was simple and clear; do whatever was super humanly possible to get their men out. The flight crews that put their lives on the line daily to recover downed airmen under extremely dangerous situations could easily be understood by the squadron's motto: *That Others May Live.*

Washington would be briefed within the hour by the Joint Chiefs as the rescue force hastened toward the *Fishhook.*

The gunships AN/APQ-135 Forward Looking Radar guided the two aircraft along the contour of the earth, avoiding detection by enemy radar that might have been positioned in the area. Marks aircraft bounced up and down from the heat thermals. Ten miles out, the Major instructed the navigator to contact *Taino*. As Vaquero looked toward the nose of the aircraft, he could see large plumes of black smoke rising through the jungle canopy where the raging battle ensued. An AC-47 Spooky and a AC-119 Shadow gunship had just left the *Fishhook* after having showered *Taino's* tree line with thousands of 7.62-mm and 20-mm fire, keeping the NVA at bay. Spooky 20 fired its full load of 21,000 rounds of 7.62-mm, saturating the recon team's perimeter. Out of *Phan Rang*, the AC-119G Shadow tore gaping holes through the jungle canopy, concentrating their barrage on silencing NVA mortar fire.

"*Taino*, this is Spectre 07, come in, over." The navigator encountered radio interference as static mixed with voices cracked over the radio.

"Spectre 07, this is *Taino*." Good to hear from you again." Ray Vaquero tuned into the navigator's communication channel with *Taino*.

"What's your situation?" Chris Andrews asked.

"We're OK, just a few cuts and bruises," Rodriguez replied. "What's the game plan, Spec'?" Manny knew something had to give sooner or later. The NVA were dug in with no intention of moving. His last communication with Nest had forecasted a low fog by nightfall. If they were going to get out of there, it was going to be now or…never.

"Keep your heads down *Taino,*" Marks interjected calmly. "SAR inbound in one-five. You copy, *Taino*?"

"Roger Spec', we copy," replied Rodriguez. "Hey Spec', is Vaquero with you?"

"Roger that, recon. He's here. Stand-by one," replied Marks.

Vaquero went into the booth and connected to Eric Castillo's com line while Gramps covered for him on the ramp. "Make it quick, we're almost there," remarked Andrews.

"*Taino*, this is Vaquero over," said Ray.

"Glad you could make it back, *mano.*" Vaquero sensed a tone of apprehension in Rodriguez' voice.

"Everything will be OK, just hang in there a little longer." Vaquero couldn't think of anything better to say.

"You were always there when we needed you, Ray…" remarked Rodriguez. Static crackled over the radio again disrupting the communication.

"We're losing you, *Taino*. We'll be in contact later, over." Rodriguez was barely audible as he signed off. Vaquero let out a nervous sigh as he walked back toward the ramp.

The Black Panther team silently spread out a hundred yards apart, concealing their positions in the trees and thick jungle brush. Before they knew what hit them, fifty NVA fell dead; the ARVN snipers swiftly picked them off at fifteen hundred yards with their M21 sniper rifles mounted with silencers.

The roar of Spectre's Vulcans engulfed the jungle as the two gunships suddenly appeared with their cannons blazing banking steeply over *Taino,* forming a ring of fire. A massive cloud of dust swallowed the battle scene as acres of trees, brush, and bodies were neatly sheared by the sudden burst of four thousand rounds from the twin cannons. Hundreds of green and red tracers filled the sky as the NVA angrily responded to Spectres presence. Vaquero could hear the loud metal thud of AK-47 rounds slam into Spectre's protective armor plating along the left side of the aircraft fuselage. After the initial gunship assault, three Wolfpack F-4 fighter escorts rolled in on NVA positions releasing silver napalm canisters across the terrain. Rolls of flames burst through the jungle canopy as the immense heat singed the faces of the concealed recon team. Cano continued to throw colored smoke grenades to mark the enemy's position for the Spectres. As he exposed himself above the bunker to hurl another smoke grenade, he was struck in the left shoulder by a sniper round. *Tuan* rushed over to him to check out the injury. His right shoulder was shattered.

"I'm OK, *Tuan*. Get that motherfucker for me." Cano winced as *Tuan* applied pressure to the wound with a large bandage.

"You OK, *mano*?" Rodriguez raced from his M60 machine gun position to check on Rincón.

"Shit, it hurts like hell." Cano let out a painful laugh while Rodriguez tied a bandage around his shoulder. The bullet had gone straight through after shattering the bone.

"Sweet dreams," Rodriguez said as he injected Cano with morphine. He dragged Cano toward the mouth of the cave, leaning him up against the wall so he could keep on eye on him.

"Hey," Cano whispered as Manny crawled to man the M60. Manny came back and squatted down next to him. "Give me a cigarette, Manny."

Rodriguez pulled the last two cigarettes from a crumpled pack. He lit them both then placed one between Cano's lips. Cano coughed, spitting the cigarette to the ground. "That's a nasty habit we have, Manny. We oughta give it up when we get back to the *world*." There was an uncomfortable silence, something that had never existed between them before. "You know what'll happen if they get their hands on us. Don't let them, Manny."

"I won't," whispered Manny. He looked up toward the thick jungle canopy, envisioning the long ride up on the forest penetrator, exposed. "And don't forget, Ray's up there watching over us. We've got it all figured out." Rodriguez squeezed Cano's left hand then went back to his post.

NVA Snipers had set up positions in the trees one hundred yards from the bunker, hoping to pick off the team one by one. *Tuan* was enraged. He picked up his M-79 and with his jungle eyes, blasted three snipers that now swayed slowly dangling from a tether line tied around their ankles.

NVA trail watchers perched high in the trees watched in amazement as dozens of their comrades suddenly arched backwards as they were violently stopped in their tracks. Realizing that the gun fire was coming from their rear, one of the spotters quickly notified his battalion commander in a command bunker that was two hundred yards from the recon team's position.

Le Thanh quickly concluded that the Americans had somehow inserted another team in the area to draw them away from *Taino*. Obviously they were not the anticipated rescue force. What was their purpose? he thought, as he scanned maps of the *Fishhook*, evaluating where the team was hiding. Finally it struck him that a rescue mission was in progress and that the *South Vietnamese* sniper attack was only a diversion. Upon his orders two hundred soldiers marched toward the ARVN snipers spread out in a straight line, executing an NVA version of a 'mad minute,' walking toward the hidden ARVN positions, firing continuously, hoping to flush out the ARVN snipers. Pith helmets and khaki uniforms were clearly visible to the ARVNs now. Like an angry swarm of bees, the NVA sprayed the brush and tree line with a savage barrage of automatic weapons, RPG's and mortar fire. A Black Panther radioman quickly transmitted that their position had been compromised and were heading toward the extraction LZ. Two Cobra gunships circling the area headed toward the elite sniper team to cover their retreat. They were out numbered but not in courage, as they dropped another thirty *North Vietnamese* as they covered their retreat.

"We're five minutes out," Lieutenant Colonel Ward Scherr informed Crown. Two Sikorskys and six A-1 Sandy Skyraiders were now in visual range. The SAR team could see the massive plumes of black smoke rising from the *Fishhook* region, as they made their final turn toward the pickup point. Scherr was designated the 'low-bird' for the mission, while the 'high-bird' would hover above the scene in the event Scherr got into trouble. If everything went according to plan he'd have the team out of there in fifteen minutes and back at *Korat* in thirty. He tightened his shoulder harness one last time then thrusted the HH-53C to the max at 190 knots into the blurred terrain below. Scherr was a legend at the Thirty-Eighth. His HH-53 was the lead helicopter during the a POW rescue attempt at *Son Tay, North Vietnam* in 1970, but the camp turned up empty. The prisoners had been moved to *Hanoi*. Better known as "Greyhound" around the squadron, Ward Scherr was on his third and final tour in Southeast Asia. He had flown every helicopter that existed in the government's inventory, going as far back as to the Korean War. They didn't come any calmer than Scherr. Composed and invariably poised, Scherr was unflappable under fire.

Le Thanh's men kept their heads down below the zigzagging trench lines, waiting for the helicopter to lower its forest penetrator. As the rescue force approached, Sandy 01 and 02 saturated the tree line with seven thousand pounds of ordnance then raked the shattered terrain with its four 20-mm cannons prepping the area before Ward Scherr brought the HH-53 to a hover above the trees. Scherr's co-pilot was now in contact with *Taino*. Two AH1G Cobras raked the jungle with rocket and cannon fire while three UH-1 Huey's pulled the elite ARVN Black Panthers out of the *Fishhook*.

"*Taino*, this is Hound 15, over." Ward Scherr slowed the helicopter as they approached Taino's position. After authentication, *Tuan* threw a purple smoke marker outside the bunker. Scherr gracefully hovered the

HH-53C above the trees as two door gunners showered the jungle forest with their GAU-2B 7.62-mm electrically powered gatling guns.
Another crewman slowly began to lower the forest penetrator that
incorporated spring-loaded arms that parted the jungle foliage while it
was lowered to the ground. Carrying Cano's shotgun, *Tuan* was first to
leave the security of the bunker while Manny carried Cano out. He
would go up after his friends were safely in the hands of the SAR rescue
team. Then reality turned into their worst nightmare. The HH-53C violently shivered as a fusillade of automatic weapons fire struck the helicopter killing one of the door gunners instantly. Within seconds the
co-pilot was dead after multiple hits to the head and torso. The shattered windshield showered Scherr with glass as he struggled to keep the
helicopter airborne.

Taino raced back to the bunker as Scherr banked the helicopter hard
left before crashing through the trees two miles away. Rodriguez then
radioed the backup HH-53 to abort the extraction. Sandys 03 and 04
rolled in and blasted the jungle with Napalm, as plums of thick black
smoke belched through the triple jungle canopy. Dark puffs of smoke,
the size of basketballs, trailed the two Sandy's forcing them to leave the
area and terminating the rescue.

The NVA crept closer now to *Taino's* bunker to avoid being hit from
the ensuing airstrikes. A lone sapper had crept up to the mouth of the
bunker to throw a stick-handled potato-masher grenade that landed in
front of Cano. *Tuan* immediately grabbed the grenade then flung it outside the bunker taking out a very surprised and horrified attacker.
Hidden down in the vegetation, RPG teams moved silently forward in
the tree line, gauging distance toward the fortified bunker. Marks
immediately rolled in after Sandy 03 and Sandy 04 made their final
pass. Seventy-nine more NVA were literally ripped apart by the Vulcan
20-mm cannons, caught by surprise in the trench line. But there were
NVA everywhere, and they would not pull back.

"The LZ is too hot," acknowledged Marks. "Get the 105 on-line B.J.; let's bury them in the trenches while they're still in it." The attackers were so close to *Taino*, that NVA body parts were torn and tossed into the bunker as Spectre pick them apart.

"We've Winchestered and we're at Bingo fuel, sir," reported Chris Andrews. "Spectre 21 is on station, sir, we'd better head back." Marks was visibly upset along with the other crew members.

"It can't end this way," whispered Marks, frustrated that he couldn't finish the job. "Call *Tan Son Nhut* and tell em' we need fuel and munitions ASAP." He thought about the ass-chewing he'd get from Roberts for not bringing the aircraft back to *Ubon*, but he'd worry about that later.

"Roger that, sir," replied Andrews, delighted by Marks' decision. Everyone pitched in, quickly loading 96 105-mm rounds and nearly six-hundred 40-mm for the Bofors. Gramps and his gun crew rapidly loaded the 20-mm belts for the Vulcan cannons. Within two hours they were serviced and back on their way to the *Fishhook*.

The evening stood still until the team heard the screams and bugles. It was a signal that the NVA were about to launch another attack on them. Screams, shouts and whistles split the night as the NVA swept down the hillside directly in front of the bunker's killing zone. Rodriguez quickly called FSB Defiance for artillery fire, turning them loose on the already hammered jungle real estate. Three hidden NVA suddenly appeared from Rodriguez's left, spraying the bunker with automatic weapons fire. *Tuan* waited until the gunners paused between burst then fired a 40-mm round from his M-79 into the center of the three NVA, killing them instantly. As if in slow motion, two grenades landed beside Cano and Manny. Cano instantly jumped onto Rodriguez shielding his body with his own as sharp jagged pieces of shrapnel ripped into Cano and *Tuan*. Another deafening ear piercing blast as sizzling metal fragments embedded into the bunker by the force of the explosion. A loud whoosh and another explosion. *Tuan* was neatly severed in half by an RPG that had penetrated the bunker, slamming his body against the karst cave walls. A sapper came screaming out of the smoke and dust and hopped on top of the bunker in front of Cano who had been blown off of Rodriguez after the second RPG explosion. Instinctively Rodriguez lifted Cano's Remington 12-gauge and thrust it into the sappers stomach blowing a hole clear through the other side.

The jungle was suddenly silent again. Another hour went by without an attack. It was eleven o' clock and pitch black. Manny turned to Cano, who was sweating profusely; hallucinating in the darkness. He decided to inject him with more morphine. "Everything's is going to be OK, Cano. Just hold on a little longer." Rodriguez suddenly heard the low guttural sounds of a tiger lurking in the distance.

#   #   #

The chaos of the battle was unbelievable. The roar of automatic weapons, machine guns, mortars and grenades shook the thick forested jungle surrounding FSB Defiance. During the night, *Le Thanh* had dispatched three hundred men to take out the fire support base. He wasn't going to let Defiance interfere with his mission any longer. Captain Buck ordered the Howitzers lowered to ground level, aiming them at the charging maniacal *North Vietnamese*. Buck was preparing to evacuate Defiance. Choking clouds of black smoke and dust obscured the killing ground as the NVA were cut down as they charged head on against the Howitzers. During a lull in the fighting, two HH-53's landed to remove the artillery team, abandoning the FSB and leaving *Taino* without fire support. They were now on their own.

#   #   #

Predictably, Washington got nervous whenever things didn't go their way and always looked for someone else to point the finger. The politics of the moment would not permit an all out rescue of *Taino*, nor could they afford the perception of engaging in what might be construed by the international community as a hostile act even for defensive reasons. The Search and Rescue was called off, when the Secretary of Defense was said, "Wait until things cooled off." Whatever that meant, it would not comfort the crew of Spectre 07, nor the men who were willing to lay down their lives to rescue *Taino*.

#   #   #

A dense cloud cover began to slowly roll in from the east, frustrating air support targeted to keep the NVA at bay and away from Manny and Cano. *Le Thanh* went through the plan one last time with his commanders. He stared into their eyes menacingly, aware that some of them wanted the heads of *Taino* as trophies for political as well as personal gain.

"Give them every opportunity to surrender. Instruct your men that if they must shoot, it must not be to kill. Otherwise, they, as well as you, comrade…" he paused intentionally so that the words would sink in. "…will personally answer to me if they fail to demonstrate proper fire discipline." A new directive from *Hanoi* instructed *Le Thanh* to capture the Force Recon team at all costs. The *Politburo* had made plans to march the captives down the streets of Hanoi as proof to the world of the United States' aggression against the sovereign nation of *Cambodia*. The political maneuvering in *Hanoi* sickened *Le Thanh*. *Taino* was not to blame for the destruction of *COSVN*, he thought. The truth was, *North Vietnam* had violated *Cambodia's* borders for years. They brought it on themselves, and it was only a matter of time before it was found and destroyed.

Nearly five hundred of his soldiers were amassed along the tree line. Whistles and bugles echoed throughout the emerald green forest signaling the sappers to move forward.

Spectre 07 had just arrived over *Taino* when Nick Bristle informed the Major he was picking up hundreds of hot spots on his FLIR screen. Meanwhile, two Wolfpack F-4's announced their arrival, armed with eight Laser Guided Bombs to destroy enemy triple-A gun sites if the situation presented itself.

"How many Nick?" Marks asked, shocked at the numbers the FLIR operator had reported.

"There are hundreds of them down there. Looks like they're getting ready for another assault. They're lining up that way from what I can tell, sir." Vaquero was coming unglued, wanting something, anything to happen to protect his friends. *Taino* was running out of time.

"I.O., give me a flare every third orbit," Marks ordered, then signaled to B.J. that he wanted the 20's on-line. As the NVA got closer to the bunker he'd switch to the 105-mm.

"Yes, sir," replied Vaquero as he pressed the control panel launching the first LAU-74 flare.

"Chris, contact *Taino*. See if they can see what we're picking up," Marks asked.

"*Taino*, this is Spectre 07. Come in, over." After several minutes with no response, Andrews tried again. "*Taino*, this is Spectre 07. Come in, over."

"Answer Manny, come on," Vaquero pleaded into the rushing wind.

"Spectre 07, this is *Taino* over." Rodriguez voice was weary.

"What's your status over?" NVA voices began to jam the transmission with curses and loud music.

"We're down to two, Spec." Vaquero now stood on the edge of the ramp. "Cano, is hurt pretty bad." Sporadic gun fire could be heard coming over the radio. The FLIR and LLLTV tracking of the advancing NVA was becoming arduous due to the sporadic cloud cover. They needed to fire now or lose any chance they had of saving Manny and Cano.

"Can't hold it, sir," remarked Bristle. "The clouds are in the way."

"Fine, we'll take her down just a bit." Spectre 07's nose dropped slightly as the Major pushed the control column forward. Marks was going to take the gunship below the thick cloud cover. At fifty-five hundred feet, Marks was now in the range of every conceivable weapon the NVA wanted to throw at them. There really wasn't any other choice, thought Marks and his crew, driven to make the NVA pay for every inch they took toward *Taino*.

The advancing sappers were startled by the loud buzz-saw sound of the twin Vulcan cannons as they spewed fifteen-hundred rounds of red steel on them. The attackers scattered in all directions as the Major slowly dipped the aircraft's left wing deliberately spraying the jungle terrain over a wide area. On his second firing pass, Spectre 07 was welcomed with thousands of small arms fire, several reaching there mark under the aircraft's belly. One round found its way through the booth decommissioning the LLLTV. Vaquero's LAU-74 took three hits setting it on fire, forcing Vaquero to quickly jettison the launcher over the battle scene exploding when it finally hit the ground. With a twenty-five yard kill radius, Marks began pounding the NVA assault with the gunship's 105 Howitzer. The Major formed a wall of death along the bunker's perimeter as scores of sappers attempting to breach Taino's defenses. Marks fired a 105 round every three seconds, but *Le Thanh's* diehard zealots would not let up. They continued to inch toward the bunker in the midst of the gunship's barrage. Spectre 07 was quickly running out of options. The cloud cover was so thick now that the gunship was unable to lock on any targets.

Rodriguez' M60 jammed. He tossed it aside then quickly grabbed the 12-gauge blasting two sappers that began to climb over the sandbags. Manny raced to get the other M60 at the other end of the bunker. Taking it off its tripod, he braced it tightly against his side then fired across his perimeter forcing the NVA to retreat for the moment. A thick cloud like wall formed a blanket over *Taino's* position.

Rodriguez hopelessly gazed skyward and muttered, "so this is how it all ends." Stoically, Manny prepared to execute his final directive. Frightened, Cano called out to Manny.

"I'm right here, *mijo*. I'm right here. It'll be over real soon, Cano," Manny whispered reassuringly. He then dragged the radio toward the middle of the bunker so he could keep an eye on the NVA with the M60 while he called Spectre 07 again.

"Spectre 07, this is *Taino*. Come in over." Rodriguez bent down and picked up the M-79 grenade launcher, slamming a white phosphorous round into the chamber then resting it on top of the sandbag.

"Roger *Taino*. this is Spectre 07. What's your situation, over?" The gunship skimmed the cloud cover as it frantically searched for a break in them. Rodriguez let out a long sigh as he looked at Cano's broken form.

"Not good Spec. A fog has begun to roll in, NVA getting closer, over." Tears welled in his eyes.

"Roger Taino, we'll stay over as long as we can. Another Spectre will be on station in one-five. You copy? Over."

"Can't wait that long, Spec," shouted Rodriguez. "They're almost on top of us." The gunship's crew heard the quick burst of machine gun fire coming from inside the bunker.

"Prairie Fire! Prairie Fire! I've got sappers in my perimeter, over!" The crackling sounds of RPG's and automatic weapons fire reverberated over the radio as the *North Vietnamese* launched their attack again. Rodriguez invoked the code word authorizing a bombing run on his position. "Repeat, Prairie Fire, you have authorization. Lock in on my Willie Pete. Firing…now." Rodriguez fired the WP on the other side of his bunker setting the far end of the bunker ablaze.

"Do it!" Vaquero shouted over the intercom. Marks contacted Wolfpack 17, loaded with four laser guided bombs under its wings. Spectre would irradiate the bunker with its Laser Ranger Designator.

"Hurry Spec', they're in the bunker." When the M-60 ran out of ammo, Rodriguez grabbed the Remington shotgun, firing multiple blasts at three NVA that leaped into the far side of the bunker attempting to extinguish the blaze. Rodriguez then turned his plea to Vaquero. "I'd do it for you, Ray. *Any time anywhere*, remember?"

"Do it! Do it now Marks!" screamed Vaquero over the intercom as he slammed his fist on the ramp floor with uncontrollable rage.

"We hear the music Spec," responded Wolfpack 17, releasing the 2000 pound bomb. The sensor in the warhead locked in on Spectre's illumination as it glided silently toward the bunker.

CHAPTER FIFTEEN

When they landed back at *Ubon*, everyone was quiet. No one said a word to Vaquero, not even Marks. Ray Vaquero walked purposefully to the back of the bus, saying nothing, yet conveying everything.

Le Thanh withdrew his troops out of the *Fishhook* to let the Americans retrieve *Taino*, permitting a joint service recovery force to recover the bodies the next day. Manny Rodriguez' and Cano Rincón's remains were taken to Graves Registration in *Da Nang, South Vietnam*. *Tuan* was returned to the *Jeh* for burial.

Tears streamed down his face as he sat silently across from the two caskets as vivid images of his friends raced through his mind; of childhood adventures and simpler times. Their love for the barrio and Puerto Rico, and their eternal bond. But worst of all, there was the guilt and anger and his inability to save them when they most needed him. Ray Vaquero was overcome by a raging storm of grief as he escorted Manny and Cano home. Placing his hands on the caskets, he knelt beside the flag-draped gray coffins, petitioning his Maker, his friends, and Suzanne Logan, "please forgive me."

#   #   #

The flight to Ramey Air Force Base in *Aquadilla, Puerto Rico* took twenty-three hours on the C-141 Starlifer. Dressed in black, Manny

Rodriguez' and Cano Rincón's parents stood silently in the hot morning Caribbean sun as twelve Marine Corp pallbearers loaded the caskets into two separate vehicles.

Rosa and Miguel Vaquero fought back tears of sorrow, embracing their son when he walked over to stand beside them. Ray didn't say much as they drove to the Island's national cemetery in *Bayamón*. But he felt a peace and tranquility that he had not sensed for a long time, proclaiming that life was good and still worth living despite his personal failures and miscalculations. You just learn to live with them, he reasoned now. Rosa turned and looked at her beloved son, still fighting back the tears as she tried to smile for him. Ray leaned forward and pressed her arm to comfort her. His smile was radiant and blissful.

"I love you *mami, papi*. It's good to be home." Miguel Vaquero struggled to get his white handkerchief from his coat pocket to dry his eyes.

"It's OK Miguel," Rosa said, rubbing his arm, comforting him. "It's good for a man to cry."

Manny and Cano were buried on the Island's national cemetery, on a beautiful hillside overlooking the Atlantic Ocean. In the distance, Vaquero could see *Old San Juan* and the *El Morro* Fort as it jutted into the sea. As shots were fired into the air honoring the dead, Manny and Cano were laid to rest next to the Island's two Medal of Honor recipients. On Manny' and Cano's white stone marker, it read:

Deeds of great courage in the darkness
never seen or recorded

When they got back to the house in *Fajardo* later that afternoon, Rosa cooked up a quick meal, as only she could. There was a long silence before Miguel asked, "When do you have to go back, *mijo?*" Rosa stood behind Miguel, holding on to his shoulder.

"In about a week." Ray's smile was comforting and serene. "I'm OK" he said, assuring them that he would be back. Ray turned to look out the wooden screened door, drawn by the sound of a closing car door. He walked slowly toward the covered porch squinting his eyes from the late evening sun. And then he saw her. At first it was like a silhouette, a faint outline that caused his heart to beat rapidly at the cruel thought that it actually might be Suzanne. He blocked the sun with his left hand, but, it *was*, her.

Suzanne nervously opened the wooden gate, walking slowly toward him. Vaquero walked toward her in overwhelming shock and disbelief. And without uttering a word, they embraced. Neither of them spoke nor did they look into each other's eyes. They just simply embraced each other with all the love and passion they could summon, assuring themselves that this moment was real. Suzanne firmly clutched Ray's shoulders with both hands, while tears seeped into his uniform. "I'll wait for you, Ray. No matter how long it takes, I'll wait," Suzanne said with a quivering voice.

"You were always there when I needed you," Vaquero said with his arms tightly wrapped around her, still in disbelief that she was there.

Miguel and Rosa looked on from behind the old wooden screened door. Rosa gently squeezed Miguel's hand as tears silently streamed down their face.

"What do you see Miguel?" She asked with her gentle smiling eyes.

"True love...is eternal," replied Miguel, caressing Rosa's face. Then Miguel and Rosa quietly walked back toward the kitchen hand in hand. When they were finally there, they embraced.

#   #   #

ABOUT THE AUTHOR

Bill Morales' novel, *The Fence*, resulted from his experiences in the Barrio and the War in Vietnam. In 1972 he volunteered to fly combat with the 16th Special Operations Squadron in Ubon Thailand. He flew more than a hundred missions and was awarded the Distinguished Flying Cross, and 15 Air Medals for combat missions in South Vietnam, Laos, and Cambodia.

To contact author, E-mail: billmorales98647@aol.com

978-0-595-17820-9
0-595-17820-0

Made in the USA
Lexington, KY
26 January 2011